122
RULES

122 RULES

Book One in the 122 Rules Series

DEEK RHEW

Tenacious Books Publishing

Published by Tenacious Books Publishing

Copyright © 2016 Deek Rhew

Published by Tenacious Books Publishing in 2019
Tenacious@TenaciousBooksPublishing.com

This book is a work of fiction. Names, characters, places, and incidents are either the product of the author's imagination or are used fictitiously.

Library of Congress Cataloging-in-Publication Data
Rhew, Deek. Second edition.
122 Rules/ Deek Rhew
ISBN 978-0-9998978-7-4 (print)
ISBN 978-0-9998978-8-1 (e-book)

Cover Image: © ShutterStock
Cover Design: Anita B. Carroll www.race-point.com

Printed in the United States of America

www.TenaciousBooksPublishing.com

For the tenacious: **Never** give up!

PART 1

Chapter One

Monica and the three goons in the death wagon drove for what felt like an eternity. A man with the chest and shoulders of a linebacker and a face chiseled out of granite sat opposite her on the backseat. Clad in a three-piece suit and dark sunglasses, he had first captured then belted her into the large SUV. But now it seemed the fun for him had ended, and he only glanced her way on the occasional mile.

The man in the passenger front seat with the broken nose ignored her, giving his full attention to the road ahead. The hood of his sweatshirt had fallen back, revealing the bristles of a crew cut as sharp and squared away as the Super Bowl field on the morning of game day. He wiped his sleeve across his upper lip, leaving a trail of blood on the dingy gray fabric. After their altercation earlier, his groin and ribs had to be aching as well. A thin smirk of satisfaction played across her lips. If only for a moment, she'd had the upper hand.

Monica's smile faded as her thoughts returned to her predicament. She sat directly behind the driver. Maybe a chop to the neck or a blow to the temple would disable him? Would that cause him to lose control of the vehicle? Could she grab the wheel and yank it? If they crashed into oncoming traffic, would she be able to escape the twisted metal and broken glass? Though she hadn't seen the driver's face, the thickness of the man's shoulders beneath his suit jacket rivaled Granite's. This man could swat her off as easily as an annoying spider.

She couldn't out-muscle them, so surprise and distraction were her only allies. Surely these meatheads carried weapons. Could she startle one of them—maybe scream in Driver's ear since he was focused on navigating the busy city streets and would be less able to react—and grab his gun? She would hold the barrel to his neck, forcing him to pull the car over, and blast anyone that tried to stop her. The idea had merit. But Granite sat only inches away; he would enjoy subduing her.

Though the idea made her nerves cringe, she could dive out the door. They did that on TV all the time. Fall and roll, right? Looked simple enough. But she doubted it worked in real life. In the movies, no cars ever trailed behind the hero as she made her escape. Most likely, she would be mowed down by one of the insane taxis that prowled the boulevards. At the very least, she'd break a leg or twist her ankle, and they would recapture her.

But the closer they got to wherever these brutes were taking her, the faster her viable options dwindled. Seeing no alternative, she tensed, fingers wrapped around the door's release handle. Steeling herself, she took a deep breath and pulled the lever.

The door didn't budge.

Shit. Child locks. Of course these guys would have thought of that. She looked up to find Crew Cut watching her.

He pointed at her lap. "You forgot to unbuckle your belt too." Her eyes dropped to the buckle. *Duh!* The corners of his lips curled up, then he turned away to watch out his window, uninterested.

Shit.

No one said anything for a few miles. Finally, Monica turned to Granite. "Look, before you kill me, can I at least call and say goodbye to my family?"

☆☆☆☆

As time and distance slipped past, Monica ran and reran each scenario in her head. Each new option of escaping these men seemed even less likely than the last.

They surprised her when they turned into an underground garage. Driver handed a plastic card to the stern security guard who met them at the gate. Another guard stayed back but kept his hand on his holster. He hadn't drawn one of the several weapons hanging from his belt but looked competent and ready to go to war at the slightest provocation. The first guard, who looked like he drank from the same steroid-laden stream as Granite, examined the embossed card, made a call, and waved them through.

These were not rent-a-cops.

What the hell? She hadn't known what to expect, but certainly not a military-like fortress. Maybe an abandoned warehouse—her mind refused to imagine what they had in store for her there—or a deserted pier, followed by a swim in the Hudson. At least they hadn't made her ride in the trunk.

They parked, and, in unison, the three men got out. Evidently only she required a child lock. Granite came around and opened her door, but she didn't budge. After a few seconds, he unbuckled her belt and lifted her out of the car with the same odd gentleness he had used to deposit her into the seat.

Learning from the mistakes Crew Cut had made earlier, they surrounded her as they marched to an armored, unmarked door. The entrance had no handle; instead, Driver swiped his card and typed something into the inset keypad. He looked into the lens of a nearby camera mounted in the rough-hewn rock wall. A second later, the door buzzed and clicked. Driver opened it. She glanced about, desperate for any opportunity to escape, as they ushered her inside then down a long, dimly lit, colorless hall. Granite pushed through one of many indistinguishable side doors into a narrow room. The small space, empty save two chairs and a table, had a can-it-be-more-obvious-that-it's-a-one-way-glass mirror covering half the far wall.

Granite took a position in the corner, perhaps to ensure her cooperation, perhaps for intimidation. Monica turned from him to the rail-thin woman who trailed in his wake. Her severe features were exacerbated by a bun so tight it pulled the corners of her eyes back, as though a discount plastic surgeon had arrived intoxicated to her facelift. She wore a crisp white shirt, creased blue slacks, and no makeup.

As the woman began to thoroughly pat her down, Monica grabbed the woman's arm and twisted it around. "Get your hands off of me," she growled.

The unmistakable click of a gun next to her ear made her blood freeze. Swift and silent as the wind, Granite had stepped forward to protect his coworker.

Bad Facelift yanked her arm free, giving Monica a knowing, satisfied glare. She finished the frisk, even taking Monica's watch and plucking the ring off her finger. Then she waved a wand over Monica, searching for telltale bits of metal. Granite had taken Monica's phone, purse, and satchel bag when he had first apprehended her. The stern woman had them in a large plastic sack and now added Monica's jewelry to the haul. Then both Granite and Bad Facelift left, closing the door behind them.

Monica tried the knob, but of course it refused to turn. *Shit.*

She pressed her face against the one-way glass, cupping her hands around her eyes to block out the light. If she stared hard enough, she might be able to see who watched her from the other side.

Only her own reflection stared back.

She banged on the glass. "Heeeellllllooo, anyone in there? You can't just lock me up. I get a phone call."

When no answer came, she examined the door. She'd seen a movie where the hero had escaped by punching the pins out of the hinges. But Monica had no tools and tore

off part of her fingernail after a few minutes of fussing
and grunting. She rapped her knuckles on the entrance's
surface, but it felt solid and heavy. The handle seemed the
most vulnerable to her efforts, but she had nothing with
which to jimmy the latch open. Cursing, she kicked the
door and began to pace.

The windowless room had no clock, so she had no way
to know how much time had passed. At this rate, though,
she would not be attending tomorrow morning's Legal
Ethics class. She stopped and looked around at the small
space. Maybe not the one after that either.

She went back to the window and searched for gaps
in the frame. Having found nothing, Monica pressed her
ear to the space between the bottom of the door and the
floor. Only the sound of air moving through the ducts
greeted her.

She tried banging on the glass again. "Hey, anyone
home yet? I need to pee. Keeping someone from urinating
is considered cruel and unusual punishment. I go to law
school and know about such things." She pounded again.
"Hello?"

Still no reply.

Frustrated, she slid to the floor, her back against the
wall, and started counting the holes in the ceiling tiles.
When she reached a thousand, her stomach growled.

Just as she considered throwing one of the chairs
through the window, a short, bespectacled man swept into
the room. He wore a crisp white shirt, blue tie, creased

blue slacks, and shiny black shoes. *This guy and Bad Facelift must shop at the same military surplus store.* All spit and polish.

He carried a file and an air of casual authority with him. He smiled at her, probably to put her at ease. It only kicked her anxiety up a couple of notches.

"Hi, my name is Jon Smith, sorry for the wait. Can we get you anything? Water? Tea? Coffee?"

"My phone and a cab home?"

Jon chuckled and sat down, motioning for her to do the same in the opposite seat. "So, Monica is it?"

She nodded and followed suit. Her chair—the no-frills, no-specific-color, plastic variety—reminded her of a larger version of the kind she'd had in elementary school. Unlike the one Jon sat in, hers had no rollers and didn't recline. Its entire purpose seemed to be keeping the occupant uncomfortable. It succeeded. Also, it was short.

When she settled into her seat, Jon towered eight to ten inches above her, even though, when standing, he only came up to her chin. Monica seethed at the obvious strategy for psychological dominance—he could play both sides of the coin from this position. Even when he smiled, she could see Bad Cop right beneath the surface.

Everything that had happened since they had nabbed her at the library had been designed to intimidate her—locking her in the black SUV, ginormous goons, leaving her alone in this little room for hours on end without her cell or any way of contacting the outside world. Now this little demonstration of authority… She screwed in her resolve, refusing to give in, and sat up straight in her chair, staring into the little man's eyes. She would make him blink.

"Seems you had a little meeting today," Good Cop smiled. *Please tell me everything*, his eyes seemed to say.

In her psychology classes, Monica had studied ways to get information from people. One of the most effective techniques was to make a simple, open-ended, often-wrong statement then remain silent. In response to this non-question, the other person, more often than not, would start babbling, if not to correct the inaccuracy then to fill the uncomfortable empty space. Monica didn't answer, letting the quiet spin out.

Several tense but wordless minutes passed. He seemed reflective when he continued. "Not sure what part you play in the operation. We also didn't see how you got there. We have been trailing those guys for months, waiting for a meeting just like that one. You must have slipped in before we arrived."

"You mean that little tryst between Baldy and the guy that sounded like Joe Pesci?"

He chuckled again, though it sounded forced and placating. Just barely Good Cop; more like Annoyed Cop. "Yes, that."

"Look, I don't know what this is all about. I was just reading, minding my own business, when these guys showed up and started talking. I don't know what they were talking about exactly. But it sounded shady, so I did the Good Samaritan thing and tried to help."

Good Cop vanished like an apparition. "So you want me to believe that one of the biggest drug dealers in New

York and his favorite knee buster just showed up without a care in the world and started yammering about their business right in front of you? Only a couple of people knew that meeting was going to take place, and you coincidentally happened to be there? That's what you're trying to tell me?"

Indignation fed her building rage. "I didn't know about the meeting, and I have no idea who those guys are. What I do know is I don't want any part of you"—she pointed at him—"or any part of *this*. I've got midterms to study for, so unless I'm under arrest, you have no right to hold me. I am leaving now." She stood and started moving toward the door.

"You understand that it would be easier to take you seriously if you hadn't just been arrested on drug possession."

Monica rolled her eyes. "It was only about a gram of coke. At a small get-together back in Alabaster Cove, a friend of mine gave me a little as a going-away present. I forgot about it, and when I got pulled over for speeding it fell out of my purse. I did a few hours in custody and was released. You obviously have the report, so you already know all of this."

"I see." He had opened the folder flat on the desk and appeared to be reading.

She stood next to the door, arms folded, fingers drumming against her bicep.

"Can you as easily explain the time you spent in juvie for murder?"

Oh shit. Dread flooded her veins and invaded the hollow of her gut. Monica moved slowly back to her seat—her very short seat—and dropped into it. Her eyes settled on the pictures Jon casually perused. They were upside down to her, but she didn't need to see to know what they contained. Blood on the floor. Blood on the bed. Blood splattered in a rainbow pattern across the wall. A dead man with his head caved in. A baseball bat with *Louisville Slugger* in blue script and clumps of scalp and bloody fingerprints—her fingerprints—along its sleek oak-colored length. Her body threatened to disgorge her stomach's contents right there on the no-color floor, and only by herculean efforts did she prevent the tuna salad she'd had for lunch from making a grand reappearance.

"I thought those records had been sealed?" Her voice sounded barren and deflated even to her own ears. "I thought it was illegal to access them without a direct order from the court."

Jon smiled a non-smile while his eyes drilled into her skull. "What you need to understand is that we are above the law. The sooner you get that into your genius-level head, the easier this will be."

Defeat, as thick as molasses, dulled her senses and deflated her spirit.

When she didn't answer, he continued, "So let me spell this out. Someone with a history of drugs and murder has recently traveled across the country. She allegedly 'attends' school but has no formal address and, as far as we can tell, no friends. Her instructors say she has well above average intelligence, but only sporadically attends class and speaks to no one. This woman with almost no societal ties and little traceability attends a meeting with a high-powered dealer and a hitman. You're a smart girl; do you see the picture this paints?"

The little man sat ramrod erect in his high chair in an attempt to make himself into a larger-than-life bully. *Compensating for something?* Heat and anger replaced the liquid lead that clogged every thoroughfare in her circulatory system. "Look, if you actually had anything on me, I'd already be in jail. But seeing as how we are having this little conversation and I have no cuffs on, you clearly don't have any proof. Just access to records that you shouldn't and a wild imagination for the dramatic. Thus unless you plan to formally charge me, I'm free to go." She stood again.

Jon shook his head. "I can see your law classes are paying off, but what you've learned out there doesn't apply here. As I told you, *we* are above the law. I'm afraid you're going to miss a few more lessons before this is done. A process has been started, and there are no shortcuts, no quick paths through it. Please, just relax and let me guide you."

"I don't need guidance. What I need are answers. Who were those guys? Who are *you*, for that matter? You haven't exactly explained that. Tell me, Jon, who exactly do you work for and what do you want?"

He shook his head again. "It doesn't work like that. I'm asking the questions. If you cooperate, maybe I'll answer what I can. If you don't," he paused, "we will be here a very long time." The underlying threat hung in the air.

Good Cop seemed to have left on a bus for parts unknown. And Bad Cop's mood had gone sour. Dread returned in all its syrupy thickness.

"Okay, now that we've cleared that up, are you sure I can't get you something?" Good Cop suddenly returned with a sarcastic smile.

She shook her head.

"Fine." He closed the file with the damning pictures in it, folded his hands on the desk and looked at her. "Here's what's going to happen. You are going to explain everything that went down this afternoon. Start at the beginning and do not leave anything out. Do I make myself clear?"

For a moment Monica held herself tall, but soon she slouched in her chair like an amateur boxer who had just gone three rounds with the champ...and lost. Badly. She nodded.

"Good. Whenever you are ready."

Monica took a deep breath and began. "I went to the library because I have a huge Criminal Law midterm coming up..."

Chapter Two

EARLIER THAT DAY

Monica sat in one of a thousand seats in an auditorium NYU Law called a classroom. The instructor, his gloomy voice amplified by the microphone headset he wore, looked no bigger than a Ken doll from this distance. He had somehow turned the required Criminal Law class—a subject Monica had always found interesting—into a depressing saga of oppression and despair. Among the students and faculty, the graying, squat teacher had been given the nickname Professor Doom because he tended to deliver his lectures as if they foretold the end of the world.

Whatever. She didn't have to like her instructors, just needed to get through their classes.

Just when she thought her brain would implode from boredom, Professor Doom wrapped up the monologue by reminding them about the midterm next week. "And remember," he said, holding up a finger to emphasize his point, "it's worth a full third of your final grade." A collective groan went up from the audience.

Not seeing the point of attending when she could read the material online, Monica hadn't been to class in almost two weeks. But Dr. Doom liked to throw in a few lecture-only, exam-worthy tidbits during his dreary pontifications, so she made it a habit of attending the class right before a test. Her next shift at the coffee shop wasn't until tomorrow, and since she had no more classes that day, she could use the free time to study.

Her full-ride scholarship didn't include living expenses or books, and her job only just covered her meager expenses. She'd managed to sweet-talk Tom Phillips, a fellow first-year with too much money and too many raging hormones, for use of the spare room in his apartment. But if she went there, she'd never be able to concentrate. He almost always had at least half a dozen friends over, drinking and talking too loudly. She couldn't complain though, since the lack of rent fit perfectly into her tiny budget.

On occasion, she would let Tom lure her into his bed, but only to keep her sexual frustration at bay and the rust off her lady parts. Though she suspected he wanted more, Monica had her entire life for the whole relationship thing, so she kept him at arm's length most of the time.

The school's library had little to do with academia and more about friends getting together to catch up on the latest gossip——far, far more interesting than understanding the finer points of blameworthiness as a precondition for criminal liability. So Monica loaded her backpack and hiked almost two miles to the huge New York Public Library where she could get lost in the anonymity.

The walk seeped the tension from her shoulders and cleared her mind. Compared to her little Southern California hometown of Alabaster Cove, New York had a lot more texture and gritty layer upon gritty layer of big-city flavor. The crisp air put a tangy chill in her cheeks. The gray skies drizzled a thin November mist, and by the time she passed the huge, concrete lion sentries guarding the front steps of the library, her mind had cleared.

Monica hated the open-table layout of the reading room, so she had long ago found a secluded aisle among the last rows of dusty books. She slid to the floor and cracked the first book—an in-depth review on the criminal code and interpreting statutes—and lost herself in the text.

On the other side of the shelving unit, footsteps echoed among the tomes. She waited for the wandering intruder to find what they sought and move on. They lingered, though they did not seem interested in disturbing her peace and quiet. So she turned her attention back to the work at hand.

Just as Monica became reacquainted with insanity and intoxication defenses, more light footsteps approached, and yet another intruder started talking with her unknown interloper.

Monica rolled her eyes and sighed. *Really? Inside voices, people!* She tried to tune them out. Library conversations should be soft and covert, no more than mere whispering. People could be so oblivious. The two clearly thought they were alone, but they just needed to look past the wall of Shakespeare and Marlowe to know they had company.

Morons.

"So, did you take care of the problem?" a man who sounded like Joe Pesci asked.

Focus, girl! Test looming. One-third of your grade. Professor Doom. But try as she might, she found herself drawn to the conversation.

"Yes," came the reply. This voice had a smoky rasp, tinged with a slight accent, Latino maybe. "No need to worry. Lenny has been—how shall I put it?—permanently silenced, unless of course he learns how to breathe without a head and through three feet of concrete."

Ummm... Holy shit! There is no way this is for real. Tom. It had to be him. He knew she came here and, at any second, planned to jump out. "Fooled ya! Ha! You totally believed it!"

But Tom couldn't convincingly pretend to be a pancake if a piano fell on him. A reasonable imitation of Joe Pesci? That seemed way out of his league.

Trusting her intuition, Monica slouched down until she lay on the floor. She survived because she listened to her gut, and it said to not make a sound. Most people who had been through what she had would have hunkered down, frozen, trying to stay as invisible as possible. But Monica persevered where others perished. She glanced down the long corridor, but no one browsed the aisle in either direction. She could scream for help, but if these guys were half as bad as they seemed, she would spend her whole life waiting for her turn under the blade and in the concrete. What *could* she do?

Suddenly she knew. Her smart phone, one of the few splurges she allowed herself, lay in her satchel next to Tom's apartment keys. Careful not to let her jittery fingers rattle the keys, she retrieved it. Monica had been taking notes for years from fast-talking professors and often recorded the lectures. Her fingers clicked and swiped the familiar pattern that started the dictation app. She sat up enough to slip the little marvel of technology on top of a particularly tall book on the bottom shelf, then froze as a shadow passed her hand.

"Good," the Joe voice said.

Monica breathed a sigh of relief. Joe had shifted his leg but still seemed unaware of her presence.

He continued, "Lenny's been getting greedy. He and his boys have been shorting orders, delivering sub-par product, and cutting into our profits. I'm a patient, generous man, but if I allowed this to continue, it would ruin my reputation. Did you receive the final delivery before his untimely demise?"

"Yes," the accented voice said, "and the product has been delivered, just as requested. They are waiting for word from you before sending it out. Here."

Monica chanced pressing her eye to a gap between books. Two men occupied the narrow space on the opposite side of the shelving unit. A bald-headed man with his back to her handed a thick white envelope to the one who must be the Joe Pesci sound-alike.

"Joe" opened it, thumbing through a thick stack of hundred dollar bills, closed it back up, and tucked it in his jacket pocket.

Oh. My. God. This is for real. Her heart beat so hard in her ears she could no longer understand the conversation. She could only see the back of Baldy's head, though when he turned, she thought she glimpsed a scar running from his left ear down to his jaw. She had an unobstructed view of the other man, though. He had a short, solid body and dark hair cut in a no-nonsense style. Nothing to note in the looks department until she saw his eyes: black, and as cold and soulless as a shark's. They sent a chill up her spine.

But his voice… It made the hair on her neck stand up. He sounded like Mr. Pesci but spoke with an icy authority. *Do not cross me*, the tone said. *Ever.* This personality didn't jive with the jovial little man she had come to know from movie comedies. This man was a heartless, merciless machine, about as far from bumbling as possible. How she could possibly know that, she wasn't sure. But, as always, Monica trusted her gut.

Joe continued, "Let Frankie know it's done. We can move the product to the distributors in a couple of weeks once we're sure Lenny isn't missed."

"The guy was such an incompetent, meddling asshole. I don't think anyone'll go looking for him. And if someone did find out it was us, no one would care," Baldy said.

"Don't be an idiot. How many times do I have to tell you about being careful? I do not want this coming back on us. People come to our organization because they trust our brand and our ethics. You know that. Incompetent or not, if word got out that we removed the head of the biggest supplier in New York, it could seriously hurt our reputation."

Baldy chuckled. "Removed the head. Literally. Funny, boss."

Those black, soulless eyes fixed on the underling. Ice chilled her soul as Monica stared into their frozen depths. "It's time to go. The spooks have been watching, and I don't want anyone to see us together. Wait five minutes then get out of here before someone spots you."

Baldy nodded, and Joe walked away. He turned around, and Monica jerked back from the gap. Had the mobster seen her?

When he didn't say anything, her heart slowed a little, though its rhythm remained far above its normal cadence. The killer waited a few minutes, set something on the shelf, then turned and strolled away as if he didn't have a care in the world.

Monica let out her breath and tried to calm her still-galloping heart. Had she really just seen what she thought she had? She hit stop on her phone and played back part of what she'd recorded. "I don't think anyone will go looking for him..." She clicked stop.

Oh, shit. She had become a witness.

Now the big question: What did she plan to do about it?

Nothing! You do not want to be involved in this! Do not go to the police. What did you see, really? Nothing. Nothing at all. None of it made any sense or meant anything.

Besides, would the police even believe her? Every day, millions of nut jobs in this city screamed about conspiracy theories and government cover-ups. No one would listen. Just another crazy looking for attention. But the recording... Did that matter? Would it give her credibility? With each question, her doubts compounded.

She didn't know the answers, but she did know she wanted out of the library as fast as possible. With trembling hands, she shoved her books and notes into her bag helter-skelter, tucked the phone in her pants pocket, and stood. Before leaving, she reached through the shelf and picked up the book Baldy had left behind. *The Untouchables.* How ironic.

Monica's eyes scanned the reading room as she moved out of the rows of books, looking for Baldy and Joe, but she saw no sign of them. She moved quickly past the tables thick with people reading, toward the door leading to the massive stone hallways. She had almost made it when a man at a workstation she had just passed stood.

He fell in step beside her, gripped her by the arm, and whispered, "Come with me." He pushed her in front of him, guiding her, naughty-three-year-old-like, toward the exit. *You're gonna get it when we get home.*

Stunned, Monica let him lead her away.

Just before they reached the door, she tried to pull out of his grasp, but he held her arm in an iron grip. "Don't..." he started to say, but the survivor took over, breaking her paralysis. With all her might, Monica swung her free elbow back into the man's solar plexus. He stood a head taller and arched forward in response to being sucker punched. She thrust her weight up and back, and when the back of her head connected with the center of the man's face, his nose broke with a satisfactory crunch.

Monica tore her arm free and swung around, kneeing the unprepared man in the groin. She didn't weigh a lot, but she put all of her energy behind it. He doubled over, grunting in pain, rewarding her for her efforts.

In an adrenaline-driven sprint, she bolted for the door. She would hug her best friend, Angel, for making her take that self-defense class before heading off to NYU. Jesus, how many times would that girl save her?

Monica had just reached the exit when the man caught up to her again. He spun her around and slammed her into the wall, holding both of her arms this time. Fear and anger mingled as he stepped into her personal space, preventing further attacks, and whispered, "Are you trying to get yourself killed? If you are interested in living, knock it the hell off and come with me." His voice, strained thanks to his injured testicles, carried the weight of someone used to being in charge.

He wore his jet-black hair clipped crew-cut short; sharp blue eyes stared unwavering into hers. A thin stream of blood trickled from his nose to his mouth and dribbled onto the front of his gray hoodie, but he did nothing to stop it. "Do I have your undivided attention?"

His words crushed Monica's brief feelings of victory. She gritted her teeth and nodded.

"Good, now let's go." He opened the door and ushered her out. Instead of leading her down the walkway toward the front entrance where hundreds of people milled about, he dragged her into an office on the other side of the hall. Across the small space, he ushered her out a side entrance to a deserted alleyway.

Oh my god! Dead. I am dead. Do something! Her eyes darted about, looking for an escape. She had missed her chance to get away. No way would he underestimate her again.

He led her down the steps, around the corner, and toward the inevitable large black SUV. She had to do something, but he had left her almost no options.

Almost.

Her body tensed as he relaxed his grip ever so much while reaching to open the rear door of the death wagon. In one swift move, Monica dropped her purse and backpack, yanked her arm free, and bolted.

An Olympic sprinter spurred on by the blast of the starter's pistol couldn't have taken off faster. She just might escape. That thought had barely broken the surface of her mind when a building of a man stepped out from behind the SUV. She saw the obstacle too late to avoid it and collided with what may as well have been a concrete wall. The huge, unyielding man had the chest and shoulders of a linebacker and a face chiseled out of granite.

When she hit him, she bounced, sprawling onto her backside, stunned. Before she could regain her wits, the huge man reached down, picked her up, and gently set her in the rear seat of the SUV. He then buckled her belt.

"I'm not a toddler," she informed him, embarrassed yet indignant.

"Just stay put." His voice rumbled like rock plates deep in the Earth.

With that done, he glanced at Crew Cut's bleeding nose. Crew Cut glared back at him. The big man's lips curled into the slightest of grins as he shook his head and closed her door. Monica might be about to die, but at least she got in a lick of her own, and Granite knew it.

Chapter Three

Jon hadn't interrupted Monica's monologue but instead took notes on a large yellow legal pad. When she finished, he set his pen down, leaned back in his chair, and flipped through the pages with his neat handwriting scrawled across the surface.

She waited, letting the silence spin out.

"So, you are living with this Tom Phillips?"

"Yes."

"And he does not charge you rent?"

"No."

"I see." He scribbled something else on the pad. "This is in exchange for sexual favors?"

She leered at him. "Favors for him or favors for me?"

Jon looked at her over the top of his glasses. "Favors for him, Ms. Sable. Does he let you stay there in exchange for sex?"

"You cannot be serious."

"You have been arrested for drugs and murder. What I'm trying to determine is if we add prostitution to the list of your admirable qualities."

She leaned in, her hands folded on the table. "I think Tom is in love with me in his own schoolboy sort of way. One of the ways he displays this affection is by letting me stay with him free of charge. We have sex because we are young and horny. Please be sure to add that under your Admirable Qualities category, Mr. Smith. Do you need me to spell it for you? *H, o, r...*"

"Thank you. I've got it."

To her satisfaction, he wrote *young and horny* at the bottom of the page. He continued to review his notes while she watched him in silence. "So you went to the library to study for a Criminal Law midterm?"

"Yes. It's best to study up on a subject when preparing for a major exam. Wouldn't you agree?"

Jon ignored the question. "So you are reading, and Mr. Pesci just strolls up to the other side of the bookshelf and starts babbling about someone he's killed?"

Monica sighed. "Actually, if you'd taken accurate notes you would know that I don't know who arrived first. I didn't look. Didn't care. I just wanted them to leave me in peace. Whoever it was didn't say anything until his lover arrived."

"I see."

"Do you? You seem confused. I thought my story was very linear. Here." She held out her hands for the pad of paper and pen. "I can draw stick figures or make a flow chart or something for you, if it will aid in your comprehension of the situation."

Jon set the legal pad on the table, where it lay like a flat yellow turd. He removed his glasses and placed them next to the papers. "See, and there's my problem. The whole thing sounds like a 'story.' It seems simply too fantastic. Too convenient. I'm having trouble with it."

"Which part?"

"All of it. This mystery boy lets you stay for free. You almost never go to class, yet pull straight A's. You just happened to be there when one of the biggest drug lords in New York decides to renew his library card."

Monica shrugged and continued to gaze at him.

He looked back at her for several minutes. Finally, he gathered his belongings and stood. "I need to go have a conversation."

"Oh? Am I boring you?"

He opened the door but stopped before exiting. "Do you need to pee?"

"Pardon?"

"Pee." He pointed at the mirror. "Earlier you told my people you needed to go."

Maybe she could get out of here after all. "Yes. I need to urinate."

"Very well. I will send a female agent to escort you."

"Don't think you can handle me? Got to get a real agent to do your dirty work for you?"

"In my position, I'm above having to take a dog for a squat."

"Whatever. Go talk to your goons. I'm sure they want to congratulate you on a job well done. Maybe give you some kind of commendation, Biggest Asshole at the Agency."

"Probably. Sit tight."

☆☆☆☆

Bad Facelift returned a few minutes after the door closed. "Come," she said and allowed Monica to exit.

The narrow hall felt as cavernous as a baseball stadium compared to the confining space of the interrogation room. Bad Facelift marched Monica past a series of unmarked doors to one with the female bathroom symbol. The agent followed her into the sterile space.

"Don't I get a little privacy?" Monica mocked.

"The stall has a door, Ms. Sable."

She entered the stall but could not force herself to go. She hadn't actually needed to pee, just wanted out of the interrogation room and hoped for the possibility of escape. But Facelift had kept her distance and probably carried a weapon.

"Are you almost done, Ms. Sable? We have an organization to run, and I do not have the time or the patience to sit here waiting for you."

"Maybe it evaporated. Besides, what are you going to do? Come in after me?"

"Yes," came the unhesitant reply.

This girl means business. Monica could almost hear the smile in the woman's voice. *Try me*, the tone said. *Shit.* "Fine. Fine. Whatever." She cleaned up and came out of the stall.

As they marched back, Monica asked, "Can I get some food too?"

"I was instructed to see you safely transported to and from the restroom. You will have to take up other amenities with Mr. Smith."

"I'm sure he wouldn't mind. You would be helping to keep my strength up."

Bad Facelift held open the door. "This isn't a hotel, Ms. Sable, and I'm not your maidservant. Now, if you please." She gestured toward the entrance.

Monica sighed as she re-entered the small space and once again found herself alone.

☆☆☆☆

Monica resumed her place on the floor, counting the holes in the ceiling, starting where she'd left off. She had almost doubled her original number when Jon swooped in, followed by Crew Cut. Jon resumed his seat while the man with the Super Bowl-field hair stood next to the door.

"Hey." She grinned at Crew Cut. "How's the nose?"

He didn't react or say anything but just stared at her. She studied his face a little closer. Could he be scowling more than normal? *Is somebody in a bad mood? Poor boy.*

Jon still had the yellow legal pad, which he flipped to a middle page.

"So," she asked, turning her attention back to her interrogator, "did your little conversation go well? Did you decide if I'm lying or not? Want me to tell you something else?"

"Actually, it doesn't matter."

A jolt ran through her. "Pardon?"

"It doesn't matter if you're lying or not. We are about done here."

Her body stiffened. Were they going to let her go? She had anticipated at least one more round of interrogations. "So what does that mean?"

"It means that we need you to tell your story again."

Her anger flared as they pulled the rug out from under her again. "What? To whom? You?" She directed this last question at Crew Cut.

Jon chuckled. "No, no, you have it all wrong. To a jury."

She smelled a trap. "I don't have any idea what you are talking about."

"We're going to bring charges up against Laven Michaels, and you're the star witness."

This game Jon played fanned the flames of her already lit and stubby fuse. "Who's Laven Michaels?"

"Joe Pesci."

"Joe is Laven?"

"One and the same."

Anger and annoyance merged, producing a baby so irked, it bordered on irritable bowel syndrome. "So who is Laven slash Joe?" Monica asked.

Jon shook his head. "See, I think you already know that."

Instead of leaping across the table and throttling the agent, she took a long deep breath. With her last sliver of patience, she said, "For argument's sake, let's say I don't have all the answers."

Jon sighed. "Fine. Laven Michaels is, among other things, the biggest mover of illegal and controlled substances in the city. We've been trying for years to nail him with something that will stand up in court, and until yesterday we didn't have it. But now we have a witness that places him and Tyron Erebus, a known assassin for hire, having a conversation about a murder that, until yesterday, we didn't know about but have since uncovered."

She crossed her arms and sat back. "So you want me to testify?"

"Yes." Jon smiled. "That's all we need." But something sinister lurked right beneath the surface of the man's knowing grin. "Oh," he said, as if the thought had just occurred to him, "you will be sequestered until the grand jury renders a verdict."

She sat forward in her chair. "Ummm, no. See that doesn't work for me. I have school and a life."

"Both of those things will be put on hold. You can resume your classes after Laven is locked safely away."

"No, you don't understand. If I drop out of school, even for a while, I lose my scholarship." The first ripples of real panic began to course through her. "Sorry, I can't do it. You'll have to find some other way of nabbing this scumbag. It's not my problem."

Jon leaned forward until they were almost nose-to-nose. "See, it is you who doesn't understand. One way or another, you've lost your scholarship. You are done with school for now."

A quiet dread filled her stomach, but she refused to blink as she stared into Jon's eyes. "What are you talking about? My cooperation is strictly voluntary, and I am no longer volunteering."

"That's where you're wrong. We looked into your scholarship. It's for academics and ethics."

"Yeah. So?" She had to change the direction of the conversation—sway it to an alternate course, just a few degrees left or right—because right now it was headed straight toward the rocks, and she would be smashed to bits when it hit. But as frantically as her mind worked, throwing levers and spinning wheels, no ideas materialized to turn the tide in her direction.

"The review board that oversees the funding of the award has been notified that you've been brought up on charges, one of them a felony."

She blinked. She hated herself for giving in, but the room had started to spin as her existence began to spiral out of control. They were trying to rip away everything she'd worked her entire life to achieve. "What? What are you talking about?"

She resisted the urge to smack the satisfied expression off Jon's smug face. "Obstruction of justice for one. Your little story may sound good at a book club, but it doesn't wash here."

"Obstruction of justice? I'm here aren't I? I came in willingly to help you."

Crew Cut snorted.

"Okay, maybe not of my own accord, but I'm still here. I recorded the damned conversation and gave you my phone. Have you even bothered to listen to it?" She fought the desperation that clawed at her like a feral cat.

"Oh, yes. Many times. Our techs have pulled it apart and are trying to determine exactly how you altered the recording."

"I wha…? Ummm…no. That didn't happen. You've got nothing." Though her words were sharp, the room spun faster, and she had to hold onto the table just to keep from falling over. "There is no obstruction of justice. The recording was in no way modified no matter what your 'experts' say. You've got nothing. You need to contact the review board and say there has been a mistake, and you need to do it now, or I'll hire my own lawyer and bring holy hell down around your heads."

"As for the second charge, assault…"

She reeled back as if she'd been slapped. "What assault?"

"You assaulted a federal officer." He nodded toward Crew Cut. "That itself is a felony. You claim you came here willingly, but attacking one of our agents hardly seems cooperative."

"He surprised me. Grabbed me in public like he was some kind of pervert. How was I supposed to know who he worked for?"

"Maybe when he identified himself it should have clued you in."

Monica glared at Crew Cut, who now smirked at her. "You told him you gave me your name, rank, and serial number? That's not the way I remember it." Her attention returned to Jon. "I'm single and alone in a big city. As such, I've learned to protect myself from the lowlifes that prowl the streets. He's just lucky I wasn't really pissed, or he'd be in the hospital."

Jon held up his hand for silence. "As we speak, the scholarship committee is convening to discuss the situation. I think you can imagine how that will end."

Monica's heart sank. Years of work and dreams lost. A possible career and life after the hell she'd been living——gone in an instant.

"Here's the deal," Jon said. "You will go hide away for a while and testify. In exchange, we forget about these little incidents, chalk them up to misunderstandings."

"Great. So I'll only not go to prison."

"We'll also give you a full-ride scholarship including a stipend for living expenses. No more having to bum a room in exchange for blow jobs."

If she could have shot fire from her eyes, she would have turned him to a flaming McNugget. "So my choices are jail or jail and school?"

"Not jail, Ms. Sable. Just a minor inconvenience to help us put away a very bad man. Consider it giving back to society. However, your testimony has to be rock solid. The prosecutor says if you stick with the story you've given us…"

Monica thumped the table. "It isn't a story."

"Yes, yes. If you stick to the story you've given us, you'd better not waver a single syllable. Everything you've said had better be accurate, or the charges stick and our offer is revoked. What do you say?"

She looked at Jon then at Crew Cut, who continued to smirk down at her. "What choice do I have?"

"Good, I'm glad we came to an agreement. We begin immediately. First, I'd like you to meet Hale Lenski." He motioned to Crew Cut.

"Yes, we've had the pleasure," she said. "Though until now I didn't know his name. Score a point for the 'secret' part of 'secret service.'" She turned to Crew Cut. "Gotta be kind of embarrassing for you to get your ass kicked by a girl though, huh? What are you—an accountant with delusions of grandeur you could excel in the field? That never really works out, does it?"

Jon prevented her from continuing to badger the agent by saying, "Mr. Lenski is a highly trained field operative and the head of your security detail."

So it got worse. "He's my what?"

Crew Cut gave her a grin so plastic it could have had *Made in Taiwan* stamped on the back of it. "It's my job to keep you safe by whatever means I deem necessary. Don't worry"—he leered—"I'll take good care of you."

A sense of foreboding tried to wash over her already overtaxed nerves, but Monica shoved it away. She had always relied only on herself; this would be no different. Besides, she'd kicked Crew's ass once, so she could do it again if she had to. She sat back, returned his smile, and began planning her escape.

Chapter Four

Monica pressed the phone to her ear, listening to it ring in a world a thousand miles and half a lifetime away. A familiar voice answered. "Hello." A longing for home washed through her at the simple greeting.

"Hey, it's me."

"Oh, hey hon! I didn't recognize the number. How's life in the Big Apple?"

"Ummm…fine. How are things with you?"

"Mon, what's wrong?"

Just like that, the years unwound, and within a few words, her best friend sensed something was wrong. She must have heard the anxiety in Monica's voice. "Jesus, how do you always know?"

"I'm amazing," Angel replied. "Now spill."

Monica sighed. "I need to see you. Soon."

"Okay, like how soon?"

"When can you get here?"

"Ummm, honey, I've never even been to New York. I don't know. I guess I could figure something out."

Monica shifted the phone to her other ear. "No. Not New York. I'm at Len's off Highway 23."

"Wait. You're there *now*?"

"Yes."

Nothing lined the deserted roads leading into and out of The Cove for almost a hundred miles in either direction except trees, scrub pines, and jagged mountains. But some sixty clicks north, smack dab in the middle of nowhere, Len's Little Diner eked out a humble existence off of weary travelers too exhausted and desperate to find something decent.

"Okay." Monica heard her friend shift gears like a well-tuned auto, from surprised to task-oriented problem solver. "I'm scheduled to work…gotta get out of that… I'll be there in a couple hours. Maybe a little less."

Just like that, no questions. Her friend would bend heaven and earth to be there for her. Gratitude and love soothed Monica's heart.

☆☆☆☆

Ninety minutes later, Angel's beat-up VW Beetle bumbled into the parking lot of Len's Little Diner. Usually when they met, Angel greeted her with a hug and a Texas smile. But today she slid into the booth, somber and without so much as a "hello." Time to get to business.

"I'm leaving," Monica said without preamble.

Angel cocked her head, consternation reflecting in her eyes. "What do you mean? You've already left. Where are you going?"

"I can't tell you."

"I don't understand." Angel studied her closely, like a scientist examining an unusual specimen of bacteria. "Mon, you look like crap. What the hell's going on?"

Monica took a deep breath. "Look, I saw something I wasn't supposed to, and now some people, some very angry people, would like nothing more than for me to be quiet. Forever. So, I'm going into a program that will protect me from them. In exchange, I have to testify to what I saw, but that won't be for a long time. Stupid court system takes forever. Kinda funny, me wanting to be a lawyer and complaining about the court system, don't ya think? Anyway, the government—at least I *think* it's the government, they're kinda hush hush about all that, assholes—promises to keep me alive. So we won't be able to see each other for a long time. Maybe even ever. I just wanted the chance to say goodbye to my soul sister, so that's why I'm here. To say goodbye."

Angel blinked several times after the random rush of words bombarded her. "What are you talking about? What people? What did you see? Why would anyone want to hurt you? I haven't seen or heard from you in months, and now you make me meet you out here in BF Egypt telling me you're going away or underground or whatever because someone, what? Wants you dead? That's what you're saying, right? Someone wants to *kill you*? This makes zero sense." Angel paused and took a deep breath. "Okay, honey, what *exactly* is going on? Start from the beginning, and tell me everything."

Monica regarded Angel over the diner's worn, yellow laminate table. She wanted to talk to her friend, not only because she needed to say goodbye but also because someone should know what had happened to her. Besides, she needed someone to talk over the situation with, and no one fit the bill better.

From an academic perspective, the two belonged to different leagues. Monica had natural book smarts. Angel on the other hand... If she were a bulb, her filaments wouldn't shine as brightly as the rest of the lights in the chandelier. As a knife, her edge would be duller than the other cutlery in the drawer. On the shelves in the grocery, she would be one Dr. Pepper short of a six-pack. Angel had little ambition and tended to pick men for their looks and bad boy attitudes instead of their willingness and ability to make her happy. But her heart overflowed with kindness and patience. Plus, she possessed an uncanny ability to see through bullshit.

Angel had entered the diner as a pigheaded pragmatist, and in this mode, no amount of arguing would sway her from getting to the heart of the matter.

Monica loved this part of her friend's persona, which had helped forge their lifelong bond. This would make it impossible to try and cover up what had happened. Angel would have just looked at her in that we-are-both-going-to-sit-here-till-you-stop-effing-around way until the truth came out. And out it came.

Angel's eyes grew huge and round as she listened to Monica's story about overhearing the conversation in the library, the subsequent trip with the Secret Service, and the interrogation in the little colorless office. "That's the most outrageous thing I've ever heard."

"You want outrageous? Look at this." Monica pulled back the curtain on the window next to their booth. Two humungous, black SUVs sat in the parking lot, each with a driver at the wheel.

"Yeah, I saw those when I pulled in. So they are part of…" Angel turned her attention back to the inside of the diner. Monica watched as her friend's eyes roamed until they froze on the two suit-wearing men standing next to the entrance. "Is that Crew Cut and Granite?"

"In the flesh. Charming, don't you think?"

Angel glared at them but neither seemed to notice. She craned her neck looking at the other patrons, pausing on each—several stern-looking men and two severe-looking women scattered here and there. No one else.

The isolated diner usually buzzed with gaggles of people on their way somewhere else. On any given day, at any given hour, the place brimmed with road-weary families, truckers, and bikers. All who came to this humble establishment forged a common bond through deep-fried potatoes and fluffy pancakes that bridged otherwise disparate lives. Save a small scattering of misplaced men in suits, the booths sat empty and forlorn. The kitchen was as quiet and vacant as a cave.

Monica watched as understanding dawned on her friend's face. "Oh, my god," Angel said.

"Look, honey, I don't have a lot of time. There isn't anyone else I care about, so I made them give me this chance to say goodbye."

"What? No! Mon—" she started.

"It's not goodbye forever. Just for now."

"I don't understand."

"I know, dear."

"Where are you going?"

"I don't know. They want me to testify against the goons. First with the grand jury, then the trial, but after he's convicted, it should be safe for me to go back to my life."

Crew Cut appeared at the end of the table. "It's time."

Monica nodded. "Just one more minute." He walked back to his post, but his eyes never left the two women.

They slid out of the booth and stood. Monica took Angel's hands in hers. "I'll always love you, remember that. You saved me over and over, and there is no way to repay you."

The other girl, tears streaming down her cheeks, looked on the verge of a breakdown. "I love you, too. I don't want anything from you; I just don't want you to go."

Monica pulled Angel into her arms and whispered. "Give me your best poker face. Do it now and listen closely. I'm leaving a small piece of paper in your hand; it has an email address on it. Don't look at it until you get home. Get a new email and send it to me. This is against all the rules, so put it in your pocket and never, never, never give it to anyone. Do you understand? My life depends on it."

Angel nodded, and Monica kissed her friend on the cheek.

They broke apart. Though Angel still had tears running down her face, she had sobered.

That's a girl. Sad but relieved, Monica said, "I've got to go now. Take care of yourself, and don't forget what I told you."

"Be safe and kick ass."

Monica forced a brave smile as Granite and Crew Cut escorted her to the door. She threw one last look over her shoulder as she left the darkness of the diner and walked into the brilliant afternoon sunshine.

For the next few months, Monica remained cooped up in a forgotten house in the middle of nowhere. Her goon squad blindfolded her whenever she came or went—the location so super-secret even she couldn't know where they were. Besides Crew Cut, Granite, and Driver, other well-armed, suit-wearing, poker-faced men had been liberally sprinkled throughout the house. These protectors-from-foes, the last line of defense from those that wished to do Monica harm, lurked in every nook and cranny, 24/7. Bad Facelift stayed in Monica's room while she slept, and Monica had spotted several more guards on random patrol of the grounds.

Spare no expense for the star witness.

All of these random people looked identical, like they were bred in an incubation chamber deep in a dark, underground lair. Or perhaps they stamped them out in some factory in Taiwan, the press working overtime to churn out as many soulless, plastic goons—complete with accessorizing pistol and earpiece—as possible.

Late one evening, Monica awoke to find Bad Facelift had fallen asleep in her usual chair. After weeks of diligence, the woman had slipped up. Gleeful like a mouse that had caught the cat napping, Monica crept across her bedroom, careful to not make a sound. The other guards sat in the living room, so instead of heading toward the door, she moved to the window. The goons had tried to make their patrol patterns appear random, but it had only taken her a few days to map out their routes in her head. She held her breath. Granite ambled past, and as soon as he disappeared around the corner, she unlatched the lock. Monica eased the window up. Thankfully the vinyl-on-vinyl of the frame made no more than a whisper as the two pieces slid together.

She tugged the small handle of the screen, and it popped out with a gentle *snick*. She glanced back at Bad Facelift, but the agent hadn't moved. A little puddle of drool had pooled on the woman's stark white shirt. It would have been sweet had the woman not been such a bitch.

Monica slipped on her pants and shoes then eased herself over the rim of the sill. She expected someone to shout an alarm at any moment, but the night remained silent as she landed on the grass.

She half-crouch walked across the lawn, then stood and sprinted for the bank of trees that edged the far side of the property. She'd almost made it when an alarm blared, and the whole world became bathed in brilliant light. Terror stopped her in her tracks as a dog began to bark, and several dark figures carrying what only could be large guns of some kind emerged from the trees.

An amplified voice boomed, "Freeze. Throw down your weapons and get down on the ground. Now."

Maybe she could make it to the forest anyway. Monica's heart galloped, and her feet itched to sprint as she glanced at the weapons aimed in her direction and the men brandishing them. She could run fast…but not faster than a well-aimed bullet. They'd mow her down and laugh about it while telling the tale over drinks. Defeated, she did as instructed and lay down on the hard earth, waiting.

Black shiny shoes appeared just in the periphery of her vision.

"Get up," Crew Cut's curt voice said.

She peered left and right to find several men with guns pointed at her.

"At ease," Crew Cut told them. As the men lowered their weapons, he pulled her to her feet and guided her back toward the house, cursing and swearing under his breath. She raised her chin in satisfaction and smugness as they marched. At the very least she'd irritated him almost as much as he irritated her. He pushed her into a chair in the living room, pulled up one of his own, and began the lecture she'd heard a thousand times before. "My job is to keep you safe, but I can't do that if you keep trying to escape."

"Yes, mom. But I just wanted to go for a walk. Is that so bad?"

"And last time you said you wanted to get donuts. The time before that, you needed your hair done. I don't even remember what it was the time before that."

"I needed Maxi pads. Girls sometimes bleed, you know." Monica gave him a sarcastic grin.

Crew Cut looked at her with an almost pleading expression in his eyes. "Members of your buddy Laven's grand jury have had an unusually high number of accidents. Three have died in car accidents. One fell off a cliff while hiking, and another drowned while swimming. This is why you keep having to give the same testimony over and over."

"I understand that. So the jury's a little clumsy; are you trying to make a point?"

"We don't believe those are all accidents. Individually these incidents may not look suspicious, but this group has a very high mortality rate. Look, there are people who want to see you put into the ground. We've kept your identity secret for a good reason. I don't understand why this is such a difficult concept for *you*."

"And I want my freedom back. I don't understand why this is such a difficult concept for you."

"It's not just that we have to keep you safe from the outside world. Our guys are professionals, but they're on edge. Everyone is well armed, we have dogs patrolling the grounds, and they don't know you from a hitman. Plus, you usually pull this crap when it's dark, so we don't know it's you until we're right up on you."

"Are you planning to make a point or just talk me to death?" She had just about run out of patience. If he had planned to kill her, he needed to get on with it instead of blathering like an old woman.

"Mistakes will be made."

"Did you just threaten me?"

Crew Cut sighed. "No, of course not. But this is the last time we go through this."

Granite walked up and handed Crew Cut a small box. He opened it and pulled out what looked like a large wristwatch.

"What's that?" She eyed the gadget suspiciously.

"The latest in babysitting technology." Crew Cut secured the device around her ankle. He pushed a button, and a small LED on its otherwise blank surface began to flash.

"It's very stylish, but does it come in pink?"

He sighed again. "You've given me no choice. Also for your protection, you will no longer be allowed to be alone."

"Oh yes, because I get so much of that now."

"It's been a long night. Please go to bed." He stood and walked off without so much as a glance back in her direction. Granite gave her a slight shrug as if to say, *He's the boss. What ya gonna do?* and headed out to the yard, presumably to keep the world safe from the terrorists or rogue chipmunks or something. Bad Facelift, who'd been standing in the corner sporting her usual scowl, came over, took Monica's arm, and tried to lead her back to her room.

Monica yanked free. "I know the way." And she stomped off.

She soon discovered the truth in Crew Cut's promise. Someone watched her with a distrust she could taste every second of every day. Perhaps trying to run hadn't been the smartest move. Could cooperation be the right answer after all? Living in harmony and all that?

The bathroom proved to be the only time she had re-lief from a chaperone. The little space became her sanc-tum sanctorum. She would soak in the tub for hours, each time taking her iPad with her. Monica journaled about the goings-on at the house and in the courtroom. She wrote about the night she'd almost gotten away and included a picture of her ankle, complete with the glamorous new electronic tether.

They didn't allow her access to the outside world—no live TV, email, or Internet—and the movies they brought remained on a shelf, untouched. Instead, she read.

She'd always been too busy for casual reading but now found herself with barrels of free time and whizzed through two or three books a day. Every day she filled out a *Multimedia Requisition, Document #995.2, Rev. C,* which she turned in to Crew Cut. The first one she'd handed him, he'd examined with the same scrutiny a terrorist would use when reviewing the blueprints for a new bomb vest. He then pulled out a pencil and drew a line through several of the items.

"Hey." She tried to grab the pencil from him. "What are you doing?"

He smacked her hand away and gave her a half-smile. "Media filtering."

"That's complete gibberish. It doesn't mean a thing."

"I don't have to allow you to get anything. You can sit in your room and watch the paint peel for all I care. This is a privilege I can revoke without cause." He stared, daring her to challenge him.

She wanted to punch him. Grab his arm and twist it around until the bones cracked and his shoulder dislocated. But she took a deep breath, shook her head, and walked away.

From then on, Monica padded the list, adding odd titles that would catch the FBI agent's attention. And when Crew Cut crossed one or more of them off, she rolled her eyes and glared at him. He would smirk at her but pass on the order to be filled.

Since she couldn't be at school, Monica requested the required books for each of her classes, including the Criminal Law class that had started the entire fiasco. She studied, taking notes and ordering supplemental material, as though preparing for finals.

She struggled to endure the constant, unbearable tension. If she hadn't had her reading and her studies, she would have gone bonkers.

After over a year of her being sequestered, a Town Car pulled into the driveway, wheels crunching on gravel. The guards, as always, appeared tense, ready for the worst. As the car came to a stop, the rear door swung open. A gleaming, black-polished shoe touched the ground, then a figure in dark sunglasses stood. The guards had been right to be apprehensive; the worst thing imaginable had arrived.

Jon waltzed into the house, taking off his sunglasses as he did so. Arrogance cascaded off him in waves. "Hello, Monica. How have you been?"

"Just great," she said, not bothering to hide her sarcasm. "I've been hanging out here with the fun squad waiting to get killed."

"It hasn't been that bad. This is one of our better safe houses," he said, looking around.

"Oh, yeah, it's splendid. Let me give you the grand tour. Here's the kitchen; there's the living room." She looked around. "Yep, that's about it."

"Always the sassy one."

"Always the smooth political puppet." Monica glared at him. "Getting what you want, when you want. You're good, but I've had time to think. You're not the one pulling the strings. Crew Cut told me there's nothing in the news about Laven's potential trial. Why is everything under such tight wraps? Keeping the press away from a story about an infamous mob boss who may be standing trial for his crimes? Not an easy undertaking."

"You've been here too long." Jon patted her check. "You're overthinking things. Our primary objective is to keep you safe. As a law student, you should already know that grand juries are almost always held in secret."

"Well, maybe if someone hadn't yanked me out of school before I got to that part in the curriculum, I would."

He gave her his best placating smile. "Besides, if the press got word of what was going on, they'd be hunting for you and sniffing out every lead. Eventually someone would figure out who you were, then they'd turn over your life trying to get their two-minute sound bites for the six o'clock news. Keeping this out of the press makes it easier to protect you and your friends…er, friend. One friend. Anyway, that's not the point. The point is the jury is done. It's time for the next step."

Monica stared at him in disbelief. "It's over?"

"Yes."

"Well?"

"They delivered a true bill. With your testimony, there's enough evidence for a trial. Laven's been arrested. And since the judge determined he's a flight risk, he's been denied bail."

She sighed. "So he's in jail, and I can go back to my life."

"Yes and no."

Every nerve in her body went on full alert. "What do you mean 'no'? The bastard's in jail. That was the whole point. That's why I had to leave school, my friends, and my life. He's locked away now, so I'm safe."

"Well, that's the thing. See, yes, he's in jail. But even from there, he will still be able to run his operation, just at a limited capacity. Before the trial was set and the witness list released, no one knew who you were. But now word is out, and you have a very large price tag on your back. And when we get a conviction, don't think that goes away. The reward for your head will be there for as long as he breathes. I thought I explained this to you last year? If you go back to your old life, they will find you."

A sinister wave of having been manipulated washed over her. Monica glared at him. If she could have struck him dead with her thoughts, he would have burst into flames.

"Come now. I bring good news. The trial's about to begin. That should give you some relief."

She snorted. "Relief? Really? You kinda failed to mention that I would need to spend the rest of my life looking over my shoulder. It's something that I would have remembered, *special* agent. In the end, you get what you want, but what do I get?" She didn't wait for an answer. "I get screwed. That's what. Any chance at a normal life? Gone."

"We've talked about this. You still get a life; it's just not necessarily the one you planned. I came here to bring you in. As I said, it's time for the next step."

She waved her hand around. "What? What's the next step?"

"Patience. Let's go; we've got a lot to talk about."

Chapter Five

Jon's driver took them back to the headquarters, or base, or whatever they called it—Monica still didn't know and didn't care. The black sedan remained sandwiched between two SUVs full of the security detail that had been assigned to her. Same garage, same steroid-laden guards at the gate, same door and dark, colorless hallway, but this time, he took her to a spacious conference room.

The chairs, crafted of deep leather, stood at the ready next to the dark mahogany table, whose glossy surface shined in the soft lights. She sat at the head of the table while Jon fetched her a cup of coffee.

He came back with a paper cup. Monica took a sip and grimaced; the black sludge barely met the technical definition of coffee. It tasted like a mix of weak, used motor oil and garden mulch.

He sat down, placing a file in front of him. "Coffee okay?"

She narrowed her eyes at him as if to say, *really?*

He chuckled. "Budget cuts. Okay, so first thing's first. Your identity." He opened the file and pulled out some documents. He handed her an Arizona driver's license.

She squinted as studied it. "Susan Rosenberg? Really?"

Jon shrugged. "Yes, we thought you'd enjoy the parallelism."

"She was a human rights activist."

"But if you recall, before that, she was a murderer and a thief. We, the FBI, caught her, and she was sentenced to fifty-eight years in prison. Are you saying there's a difference between the two of you?"

Monica saw no point in resuming that old argument, so she remained silent.

He slid other pieces of identification across the table, naming each. Social security card. Voter registration. Insurance. On and on, all the little things that make a person who they are in a modern, electronic society.

She interrupted his dry list. "So what do I do?"

"What do you mean?"

"For a *living*?"

"Paralegal."

Monica sat up straight. "Um, no. I'm going to be a lawyer. I have plans. Other kids grew up like I did. I'm going to fight for them."

He relaxed into the back of his chair. "No, I'm sorry, that's not going to happen. You're going to have to adjust those plans."

"For how long?"

"At least until the trial is over. Then once we feel it is safe for you to do so, we can discuss it." A trap loomed.

"How long will *that* be?"

"Like I said. Until we feel it's safe." He slid another piece of paper across the desk.

She glanced down at the paper, then back at the man who held her life in his hands. A white-hot flame of anger burned through her. They had done it, screwed her just as she always knew they would. "A certificate of paralegal studies from a backwater trade school in Arizona? What is this?"

Jon smiled a knowing grin. "We examined your life's ambitions and determined that this was as close to it as we felt comfortable. We found you a job and a house. You start next week at a law firm in your new hometown. It's not a huge, prestigious place like you were hoping for, but there isn't anything we can do about that. Your new life is different than what you'd planned. Not worse, not better… Except, of course, unlike other kids right out of school, you'll be starting with a job and a very healthy stipend. Oh, and you'll have to fly out on 'vacation' every so often to testify at the trial."

She stood and shouted in his face. "This is complete and utter bullshit! You promised me an education and a life. This is a certificate from a trade school."

"As I recall, you've been studying while you were sequestered. And I am delivering a life to you as promised. Do I have the facts wrong? Haven't we given to you what we said we would?"

So much anger flooded her veins that Monica couldn't even formulate an argument. She lifted her leg and placed her foot on the desk, exposing her ankle and the monitor on it. "What about this?"

"We discussed it at great length. For your own protection, I'm afraid that will have to stay. If all seems to be well and you're behaving yourself, then we'll discuss removing it. You're a witness in a high-profile case. It's in the best interests of everyone involved to ensure your security…by any means necessary."

Monica seethed. She wanted to explode with rage, but leaping across the desk and punching Jon in his stupid face would only give them a reason to lock her away and lose the key. Not that this seemed much different. She would play along…for now, because she didn't have any choice. Wait them out and grab her chance. It would come. She knew it.

Monica smiled at Jon. "When do we leave?"

"There's a private plane waiting to take you to Arizona."

Chapter Six

Susan stared at the pile of papers before her. The desk she'd been given at Bunder and Associates looked as though it had been ransacked. Lisa, her boss and the sole remaining owner, had been trying to make Susan organize the jumble since the new paralegal had arrived. But she had resisted, remaining adamant that order existed among the chaos. Each time Lisa had asked her for a document or slip of paper, Susan had extracted it with the ease of a magician pulling a bouquet of silk flowers from his sleeve, thus proving the filing system worked.

She had only allowed herself this one little rebellion, because *they* were watching and listening. This wasn't paranoia. When she'd moved in to her new little bungalow, she had searched the house and found listening devices hidden in the lamps of the living room, in the picture frames of the hallway, under her bed, and in the bathroom. Another had been found, along with a tracking device similar to the one on her ankle, under the driver's seat of her car. A search of her office turned up several bugs randomly spread out around the small workspace, including one under her desk.

To combat this constant monitoring, she'd developed a regimented routine, designed to drive any listeners to the brink of insanity with boredom.

Monday through Saturday, she woke at six fifteen on the dot, showered, dressed, had breakfast, and arrived at the office at seven thirty. She ate lunch at her desk and went home at seven. She ate dinner and read or watched TV until ten then went to bed, where she often moaned as though masturbating enthusiastically, but usually just flipped through magazines until she "climaxed."

On Sunday, she had coffee alone at the little shop up the street. Then she grocery shopped and cleaned her house. She never went out and never met with friends. Lisa proved to be the only deviation from this schedule. She and her husband had a rough and volatile relationship, and she often stayed in Susan's spare bedroom. Susan had considered refusing the first time Lisa had asked her to stay over but wanted the eavesdroppers to think she'd fully immersed herself into her new life.

On the job, Susan performed her duties of paralegal with ease and diligence, taking on more and more of the responsibilities until Lisa simply rubberstamped her signature on anything Susan had worked on.

This morning had started like any other, but as she sipped her coffee, preparing to leave, a solid knock on her front door echoed through the little house. Crew Cut stood on her stoop—no smile, no real greeting of any kind. He'd stayed for less than five minutes, leaving with as much fanfare as when he'd arrived.

For the tenth time that day, Susan rubbed her ankle where the tracking device had been for the last six months. Now that she had freedom, she needed a distraction.

Susan heard the motorcycle long before she saw it pull up in front of the building. She went back to staring at the legal brief in front of her. A few minutes later, someone pushed through the door.

"Have a seat," Lisa called from behind her.

Susan didn't look up until she'd finished reading the document. "How can I help you?" she asked.

The man stood and approached the desk. His well-loved leather jacket and faded jeans covered a superbly built frame, giving him a hard-working, salt-of-the-earth tone. His dark hair had been mussed up from the bike helmet. The imperfection on this otherwise unrivaled specimen gave him an almost palpable, aw-shucks vibe that sang to her heart. He smiled, his flat, blue eyes warm and inviting, and she couldn't prevent a replying grin play across her lips.

Taking the seat opposite hers, he said, "I'm thinking about signing a lease on a piece of property, and I wanted someone to review the paperwork for me before I do. The real estate agent seemed a little..." He seemed to be searching for just the right word.

"Trustworthy and on the up and up?"

"Ummm, not *exactly* what I was thinking."

She pretended to ponder it over for a moment then offered, "Smarmy?"

"Exactly."

She crossed her legs and touched her chin. "Yes, well, we only have one real estate agent in town, and as hard as it is to believe, Mr. Cooper has been known to try and take advantage from time to time. Let me see what you've got."

He handed her a thick stack of papers. "I'm Peter Morrell." He extended his hand.

She stood. "Susan Rosenberg. Nice to meet you."

"Oh, Susan. You're the other newbie in town."

For the first time since she'd arrived in Walberg, a bolt of fear flashed through her. She paused halfway into her chair, then resumed her seat. "And how exactly do you know this?" She tried to make her voice sound interested, but not too interested.

The man laughed, the timbre both easy and relaxed. "The first place I went to when I got to town was the coffee shop, where I met the proprietor's fiancée, Mary Beth. It took Cupid all of about five minutes before she was trying to pair us up. I probably have far more insight about your coffee habits, marital and dating status"—he ticked off the points on his fingers—"your new house, your job, basically your entire life." He coughed into his hand. "It's far more than I have any right to know."

Her shoulders and back relaxed, the tension easing its way out of her body as Susan laughed with him. Mary Beth. She should have known. The local gossip and busybody had her nose in everyone else's business. "My god, that woman is presumptuous, isn't she?" she said, shaking her head. "Guess I'm not really surprised. She has been trying to match me with just about every eligible bachelor in town. Now that we have about tapped that pool, she's been hitting up random strangers."

"She is a fountain of information. Though, if my good friend Mr. Cooper is an example of the *eligible* bachelors, it's no wonder you're still single."

"Oh, I know, right?"

"They all that bad?" he asked.

"You have no idea. So nasty."

"On behalf of my gender, I apologize."

Susan laughed. "Well, thank you." She turned back to the business at hand. "Let me review the documents, but you should be just fine. Bobby simply isn't creative enough to do anything funky to the fine print of his contracts."

"That's a relief. When can I come back for them?"

She thumbed through the papers. "I should be able to get to this by late afternoon. Why don't you stop by around five? I'll have an answer for you then."

"Oh, I don't know if I can wait that long." He shook his head. "A couple from Florida is real serious 'bout this place. It'll be gone fer sure you know."

She laughed again at his impression of the smarmy little real estate agent. "Well, I wouldn't want you to miss out on a once-in-a-lifetime opportunity. I'll give it top priority and have it done by three."

"Perfect. See you then." He got up and gave her one last smile before pushing through the door. Susan admired his physique and…well, just about everything else about him through the front glass of the office. Her heart skipped and her palms sweat as he climbed on his bike and drove away.

Chapter Seven

The office of Bunder and Associates still echoed with the sound of the closing door when Lisa came out from behind her wall of papers. "Who was that?"

Lisa had become the sole owner of the law office when the last of the partners, Jesse Ridel, left three years before. Jesse, a frank, no-bullshit kinda of guy, had stayed on for two years after the previous partner cashed out his shares of stock. He had grown up in Walberg and openly admitted he hated the thought of abandoning his hometown. But Lisa thought he had really stayed because of his feelings for her. They had dated for a short time, and when she broke it off, he appeared to have never lost hope they would re-unite. He brought her coffee in the morning, took her to lunch in the afternoon, and asked her to out more times that she could count. But as more businesses boarded up their windows, romantic prospects or not, he too abandoned the town.

"Close the place down, move, and invest in something with a future." He handed her his office keys. "The town is in a shit spiral, and in a few years there'll be nothing left. Get out while you can."

"Thanks, Jesse, but I'm going to stay. Things will turn around. You'll see."

He shook his head. "You're either the world's biggest optimist or the world's worst business owner. Good luck." And with that, he had packed his bag and left.

It hadn't just been optimism about the town's prospects that kept Lisa in Walberg. Shortly after Jesse, she started dating a guy with good "husband potential," and if she left, she didn't think the man would follow her. Unlike Susan, who never seemed to want to talk about her past, Lisa spent hours reviewing the sordid details of her many failed relationships—who said what, who did what, and the underlying reasons for *everything*.

Even after marrying her boyfriend who'd offered to run away with her, Lisa stayed because she liked being in charge. With everyone gone, she could make up all the rules and didn't have to answer to anyone.

Susan checked the contract still in her hand. "Peter Morrell."

"He's really cute."

Susan waggled her finger at her boss. "Now, don't you start. I have enough trouble with the lowlifes Mary Beth is always trying to hook me up with. Jesus, what's up with that? Doesn't she have anything better to do than meddle?"

"Seriously?"

Susan sighed, shaking her head.

Lisa continued, "I'm just sayin' you could do worse. It's rare a good-looking stranger comes to town, and when it happens, you should try and make an impression. Come. Stand. Let's have a look at you."

Susan rolled her eyes but did as instructed. Her boss inspected her, examining her shoes, her outfit, and her hair. Lisa scrutinized Susan's makeup with the intensity of a biologist studying a new strain of bacteria. "It wouldn't hurt to fix yourself up a bit, you know."

"What do you mean by that?"

"Hon, you don't exactly look ready to be on *The Bachelorette*. You're pretty, maybe not as pretty as me, but still, you've got something to offer."

Susan put her hand on her hip. "Gee, thanks."

"You know what I mean. Now turn around," Lisa said.

Susan rolled her eyes but spun. Lisa started fussing with Susan's dark hair. She experimented with a braid. "Hmmm… What we really need is a brush. Go get me yours."

"I don't have one with me."

Sighing, Lisa went to a nearby metal desk, opened one of the large bottom drawers, and started rummaging through it. In the original configuration, the office had been set up for eight employees, but with just the two of them left, she had been able to allocate one of the empty workspaces to house her many beauty products.

"You know, I have these drawers for just such emergencies. You could"—Lisa stopped the search to look up—"and *should* use them."

Susan rolled her eyes again.

Lisa found the brush and started running it through her friend's tangled, twisted hair.

"Ow!" Susan yelped as Lisa worked her head over with the industrial-sized implement.

Lisa stopped to look at the brush. Black chunks and some kind of awful residue now coated its teeth. "What did you use for dye? Shoe polish?"

"I don't remember. Whatever was on sale."

Lisa threw her hands in the air. "Whatever was on sale? Really? Oh, honey, there's no way this is going to be enough. Okay, we're closing the office for a couple of hours. Time for an extreme makeover!"

"But there's so much to do." Susan gestured toward the boxes of paperwork.

"You're right. I suppose I should run it by the board first. Wonder if I can get them all together on such short notice?" She put her hand to her chin as if thinking it over then nodded, as if by sheer determination she could make it happen. "Yes. Yes, I think I can. I summarily declare the board meeting in session. All in favor of closing the office to deal with this emergency… Aye! All opposed?"

Susan raised her hand.

"Sorry, dear, you aren't a voting member. Looks like the motion has been passed by an overwhelming one hundred percent of the senior staff."

"Lisa, I can take care of myself."

"Can you? You come and go and do and wear the exact same thing every single day. I'm tired of being the only one who has any fun around here."

Susan laughed. "Your life is fun?"

"Well, honey," she said while smiling mischievously and touching Susan's nose with a finger tipped with a perfectly manicured nail, "it sure ain't boring. Look, I'm not talking about kids and a white picket fence. That guy isn't going to stick around. You saw him. He has 'short-term' written all over him. He was flirting with you, so use that. Have a little fun then cast him aside. That's all I'm sayin'."

"You think he was flirting?"

"Honey, you have been out of the game so long you forgot the rules. God, yes! He barely even glanced at me; his eyes were on you the entire time. Little more makeup, some different clothes, and a dash of charm, and he'll be putty in your hands."

Susan nodded. "It has been a while since I've gone out."

Lisa's newest employee had worked in the office for over half a year, and in that time, she had never gone out. Susan, both smart and a hell of a hard worker, epitomized the perfect employee but remained guarded about her past. She only gave the vaguest of answers when pushed for details of family and friends: deceased parents, no siblings, graduated from Phoenix High, only dated "sporadically" in college—whatever *that* meant—and no long-term relationships. It was odd the way her friend recited her history. As if she hadn't lived it but instead memorized a list of facts and dates.

Susan was the social equivalent of a court memorandum: dry and uninteresting. Maybe if the girl got a little action, she might be looser with the sordid details of her past. There had to be something, right? Besides, then they could focus on a different topic than Lisa's own…spirited love life. "See, that's what I'm saying."

"But, what if someone comes by and the office is closed?"

"Really? Other than your boyfriend, we haven't seen a client all day. Do you think there's going to be a sudden rush of lawsuits?"

Susan shook her head. "I suppose not."

"That's what I'm talking about. Now let's go." She ushered Susan out the door.

Chapter Eight

For the tenth time since returning from her makeover, Susan examined her reflection in the small mirror. Heavy powder, dark eye shadow, bright-pink lipstick, big hair. *Gawd, was Lisa's goal to make me look like a 1980s prostitute?* She nabbed a couple of her boss' cosmetic remover cloths and began to wipe the worst of the residue from her face. She glanced at the clock. Ten to three. If she started her makeup over, she'd never be able to put herself back together before Peter returned. Best to go natural rather than look like she earned extra scratch by turning tricks.

But by three thirty, he still hadn't shown up. At least his tardiness had given her time to apply a light layer of makeup. Sighing, she tucked the cursed mirror into her desk drawer and focused on the jumbles of paper before her. To keep herself busy, she caught up on some filing she'd meant to do. By four, that task had been completed, and she sat doodling on a pad.

Lisa had given Susan some parting instructions before leaving for the afternoon to give her privacy. "Lock up when you go. Have fun, and don't do anything I wouldn't do. Oh, and I expect a full report." She'd winked and headed out into the sultry afternoon heat.

Susan sighed. It wasn't as if they'd set up a date and Peter had stood her up. She'd always been the one to call the shots, making the man wait for her. She hadn't been with a lot of men, but in her former life could have—and in Tom's case, had—gotten what she wanted and only given back what she chose. Yet now she found herself wondering when and if Peter would return. She glanced at the clock again. The closer it got to five, the more likely she'd be spending her first evening of freedom alone.

At half past four, she heard the rumble of a motorcycle and dared to allow herself to hope. As he pushed through the office door, Susan pretended to be sorting a stack of documents while her heart picked up its cadence. She shot a disapproving look at his smile in an attempt to cover the effect he had on her.

"Thought we agreed on three?" she told him.

"Sorry, traffic was a bitch."

Had he no shame? Waltzing in like he didn't have a care in the world. Although, something may have come up. She would give him this pass and see if he explained it later. "Yeah, well it *is* rush hour, so next time you have an important meeting scheduled, please plan for extra travel time."

"Noted. So, I guess I missed my time slot. Can you look at your calendar and see when the next available appointment is?"

"Hmmm," she said as she flipped the pages on her all-but-empty day planner. "Wow, I'm just not seeing anything. How about next March? Yeah, no, sorry, nothing sooner. Can I put you down for, say, three? Oh, wait. It's you. Best make it four thirty." She allowed herself a grin.

"Cute. Unfortunately it means I'll miss out on the once-in-a-lifetime rental that...ummm...what's-his-face is offering me. It's probably gone by now anyway. Snatched up by the Florida couple." He sighed. "Guess I'll have to keep looking."

"That would be Bobby, and yes, your tardiness has probably cost you the bungalow. So sad. It would have been nice having someone new in town."

"Maybe it's not too late? If I buy you dinner, can you fit me in then?"

"Are you bribing me or hitting on me? Maybe I should be recording this..." She started looking through her desk drawers as though searching for a hidden a tape recorder.

"Oh, no, no, no." He held up his hands. "I'm a law-abiding citizen! I'm just seeing if there is a way to work something into your schedule. Besides, you need to eat."

"I don't know. This is a very small town, and as soon as Mary Beth gets wind of it, word will be all over."

"Yes, but she was trying to pair us together to begin with."

She folded her arms, trying to appear relaxed though an electric current zinged through her body, making her nerves tingle and dance. "True, but I think you understand the need for discretion. We are trying to run a respectable business. You are a client after all."

"Add to that, I don't want to give that old busybody the satisfaction of being right. We'd never hear the end of it. Tell you what, how about I make you dinner? I couldn't stand the thought of eating whatever roadkill the diner has on its menu. I picked up some supplies, and there's more than enough for two."

What exactly had Mary Beth said? Oh, that woman was infuriating! Susan suspected her own network of being monitored by the FBI, so she went to the little coffee shop to use the free WiFi for a modicum of privacy. But the little know-it-all waitress used the opportunity to bombard her with questions. Susan replied to these inquiries with polite, but succinct and evasive, answers.

She had wondered if Peter would ask her out but hated that Mary Beth had been the one to arrange it. Maybe she should say no just out of spite? He'd offered to make dinner too, and that alone warned her away. But then she thought of this man wielding a pan and spatula, and a little thrill ran through her body. She didn't know him, but she could handle him if need be. Ask Crew Cut. "So, there are some problems with that. The first is that I don't even know you. You could be a lunatic. A girl needs to be cautious."

The timbre of his laugh strummed delicious rhythms across her eardrums. Each pulse caressed her, sending little jolts of electric pleasure to every fiber in her body. "Well, I suppose I could be a lunatic. What does your intuition tell you?"

Even though she'd already made up her mind, she made a point of looking him over. "That you probably *are* crazy...but not dangerous."

"What's the other problem?"

"You're looking for a place to live and thus are probably staying in a hotel. The out-of-towner accommodations in this shitty little burg leave something to be desired." She touched her chin with her fingers. "And though I haven't personally stayed at any, I'm pretty certain that none of them have kitchens. I feel quite sure that you have missed out on the rental, so no luck there. And even if you *did* have the new place, did you also pick up pots, pans, plates, and so on?" She leaned across the desk and cocked her head at him. "You look like a smart man, so tell me, where exactly were you planning to cook? Really, Mr., ummm…what was your name again—Morrell—what is your agenda?"

He held up his hands. "Very well reasoned, Counselor. You've got me. I don't have an agenda, per se. I was just hoping that someone might let me use their kitchen. I really am a good cook, and I clean up after myself. You won't even know I was there."

She raised her eyebrows. "Really? And so you thought, 'Oh, small-town hospitality and all. Surely someone will invite the handsome stranger into her house.' Is that pretty much it?"

"So, handsome, huh?"

"You're avoiding the question, Mr. Morrell," she admonished while heat bloomed in her cheeks.

"Well, everyone seems so friendly, I thought surely *someone* would show some small-town hospitality. Maybe I'm wrong. Perhaps I should just go down the street, get a cat burger, lie in my hotel room, and listen to the sound of it clogging my arteries. Such is the way of things."

"Gross."

"Tell me about it. Have you seen the menu at the diner?"

She looked at him for a drawn-out minute, even though she already knew what she'd say. "So, you do the dishes?"

Chapter Nine

Monica lay in bed and tried to ignore the rowdy laughter coming from the front room. She didn't know the hour—either very late or very early. Her Mickey clock hung on a wall, too far away for the light from her reading lamp to penetrate the thick shadows hiding the mouse's circling arms. One thing she did know for certain: she hated the sound of her mom's obnoxious, drunken conversations and loathed the men she had them with.

For the millionth time, her gaze flicked from her paperback's acid-brittle pages and came to rest on the nightstand picture. In the black frame, whose plastic corners didn't quite mesh, a slim man knelt, his arm wrapped around his pig-tailed date. In the image, a twelve-year-old Monica held a glutton-sized bag of carnival cotton candy and a just-won-for-me stuffed animal of indiscernible species, while in the background a Ferris wheel forever lit up a dark summer sky. Captured by a willing passerby, the identical hazel eyes and matching, ridiculous smiles beamed from the final image, taken just hours before a teen, glancing down to adjust his radio, crossed a pair of double yellow lines.

The distracted boy had hobbled away from the carnage on route 70. But the kind man with the hazel eyes and easy laugh had left in a somber, silent ambulance, destined for his new residence at Alabaster Cove Cemetery.

Another round of raucous laughter.

Monica sighed. The inebriated couple may as well be in the same room with her for all the good the thin walls did to filter out their conversation. The man said something she could not make out, and her mom laughed loud and long. It sounded like screaming, on the verge of hysteria.

Monica wrapped the blankets tighter around her narrow shoulders and rolled onto her side, trying to focus on her book. After a while, the words pulled her in, and she found solace in the story.

She flipped the page, starting a new chapter, and had only read the first passage when something caught her attention. At first, she couldn't figure out what had interrupted her concentration, but then her mind registered the quiet. Not even the rhythmical moaning and squeaking of bedsprings that echoed through the apartment on so many nights disturbed the heavy stillness. The ominous silence caused the hairs on the back of her neck to stand on end, and she turned over, staring at the ceiling, waiting for something to happen.

She didn't have to wait long. Heavy footsteps echoed just beyond her door. They stopped. Cheap hinges squeaked, a quiet grunt, a latch clicking shut, and then the footsteps resumed. In the center of the narrow, three-door hallway hung a single bare bulb on a short, kinked wire. She imagined the man as he walked under that light, the chain Monica had to stretch on tiptoe to reach brushing his shoulder as he passed beneath it.

The light from the naked bulb spilled under her door, creating a luminescent mat that quickly faded to darkness as it misted across the grimy linoleum. Two heavy shadows that could only be a pair of very large feet broke the illumination.

Monica moved to the far side of the bed, back against the wall. She shut her eyes and willed him to move on down the hall, out of the apartment, returning to whatever rathole he'd crawled from.

It didn't work.

The cheap brass handle rattled then turned. As her door eased open, the quiet screech of unoiled hinges echoed louder than anything she'd ever heard in her life. Amplified a thousand times over by her electrified nerves, the sound screamed through her head, so loud it muffled the rapid beat of her heart.

She opened her eyes. The large man stood backlit by the bare bulb on the thin, kinked wire. The face, cast in shadows, had no distinguishing features, but she didn't need to see it to know what it looked like. She'd seen it a thousand times before in the line of empty-eyed men her mother paraded through her life. Each of them bore the same knowing, lecherous grin of a predator making an easy score with the pretty widow.

The faceless man stepped across the threshold and closed the door behind him. The quiet *snick* of the latch in the jam resonated as ominous and final as the sealing of a sarcophagus. She didn't know what he wanted, but her mind offered up a half dozen possibilities, not one of them a day at Disneyland.

Time slowed to a gelatinous pace.

She looked deep into the gloom, but no matter how hard she peered, the blur refused to focus, as if he were not a man at all, but the *idea* of a man. As if the artist of this image, unsure of how to accurately reproduce the intricate contours and angles of the human face, instead chose to leave the details vague. The man's eyes, the mere intentions of orbs, lacked definition, but nevertheless, their cruel intent was implicit as they gazed out of the dusty light, watching her.

Just as she started to wonder if maybe his perversion stopped at the observation of children as they slumbered, time slipped forward, making up for its previous sluggishness, and he appeared at the edge of her bed. He hadn't taken a single step, but the ghost now solidified and towered above her.

It invaded the small circle of light cast by her gooseneck reading lamp, and the man's features came into focus—long, greasy hair pulled back in a thin pony tail, three days' of scruff flecked gray on a weathered face. He wore a workingman's jacket, ironic since he probably hadn't had a job in years, and a pair of dirty jeans held up with an oversized Texas Rangers belt buckle. The textured gold star glimmered and flashed as it caught the weak light.

"You need to leave," Monica said, her voice no more than a whisper.

"You look just like your mom, only younger and prettier. Not all used up."

Even from a distance, she could smell the booze on his breath as he swayed ever so slightly. She tried to yell, but her dry throat refused to function properly. "Mom!" Her voice rasped in a high-pitched wheeze as though she were asthmatic.

He laughed, low and mucousy, reminding her of the way her grandfather sounded in the weeks before the throat cancer claimed him. "That dried-up cunt can't hear you. She's passed out, so *you're* going to have to play hostess. I was thinking we could be friends." Pausing, he pounded his chest with his fist and belched.

The stench of half-digested gut-rot alcohol hit her full in the face. "Real classy," Monica said. She dared to make eye contact. "Now, why don't you get the hell out?"

"You're a feisty little bitch. It's gonna be fun teaching you to respect your elders," he said, grabbing her blanket.

Nope, not Disneyland.

She reached into the narrow gap between her bed and the wall, bringing out a baseball bat with *Louisville Slugger* written in blue script along its sleek, oak-colored length. She hopped up on her mattress, eye level with the drunk. Cocking the bat over her shoulder, she said, "One last warning, asshole. Time for you to leave." Icy resilience had replaced the blood flowing in her veins.

He paused as his alcohol-addled brain processed the change. Then he shook his head and laughed again. "I just thought we could play, princess, but you're turning out to be a fun little tease. I knew it. Deep inside, you're just a whore." He seemed to sober for a moment. She could see the predator that lurked just beneath the surface when he locked eyes with her and said, "Just. Like. Mom. Now why don't you be a good girl and put the bat down? We both know how this ends." He reached for her.

Before her dad became a permanent resident of Alabaster Cove Cemetery and her mom a drunken slut, Monica had been something of a softball prodigy. With superb hand-eye coordination, uncanny reflexes, and a natural athletic ability, she almost always put the ball over the fence no matter what the opposing team threw at her.

This swing would have left her old coach breathless. Nothing had been lost in the year since she'd last stepped up to home plate.

For a split second, she stood back on the diamond, cleats on her feet, dirt-streaked uniform, the smell of fresh cut grass. Her lean muscles remembered the familiar movement—the same pull and coordination, the same wicked swoosh as the thick end of the bat arched gracefully through the air.

But the similarities ended there.

The satisfying crack of wood on leather was replaced with a blunted, branch-snapping *thwack*.

Her swing caught the 250-pound drunk just north of his left ear. He paused as if in quiet contemplation then dropped like a sack of wet cement, blood immediately pooling beneath his ruined head.

She stared wide-eyed at the small clump of scalp with a few bloody hairs sticking out that clung to the end of the bat, then dropped the vile chunk of wood, and started screaming.

Chapter Ten

Susan woke with a start and sat up. The cry that had started in the nightmare pierced the night.

"Are you okay?" Peter asked, placing his hand on her lower back. She had to force herself to not shrink away from his touch.

Wake up, girl. You are with Peter and safe. He won't hurt you. Her sweat and tears had soaked them both, and the blankets beneath.

"Nightmare," she replied and reached for the cigarettes and lighter on the nightstand. Her hands shook with such fierceness that she dropped several before Peter took them from her.

He pulled one out, placed it between her lips, and lit it. "It sounded like hell," he said. "You were talking in your sleep. I couldn't tell what you were saying, but the longer it went on, the worse it got. I thought you were angry, but then you started crying. I was about to wake you up, but you screamed and about scared the crap out of me."

"I hate that dream. I have it all the time."

"What happens in it?"

The lunar light spilled in through the window, casting shadows around the small room. In the darkness, his skin glistened with her sweat. She could tell him she couldn't remember the details or that she didn't want to talk about it. But then again, there were people listening.

The night before, Peter had taken her out on his motorcycle, driving way beyond the city limits into the desert. Her first taste of freedom had been sweet as they sailed past cacti and armadillos. She'd pounded on his jacket, yelling, "Faster, damn it, faster!" He had indulged her, until the wind and the vibrating engine were the only things that existed in the universe.

After they'd come back to her place, she'd put on a good show, laughing and chatting, then later she'd been very vocal in her passions. Not that all of it had been for display. She felt better, freer than she had in years. Plus, Peter had certain skills and talents that she appreciated.

She'd imagined Crew Cut listening to their antics, jotting down notes in a large yellow legal pad, which he would then turn over to Jon. The little prick would file a report full of her moans and gasps of pleasure. But she'd been doing that for months; if they really wanted something to talk about, she'd give it to them.

"I killed a man," she said.

"Ummm, what? Really?" Peter appeared startled. "What happened?"

"That's what the dream is about." The sadness still haunted her. After all these years, it still gnawed on her bones as if it had happened the day before. "After my dad died, mom decided to drink the county dry and screw every

85

lowlife on the western seaboard. One night, she passed out, and the bastard she'd brought home decided to pay me a little visit."

"Oh shit."

"Yeah. I was only twelve, but the perv wanted some more action. I disagreed and sent him to the big bar in the sky."

"How'd you do that?" Peter asked.

"He was drunk, and I had gotten a Louisville Slugger for my eleventh birthday. He came at me, and I nailed him instead of the other way around." Did Crew Cut already know all of this? He had access to her files, so probably. Still, it might sound a little different coming from her instead of the pages of a police report.

"So the dream isn't a dream at all, but memories of that night."

"Yes. I spent a bit of time in Juvie. I was found innocent of any wrongdoing, and they released me after my mom kinda got her shit together, but I never forgave her. After that, she did her thing, I did mine. You know how it is when you can be together but not really."

Peter nodded. Something in his eyes—a sadness—told her he might understand.

"She didn't show up when I graduated high school, top of my class, I might add." She spat the words as if that could remove their bitter tang.

"Congrats. That's not easy in the best of circumstances. Sorry about your mom, though."

"Yeah, I wasn't surprised or really disappointed. My best friend, Angel, her mom more or less adopted me. They were the only ones that I cared were there."

"Still, it had to sting."

"Well, that's life, isn't it? Things don't always work out the way you want." Monica traced the deep pattern of scars on Peter's leg with her fingertip. "What about you? Why are you here?"

"Since my wife left me, I've been a bit lost. I'd planned out my life with her, kids, a house, a dog, the whole American dream. But plans are just that, and it turned out she had something different in mind...with someone different. So after she left, I finished my stint in the military with a small vacation over in sand land. I dedicated my future to the Marines, but my career got cut short when I got that parting gift from the grateful people of the Afghanistan nation."

She frowned. "That's not really an answer."

"Fair enough, Counselor. After I recovered, I got lost. I don't have any family. My folks are gone, and most of the people I knew that were my friends before the divorce, sort of drifted away. When you split up, it gets a bit awkward for them. They have to choose sides, and I guess I was the less popular option. I've only had a few people in my life I truly cared about; the first was my wife."

"And the second?" she prompted.

"My brother. He was my absolute best friend."

"Was? What happened? Can you go stay with him?"

"He's dead."

She knew loss and longing better than anyone, so she didn't say anything, letting him gather his thoughts.

"So anyway, after I finished physical therapy, I tried to figure out where I was going and what I wanted to do with my life. I got a little money because of my injury, not a lot, just enough to get by for a while. Started traveling the country—Chicago, D.C., New York, California, all the big exciting places everyone always says they want to see—but so far, no place has struck me as home. So, here I am, trying the opposite of everything else."

"The opposite being small, remote, and decrepit, with no hope of a job or future?"

He laughed. "Suppose so. I actually didn't know anything about the town before I got here. I was driving and found this wide patch in the road. My bike took the off ramp, and here I am. My life has been turned upside down so many times I don't know which way is which. So, I thought, 'Why the hell not?'" He fell silent for a while, then asked, "So you graduated top of your high school class, then followed your dreams to be a lawyer?"

A stab of anger pierced her heart. Not at Peter, who also seemed to be one of life's misfits, but at Crew Cut, Granite, Driver, Jon, Bad Facelift, Laven—all of the bastards that had taken her life from her. She'd told them the truth and cooperated, but they had presumed her guilty and given her no chance to prove otherwise. The FBI had locked her up and treated her like a criminal trying to skirt her punishment, while they got their witness. They always seemed to be one step ahead… Only, perhaps not. Maybe she could finally get a leg up, make them pay and hurt, if only a little. Crew Cut needed something to put in his report, so she'd give him something that would really make his life interesting. "Well, that was the plan."

Peter hesitated. "But it didn't work out? Looks to me like you're living the dream."

"Well, looks can be deceiving. I went to NYU on a full scholarship and was all set to be a big shot lawyer. But then I overheard a conversation I wasn't supposed to." She envisioned Crew Cut sitting up straight, frantic to call his boss. The image gave her a glimmer of glee, and she just managed to contain the laughter threatening to burst from her lips.

"What kind of conversation? Who was it?"

"It was between a drug lord and his hitman. Maybe you've heard of the Laven Michaels case?"

"Oh yeah. Who hasn't? It's all over the headlines and on every news channel. They have some star witness though that doesn't seem to be enough because, by all accounts, the case seems to be falling apart." He looked closer at her in the weak light. "Wait. Is that you? You're the witness?"

"One and the same. They wanted to 'protect' me, so here I am in witness protection, though I think witness prison is a better name for it. They locked me away, using me when they wanted and forgetting about me the rest of the time."

"So what happens when the case is over?"

"Well, they promised me an education and that I could continue with my life. Instead they gave me a certificate of paralegal, stole my identity, and sent me away to this little shithole of a town."

She turned toward the hidden microphone so that it would pick up her words clearly. "There's this bastard, Hale Lenski, who is supposed to be protecting me, but basically he's a demented dictator with all the charm of asparagus. I call him Crew Cut, because he looks like he has his hair done at a lawn and garden store. He's locked me up, and jumps on my ass the second I do anything, so I'm more prisoner than the guy they're trying to convict. Other than Crew's remarkable lack of personality and snow-shovel good looks, there isn't anything attractive about him."

"No love lost there," Peter remarked. "So, they stole your identity?"

She turned back to him. "Witness Protection, baby."

"Wait, so you're saying your name isn't Susan?"

"Nope. Monica Sable, star witness and slave to the system." She held out her hand. Peter looked stunned as he took it, and they did an awkward lying-in-bed-naked shake. "Pleased to re-meet you." Pleasure rippled through her body at the thought of Crew Cut and the galley shitting monkeys and making angry phone calls.

"Wow. I don't know what to say to that," Peter said.

She laughed. "You don't *say* anything." She rolled over on top of him. She kissed him, the smoke in her lungs passing to his. She took another hit off of her cigarette then stamped it out in the tray. They shared this last breath from a dead cancer stick as Monica ground her hips against his. She adjusted her pelvis, and he slid inside of her. She lay down flat against his chest as she continued to rotate her hips, setting a slow and deliberate tempo.

As they moved together, their rhythm and intensity increasing, she let out little moans and gasps. As she neared orgasm, she sat up, leaned back, and put her hands on his chest, riding him harder. A cry emanated from deep in her throat as her release went on and on, and she felt him push up as he followed her.

She lay down on top on top of him, not releasing him but instead holding tight. She drifted off to sleep with a smile in the stuffy little room.

☆☆☆☆

The next morning, Susan woke at her normal time, donned her robe, and padded barefoot to the kitchen. A half hour later, she returned to her room with two steaming mugs of coffee and a small plate of cinnamon rolls from a tube she'd found in back of the fridge.

"Good morning," Peter said, sitting up.

"Good morning to you. Hungry?" she asked, irritated he hadn't gotten dressed and, in fact, continued to linger in her bed.

"Starving."

She handed him the coffee, a pastry, and a napkin.

"Thank you." He took a sip.

She nodded, disrobed, and started pulling on her office clothes. *Take the clue, boy. Time for you to go.*

He watched her for a minute. "What's on your agenda for the day?" he asked around a mouthful of pastry.

"I need to go to work."

"You work on Saturdays?"

Crap. Duh. It's Saturday. Okay, no problem. That makes perfect sense; we've got a busy office and lots of pressing matters. "Yep, and though I've had fun, you need to go. Here." She tossed the stack of documents she'd reviewed for him onto the bed.

"Oh, sure. No problem."

"There are a few notes you should pay attention to, but overall it looks good. May I give you a little advice?"

He took another sip of his coffee. "Sure."

"Leave town."

"Pardon?"

"Leave. This place is a cesspool. The town is dying. The economy's in the toilet. There're no jobs and no prospects. It would be impossible to build a life here. Save your money and save yourself. Get out before it drags you down and sucks out your soul."

"What if one has a romantic prospect?" He gave her his warm and inviting smile.

She'd considered it. Thought about it at great lengths while the rolls baked and the coffee brewed. Thought about asking him to take her for another ride on his bike, but this time, they would leave town and never come back. But no matter how much she'd laughed at his jokes and gave herself to him in bed, she couldn't see them sharing a life on the run. He had a reserved, rule-following nature about him, that wouldn't meld itself to life with a fugitive. She'd had her fun, given the FBI the finger, but now she needed to seriously consider getting out of town, and she couldn't do that with this man around.

"No. That's not going to happen. I had fun, but this was a one-time deal. I have to stay here, but you shouldn't."

To his credit, Peter's expression did not falter when he nodded. "Okay, I understand. I'll get dressed and get out of your hair." He stood and pulled on his clothes. Finishing his coffee, he headed toward the front of the house.

She opened the door for him, grateful to be almost done. "Thank you. I had a nice time."

He turned on the stoop, touched her chin, and kissed her gently. "Thank you. If I don't see you again, I hope things work out. I really do."

Goosebumps broke out on her body at the touch of his lips and the earnest pain in his eyes. The thought of asking him back into the house flashed through her mind. Something about the moment had touched her deeper than she could have ever imagined, and she longed to talk to him about it. She wanted to know what he felt at that instant. But before she could even consider formulating the words, he donned his helmet, climbed on his bike, and drove away.

She watched him until he dwindled from view.

Chapter Eleven

The Monday after Peter Morrell stopped by their office, Lisa Bunder arrived at work anxious for date-night details. Susan filled her in on her clandestine evening with the dark stranger. Lisa's mouth literally dropped open in astonishment at Peter's abrupt departure. She'd always known her friend to be cool and levelheaded, but she couldn't have predicted such an outcome simply because she couldn't fathom herself ever being so bold.

"Wow. Yeah, you're right to ask him to leave. But wow… Maybe that's for the best. You don't need the complication of a man in your life." Lisa shook her head. "They ain't nothing but trouble. Speakin' of which, since you're alone again, I was wondering if I could stay for a spell? Me 'n' Jeb been fightin'. Just 'til things blow over."

"Yes, of course," Susan said, as she always did.

"We've just been going through a rough patch." Lisa began a long, rattling monologue on dramatic events that would have rivaled the best of daytime television.

☆☆☆☆

While the two women filed briefs and discussed the intricacies of Lisa's marriage at the office, a white telephone company van pulled up in front of Susan's little bungalow.

No one had heard of this particular company before, but later witnesses would remark this unworthy of note. In the depressed economy, even the utility companies struggled and often changed hands.

The man wore blue coveralls, work boots, a baseball cap, and a utility belt. Descriptions of him varied from five-and-a-half feet with blond hair to over six-feet tall with a long, shaggy mane and a mustache. No one got a good look at his face, and after several frustrating attempts, the sketch artist gave up, exasperated.

He carried a clipboard and a small toolbox when he walked around Susan's humble dwelling to the point where the phone line veered off the main cable and met the side of the house. He disappeared around back, perhaps to go do some technical telephone maintenance task. A few minutes later, he put his tools back in the truck, wrote something on the clipboard, climbed into the driver's seat, and drove off.

No record could be found in the local telephone company's system of any maintenance ordered for that address, or any other in the area.

☆☆☆☆

Long after the sun had set, Lisa locked the office doors, still prattling about her husband and their life. How, Susan wondered, could there be *so* much to say? She tuned out, thinking instead about a simple dinner and a hot bath. She really wanted some alone time. It had been an emotional few days, but she could see no quiet moments in her near future.

Susan placed her hand on Lisa's shoulder, interrupting the monotonous monologue. "I'm going to run to the store and pick up something to eat. Need anything?"

Lisa halted mid-sentence and seemed to think it over. "No thank you, love. I'm going home." By "home," Susan's boss did not mean the one she shared with her husband. "I'll read a book and drink myself to sleep."

☆☆☆☆

Lisa drove the four miles to Susan's modest, single-story house. She parked on the street and sat in her car listening to a sappy love song and mooning over her marriage to Jeb.

They'd had a rocky time of it lately, and she had started to wonder if they would "make it." Having Susan as a friend had been a godsend. She loved how the girl listened—almost never giving advice—and helped her pick through the details, ad nauseam, of the fights with her husband. Their arguments had become far too frequent.

Despite encouraging Susan to form a relationship with the dark-haired stranger, Lisa had been more than a little relieved when she found out he'd left town. She had encouraged Susan to have a fling, but it hadn't taken Lisa long to realize she needed her friend single and attentive, not tied down with obligations and a life of her own.

✩✩✩✩

FBI Investigative Report
Entry #0908.3
Reporting Agent: Hale Lenski

Subject, Susan Rosenberg, remained at work until approximately 6:43 PM when she left in her Subaru wagon, heading east on Desert Scape Avenue (see town map, entry #19). She entered the grocery store, "Quickie Mart," where she purchased beer: Michelob Light; cheese: cheddar; and a loaf of day-old French bread. At 7:05 PM, according to an interview with cashier, Erin Trusk, she exited the store. Presumably driving home.

✩✩✩✩

When Susan pulled into the driveway, Lisa got out of her car and headed across the street. Lisa often sat and listened to music while thinking about her wreck of a home life, so it didn't surprise Susan to see her boss hadn't yet made it into the house.

Susan got out a bag of groceries in one hand and the six pack in the other.

Lisa unlocked the front door then turned. "Hey, be a dear and grab the files from the back of my car." She tossed the keys.

Having both hands full, Susan had no way to catch them, and they slid under the Subaru.

"Oops, sorry," Lisa said but made no move to help.

Susan swore under breath. Lisa could not transition between personal and professional, telling Susan what to do and making her run errands—getting the files from the damned car for instance—as though they were still at the office.

Sighing, Susan set the groceries down and knelt behind her car, reaching under it for the keys. Her fingers searched and came up empty, so she crawled further under the Subaru until only her feet stuck out. Finally, her fingers grasped the fob to Lisa's Audi.

"Gotcha!" she said as the front door of her house clicked shut.

☆☆☆☆

Lisa leaned her back against the door, pausing to think about the cold beers Susan had pulled from the car. She slipped off her shoes and started down the shadowed hallway, nylon-clad feet whispering on cool linoleum. She had taken only a few steps, the odd smell just registering in her exhausted mind, when she flipped on the entryway light.

A small spark in the cheap, ancient chandelier ignited the gas that had been filling the house all afternoon. The resulting explosion vaporized the skin from Lisa's body as it slammed her back into the closed front door. A wave of heat from the trailing fireball liquefied the underlying flesh then began to turn her bones to ash. Later, there wouldn't be enough of her left for a DNA sample, though agents wouldn't believe they needed one to make a positive ID.

The blast lifted the little bungalow's roof, intact. It hovered a few inches above the studs for several seconds, riding a wave of heat and flame. When it came back down, it crushed the already weakened and crumbling walls, and the entire structure collapsed in on itself.

The force of the explosion shoved the car to the bottom of its struts, driving Susan into the concrete, almost crushing her. The oppressive weight of the vehicle felt as though someone had dropped a piano on her back. After the initial blast, the weight of the car lessened, and Susan wriggled out from underneath it.

She stood staring in disbelief at the destruction of the place she had, begrudgingly, called home. She remained paralyzed for a full minute by the overwhelming sadness that her friend had been inside when the house blew up.

She shook her head, trying to clear the buzzing in her ears. The sound from the blast had almost deafened her. What rang clear: someone had just tried to kill her. If she didn't get out of there, another message like it would arrive in short order. This time, she doubted they'd miss.

This was what the FBI had been trying to protect her from.

She looked at the hulk of burned out metal that, up until a few minutes ago, had been a Subaru wagon. The car bore the brunt of the violence, becoming her unlikely savior. If she hadn't been under it, she would have been killed. Grateful for the little Japanese vehicle that had protected her, she nevertheless had been left without a means of escape.

She tried to look around, but the fumes and intense heat burned her eyes, making them itch. When she tried to rub them, she almost jabbed herself in the face. The key. She still had Lisa's key. Monica ran across the street, climbed into the Audi, and drove back to the office.

Fearful to turn on the lights and draw attention to herself, she picked her way to the rear corner where Lisa kept the safe. Her hands shook so hard she mis-entered the combination twice. Before trying again, she forced herself to take a deep breath, willing her rattled nerves to settle down. Three incorrect entries and the safety mechanism disabled the keypad for fifteen minutes. She'd be forced to wait.

She punched in the ten-digit code again. Relief flooded through her as the little indicator light changed from red to green. Monica opened the door and stuffed the cash, company checkbook, and company credit card into her purse. She closed the safe and locked the front door before climbing back into the Audi and speeding off into the night.

FBI Investigative Report
Entry #0908.7
Reporting Agent: Hale Lenski

Fire crews arrived on the scene but were unable to prevent the complete loss of Ms. Rosenberg's house. They sprayed down the surrounding terrain in an attempt to keep the fire from spreading to other dwellings. Efforts that proved largely successful, although a nearby abandoned structure to the east received minimal smoke damage.

Fire chief Ryan Zyresk, of the Walberg Volunteer Fire Department, had been cited as saying, "There was no need to waste valuable resources trying to save something that clearly isn't worth the effort." The blaze seemed to be started by a gas leak, though it is unclear what triggered the explosion itself.

FBI Investigative Report
Entry #0908.7.2
Reporting Agent: Hale Lenski

It is possible that Lisa Bunder may be a witness. Interviews with members of the community, including Mary Beth Sanders, reported that Ms. Bunder and her husband were having marital disputes and had been witnessed in "screaming matches" on their front lawn. It is the opinion of said witness that Ms. Bunder saw the explosion and "simply drove away." Attempts to reach Ms. Bunder have been unsuccessful. Ms. Bunder is not considered a suspect at this time.

FBI Inquisition Investigation
Entry #8812.7
Official Disciplinary Action

...it is therefore found that Hale Lenski is guilty of egregious breaches of protocol and procedure, resulting in the loss of a valuable and key resource. He has been formally held responsible for failure to perform his basic duties. This failure resulted in the death of the person under his protection. He is to receive a suspension from duties for no less than one year, during which time a formal hearing will be held to determine if he can be reinstated or will be permanently dismissed...

PART 2

Chapter Twelve

FOUR DAYS EARLIER

The phone rang at just past six in the evening. Angel Humbolt sat eating dinner, alone. Again. "Thanksgiving Feast" from the freezer and *Wheel of Fortune* on the boob tube. This dinner-and-movie combo had become such a regular part of her routine that she now associated Vanna White and Pat Sajak's awful toupee—could that possibly be his real hair?—with watery gravy and the smell of scorched aluminum.

The faded blue wall phone rang a second time. She debated: talk to her mother who, for whatever reason, always called during dinner, or rate the intelligence of the game show contestants—were they smart enough to figure out *Declaration of Independence* was the answer to the puzzle?

"W," Nancy, the perky homemaker from Philadelphia, said.

Nope, apparently not. Loser. Seriously, where did they find these yahoos? She would *rock* this show if she were on it.

Six rings now. Only two more before the answering machine did the job for her.

What to do, what to do?

Angel didn't have to actually talk to her mother, whom she loved more than life itself but who drove her completely bonkers, to be able to tick off everything that would be discussed, point by agonizing point. Each of these conversations made her feel as though she had cracked open her diary and re-read the worst, most depressing chapters over and over and over.

*Are you seeing anyone? Have you considered giving up the grocery job for school and getting a real job like your brother? You know he just got promoted (again) to x—*fill in the blank of Richard's astounding career. *I'm not getting any younger, and neither are you, for that matter. Tick, tick, tick, dear. I would love to meet my only daughter's children before I go spend eternity with the good Lord in Heaven.*

Emphasis on the word "daughter's" since Prince Richard had already given their mother three "little cherubs."

Gag.

She had no new answers to give during these inquisitions, and none appeared to be forthcoming in the near future.

Her mom, an expert manipulator, knew every inch of Angel's mental blueprint. With the precision of a reverse bomb squad technician, she dexterously used her knowledge to cross the wires of doubt and push the buttons of guilt, twisting her daughter's thoughts and emotions until Angel thought she would scream in frustration.

On the rare occasions when Angel called her out on these devious bids at mental domination, Mrs. Humbolt would deny any knowledge of wrongdoing. "I am just expressing my concerns because I love you, honey, and I don't want to see you waste your life."

Jab. Twist. Parry.

The bitch about it, the thing that just sucked so bad, was her mom had a point. Angel, who'd just finished her shift at the market, also wondered how long this position could be referred to as "temporary."

Against her parents' objections, Angel had dropped out of college. It just wasn't her thing. She'd needed time to find herself; plus, she had plans. Big plans.

This part of her life should have been a gateway to something more fulfilling, a transition to a promising career, a family, and the whole nuclear package. But almost five years later, she still worked at the same crappy place, lived in the same dumpy apartment, hung with the same loser friends, and hadn't done a thing toward achieving her life goals. Of course, before she could go about achieving her goals, she first had to figure out what said goals were.

Okay, maybe she didn't have plans—not quite. More accurately she had plans to have plans. Maybe she just needed to meet someone to get her life on track?

She looked at the phone again. Sighing, she reached for it. "Hello."

"Hi, my name is Tom Phillips. I'm looking for Monica." The male voice, so not what she'd expected, stunned her, making it necessary for her to go back and replay his words in her mind.

Angel stiffened. "Monica isn't here. Who did you say you were?"

"Tom. Tom Phillips." He hesitated. "I went to NYU with her, and she stayed in the spare bedroom of my apartment. Well, at least she did until she disappeared. When we wrapped up the fall semester, I figured she'd transferred or dropped. People do that. Get burned out and quit, or change to a school that's less...academically stressful. Though, she had straight A's, and really, school didn't seem very difficult for her...so that doesn't make sense..."

He took a deep breath before continuing, "Anyway, I thought, okay, maybe she's just avoiding *me*. It's a big school and all. But there are a couple of required courses that are only offered this spring, so I figured I'd at least get to see her then. But class started last week and so far no Monica. I checked around, and no one's seen her in months. When she moved out, she left a note saying she'd found somewhere else to stay. Thanks and goodbye. That's it. No forwarding address, no nothing. But it's less like she moved on and more like she dropped off the face of the Earth." He sounded perplexed. "I can't find her anywhere, and, well, she told me you were her best friend, and I was wondering if you could help me."

The hopeful, optimistic timbre in his words seemed genuine, but Angel would never just turn her friend over like that. Not to a stranger; not on the phone; not to anyone. "Look, it's Tom, right? I don't know where she is. I haven't seen her in a long time. So, I really can't help you."

"Oh," he said, the hope deflating from his voice like air escaping from a ruptured tire. "So you have no idea what happened?"

"No."

"Maybe if we put our heads together we can figure this out? Somebody must be in contact with her, right?" He paused for a few heartbeats. "I'm...I'm just worried something happened."

"Why are you looking for her?" Tom hesitated, and it dawned on Angel why he'd called. "Oh. My. God. You're a freaking stalker! Damn, I told her she'd meet crazies in New York. Look psycho boy"—her voice had gone icy—"you'd better back the hell off."

"No. No. No, nothing like that. I guess I can see your point. But it isn't like that at all."

He hadn't convinced her, but when she spoke again, she let her voice thaw, only a little. She wanted the chilly undertone to convey her skepticism. "Start talking, NYU boy, you have two minutes before I call the cops."

She needed to sound in charge of the situation, but if Tom knew anything about the town, he could call her bluff. Stoner Sheriff Austin wouldn't do shit about a phone call.

"Look, I can be accused of being a lot of things, a dumb-ass weakling, a moron, whatever, but not a stalker. We had some classes together, and like I said, she lived with me. We, you know, hung out, and I wanted to ask her out, but the girl was seriously heads down. I was pretty sure she would tell me no. She wasn't interested in going to parties, or having fun, or any of the things you're supposed to do in college. So I took the long approach, you know, being friends and getting to know her, hoping for my chance. She would spend time with me because I'm straight A's too, and, well, like I said, we occasionally hung out if you catch my drift. At first, I think she only tolerated my company because she needed someplace to stay. After some late nights though, her defenses came down, and we started talking. *Really* talking. She told me about her childhood and what happened with her folks. She was warming up to me, and we were getting close. You know what I mean?"

Angel did. In fact, she had talked to her friend at great length about how hard Monica had been working at keeping people away. Angel had tried, in vain, to get her to cool it a bit and have a little fun. But she might as well have been speaking Martian for all the good it did.

She didn't answer, but she also didn't hang up. Tom must have taken that as a sign of encouragement. "So anyway, I could tell her anything, and she didn't pass judgment. I have come from, oh, let's just say, a rough childhood too, and she totally got me. Some of the stories she told me about her life..." He trailed off. "Seriously, taking down that slime in L.A. with the Louisville Slugger? I had one of those growing up, but...damn."

A tear welled up in Angel's eye. "Yeah," she said, her voice not much more than a whisper, "she had a rough go of it for a while."

"I know, and somewhere in all that time I was spilling my guts, I fell for her. It's way more than just sex. We were making love, you know? Don't know when exactly I developed feelings for her, but it kinda surprised me. Maybe I'm just a sucker for hard-luck cases? After she was gone, there was this hole in my life, and I knew that I would regret it if I didn't take the chance and tell her."

"I don't think she's ready to settle down, Tom."

"Oh, I know. Believe me. I think she has some serious demons, but I also think I understand where her mind is. Well, at least where it was before she disappeared." He didn't say anything for a minute.

Angel thought she heard a hitch in his breath, and over the line, her heart went out to him.

Finally, he continued, "Look, I don't know what's going on. She just vanished. She was there one day and gone the next. Just like that, packed up her stuff and disappeared without a word. She didn't say why or where she was going. I have to at least know if something happened. Maybe something with her mom? I have to make sure she's okay."

"You really care about her, don't you?"

"Yes. I miss her, and I want to see her. But I at least need to know she's okay."

"She's fine," Angel admitted in a whisper. "Something happened. I can't tell you what or where she is, but I can pass on whatever message you want."

"Oh, thank god!" The relief in his voice palpable. "But what's with all the secrecy?"

"Sorry, that's just the way it is."

"Well, I suppose if I don't have any other choice."

"What?"

"I really want to have the chance to tell her myself. I should have told her already."

110

Angel remained quiet as she debated, then came to a decision. "All right, look, something happened in New York, and she had to leave. I can't tell you the details; I swore I wouldn't. I won't give you her phone number, but I can't see the harm in giving you her email. You send her a message, and she can call you if she wants. That's the best I can do."

He let out a huge, relieved breath. "That would be fantastic."

"Okay, hold on, her address is totally bizarre." She fumbled through her purse until she found the old and creased slip of paper. "Here it is." Angel read off the random letters and numbers.

"Okay, let me make sure I've got it." He read it back to her.

She corrected him, "'Zd' not 'dz.'"

"Thank you so much! You're an amazing friend."

She hung up, guilt tugging on her heart for betraying Monica's trust. Angel had promised, sworn she would never under any circumstances give out that email address.

But the situation justified her actions, didn't it? How could Monica know that someone like Tom, who sounded amazing, wanted to be part of her life? Angel could sense his kindness and genuine heart. If Mon trusted him with her deepest darkest secrets, Angel could too.

She had done the right thing; she could feel it in her bones. Mon could be mad at her now, then later ask her to be a bridesmaid when the two of them got married.

Angel smiled.

Chapter Thirteen

At a secluded table in an outdoor cafe, hundreds of miles from New York University, Sam Bradford, a.k.a. Tom Phillips, smiled as he disconnected the call.

Got ya.

After the months of tedium, monotonous gathering of information, and tracking her movements, he finally had his first real lead. Score one for the *Agency's Rules*. In this case:

Rule #11:
Do your homework; always know more than everyone else.

Cunning and intelligence are no substitute for diligence and hard work. The smartest individual can be made impotent by ignorance. The most feebleminded can persevere over stronger, better-equipped foes, given enough—and the correct application—of the right information. Know all about those around you and rule them unequivocally.

—122 Rules of Psychology

He had run into dead end after dead end. Finally, he stopped and envisioned himself back at The Agency. During his training, when he found himself floundering, his primary instructor, Dr. Wergent, would admonish, "Samuel, stop. What you are doing is not working. Do you not see that? The Rules. What do the Rules tell you?"

It had been almost a decade, but he still remembered the practical lessons of drifting through society as a ghost: obtaining fake documents, avoiding the police, leaving no trace of himself wherever he went. But his core curriculum had focused on the human psyche.

He had taken courses on the physiology of the body; humans were, after all, kaleidoscopes of chemical and electrical chain reactions. But the lessons on the inner workings of the mind and techniques for making human beings tick had been the most fascinating. For all people's complexities, and activists shouting about the diverse and unique needs of the individual, humans as a species acted and reacted the same given a particular set of circumstances.

The gray matter at The Agency had boiled it down to what they called the *122 Rules of Human Psychology*. In every feasible situation, Dr. Wergent had shown Sam the proper execution of these rules. They *always* applied. After months of practice, Sam had become a maestro and could strum the emotional and mental chords of everyone around him.

He'd read the police reports on Monica and perused her impressive college transcripts—straight A's, well on her way to a law degree. No partying, few friends, no dating, no indication of any social life at all. A true nose-to-the-grindstone introvert.

Sam had visited NYU, following her movements as he believed them to be on her final days in college. He'd struck up conversations with people that would have been in her classes, claiming he had recently divorced and wanted a second career and a second chance at life. What was campus life like? How hard was the curriculum? He had little to no money to live on thanks to the recent departure of his ex-wife—the bitch got everything except his underwear and his dignity; how would someone live on next to nothing? One thing lead to another and Sam met a man, Tom Philips, who just happened to have a spare room recently come available.

Though Tom proved to be useful, it had been Angel—best friend since childhood and the one constant in the hell that had been Monica's life—that proved to be the key to unlocking the missing girl's whereabouts.

He could never force Angel to betray her friend's trust. But given all the raw material, a simple yet believable tale of love and hardship would make the oyster open up and hand over its pearl.

The story.

First, create a character. In this case, cast one Sam Bradford as love-struck Tom Phillips, the underdog, someone to root for. A good story always blends the perfect balance of emotion, truth, and "fake but believable" crap.

Rule #1:
Keep it simple.

Complex stories, ones full of intricacies, are not maintainable. It simply isn't possible to keep a copious amount of details consistent. However, if the story is too vague, it isn't relatable. Told with just the right blend of emotion, passion, and angst, people will write the story for themselves, filling in much of the details on their own.

—*122 Rules of Psychology*

Second, keep it short. As a manipulative storyteller, Sam knew better than to give the receiver time to think things through and process the details. Had he lingered, had Angel talked to him longer, she very possibly would have smelled a rat. For instance, she forgot to ask him how he had come by her unlisted phone number.

Get in, get what's needed, and get out.

Sam had honed and perfected his craft to hit that sweet spot between too much and not enough. He could get anyone to write then buy their own tale, paying a premium for it in the process.

What had he told Angel, really? She'd painted the nooks and crannies in his rough sketch, adding splashes of color with the palette of her imagination and dreams for her friend's happily ever after. Sam could envision her still working on the canvas, adding in nuances such as wedding rings and rug rats.

People like Angel made his job child's play. He had the training, but his occupation mostly required patience and the ability to get the details right.

Most people wandered through life creating a path as wide and easy to follow as a two-lane blacktop. Those that "went underground" still left a trail, but theirs tended to be subtle—more like following a series of stepping-stones through the forest. Some stones sat right on top and were easy to spot, while others were covered with moss and lichen. Still others lied buried just beneath the surface of the Earth, requiring some digging and a bit of sweat to uncover.

But the path always existed. Always. Sam didn't rush the process, uncovering one stone at a time to expose his target. Every single time.

Since Angel had been so kind as to provide an email address to "Tom," Sam had his next stone. He turned his attention to the Agency-issued smartphone.

It looked like a million others of a similar model, yet every circuit and bit had been reworked, modified, or replaced, making it anything but ordinary. Unlike cell users the world over who had to worry about such trivialities as coverage, dropped calls, and the other pitfalls of being a major network customer, this one *always* worked. An encrypted satellite link ensured a consistent four-bar signal.

The camera rivaled that of the best Nikon on the market, and an advanced embedded solar cell meant it never needed to be charged.

The phone's search capabilities, rooting out then filtering information, made the ones provided by Apple and Google look like they had been designed by ungifted school children. He could type in a name or take a picture and zip it off to the central computer. Within minutes of sending in a query, the system returned a complete dossier including DMV and phone records, credit card and banking transactions, personal history, and medical records. Anything.

Yes, there's an app for that.

Walls of security protected most of these systems, but nothing prevented The Agency from gaining access to confidential information. For them, limits did not exist. No boundaries or security could keep them out. Nothing was ever unavailable. The Agency had quietly embedded resources in all corporations and branches of the government, gaining access to the most sensitive and classified areas.

Sam opened a hidden menu and entered the email address Angel had given him. A minute later, the little device beeped. He studied the screen and frowned. The road to becoming the third-ranking officer in a drug cartel would be fraught with scrapes with the law. He'd expected a major blemish—drug dealing, sex trafficking, stealing. But other than the incident as a kid and a single, small-quantity drug possession charge, she appeared—at least on paper—to be on the straight and narrow. Something didn't add up.

He entered a number he knew by heart. It rang once, then a terse but familiar voice said, "Josha."

Sam gave a thirty second update on his progress.

After he finished, the man replied, "Good. Do you need anything?"

Standard operating procedures prevented him from querying further. *Do as you're told, and don't ask questions.*

In the ten-plus years he'd been working for The Agency, he'd never broken protocol. Never asked the questions that lingered and plagued him. He knew that sort of information—in this case, the missing link to becoming a major player in a crime organization—sometimes stopped well above his pay grade for reasons he couldn't be privy to. The system had been built by those who had more insight, more knowledge, and served a higher purpose than he did. He understood and accepted his position within the hierarchy. The best he could do was check in for updates. "I want to verify."

Josha sighed, a hint of exasperation in his voice. "Hold on." Sam waited while his handler did whatever he did. "There've been no updates, retractions, or holds. We are still green. Find and eliminate. Now, I'm going to ask you again: Do you need anything?"

"No."

"Good." The phone went dead.

Chapter Fourteen

The morning after his call to Angel, Sam received the text he'd been waiting for. He put on his black leather jacket, collected his few things from the dingy hotel room where he'd been staying, checked out, and mounted his bike.

As a professional vagabond, he only travelled with the bare minimum. He fit his clothes, computer, toiletries, and essentials in the Triumph's black travel bags. The Agency offered to fly him, but he preferred to take the bike. He relished the monotonous vibration of the motorcycle's deep-throated engine and the feel of rubber on blacktop. Riding kept the central cortex occupied while giving the rest of his mind the freedom to wander and ponder.

He had a small apartment back in California but hadn't seen it in months. The 1200 square foot flat had become another vacant address for the likes of Comcast and J.C. Penney to pander to. Had the time arrived for him to give it up? A P.O. Box would be a lot cheaper. Not that he needed the money. He almost never spent any of the generous wages provided by The Agency, and the job kept him traveling and busy—exactly the way he preferred it.

Sam had set up a tracer on the email address. As soon as someone, presumably Monica, had logged onto the account, the little app set up shop on her computer. It sent him her usernames, passwords, and physical location plus allowed him full control of her system.

He entered the address into Pocahontas, the GPS on his bike, whose female voice did not in the slightest resemble that of the Native American she had been named for. She told him to head north on I-84 for 15 miles, then east on I-405 for 885 miles. If he bent a few speed laws, he could make it by nightfall.

His destination, the little city of Walberg, sat near the edge of Arizona's southern border. Why hide out in a tiny town where Monica would stick out like a man with gigantism at a midget festival? She should have faded into the anonymity of a large city.

Perhaps he worked for the wrong team. He could do a hell-good job hiding people who, for the most part, made the same mistakes over and over. People were so predictable.

As he guided the bike onto the highway and got up to speed, the unease he'd felt earlier returned.

Something isn't right here, Chet said in a quiet, ominous voice.

More than mere instinct, Sam's inner voice played the role of devil's advocate and conscience. Chet represented the raw processing of thoughts and feelings, unfiltered by what interacted with the rest of the world.

Sam didn't have schizophrenia; he knew this voice and personality to be his own. His primal instinct, most referred to it as their *gut*, had simply evolved. Whatever the label,

Sam had developed an unwavering faith in his alter ego. Chet's personification interfaced directly from a crude but cunning nub of the brain that hadn't changed since the days when sloped-headed Neanderthals drew elk and buffalo on cave walls.

During the war, Chet had warned him of danger long before his physical senses had detected anything. Listening to his gut had saved Sam's life, as well as the lives of the men he commanded.

At some point—he didn't remember when or why—he'd nicknamed his inner voice Chet. By allowing it to evolve, he could volley with it—tussling over the most difficult decisions, morally controversial situations, and complex but subtle tasks.

Yes, but what isn't right about it? Sam asked.

I don't know exactly. It just feels, wrong. Different than the other jobs… Chet's voice hesitated, very unlike his usual self.

The Agency isn't exactly forthcoming with information. We probably just don't have all the facts.

Of course. The explanation didn't satisfy either of them.

My job isn't to wonder the whys, Sam informed him. *Those decisions are above my pay grade.*

Right. Yes, sir! How high, sir? Jesus, this isn't actually the military, and you aren't a soldier anymore. They don't want you, remember?

Sam ground his teeth. *The people we find are enemies of the state. We don't know what they've done, only that we need to find them. That's all I care about.*

Well, then, G.I. Joe, you'd better stop thinking so much and do your job. Moron. Just remember, I warned you. Sam could almost see his inner voice, huffing and folding his arms, pissed off.

Sometimes he wondered if Chet could actually be his dead twin brother, Jake, a charming, confrontational, and charismatic pain in the ass.

Unlike Chet though, Jake had developed an affinity for mind-altering substances. The recreational hobby had grown teeth and wicked-sharp claws, becoming a demon that took control of and eventually claimed the man's life. The spiral had seemed long and arduous at the time, but it had only taken the monster a couple of years to eat Jake's essence, rotting him from the inside out until nothing existed but the chaff of the former all-star athlete.

In spite of Sam's conviction that he hadn't gone crazy, conversations like the one he'd just had with Chet made him wonder if his brother had decided to haunt him, continuing his mockery from within Sam's own mind. Whoever or whatever Chet turned out to be, Sam had never breathed a word of it to anyone. Not his handler, Josha; not the military; not his ex-wife when they were together. No one.

As he flew down the macadam, the feeling of wrongness didn't go away. But he trusted Josha, who had never given him a reason not to, so he would, as always, do the job.

Chapter Fifteen

Sam had planned to spend his life serving his country. But during his second tour in Afghanistan, a single bullet changed everything. Several surgeries and months of rehabilitation hadn't been enough. Of the dozen men that had gone out on the routine patrol that afternoon, two of them had returned on gurneys, and only one of the injured had returned to service. The Marines no longer wanted Sam. The truth of his insignificance had hit him like a hammer, and he'd fallen into a routine of disheartened listlessness.

Forced retirement left Sam with nowhere to go and nothing to do, so he spent hours a day in the gym, working the injured muscles of his leg. During one of these marathon sessions, a tall, reed-thin man in a dark suit approached.

"Hello, Sam."

Regarding the intruder, Sam continued working the leg extension machine without reply.

The suit-wearing man appeared nonplussed by Sam's indifference. "I am aware of your circumstances and have been authorized to offer you a position in my agency."

He loathed being treated like an invalid. He didn't want their handouts. He didn't want anything except to be left alone. "I don't need your pity position. I can take care of myself."

"I'm sure you can, but this is not some half-rate middle management job in the bowels of a government agency. We are looking for men and women with your background who are still interested in serving their country."

Sam finished his set then sat up. He studied the man's face as he wiped his neck with a grimy towel. The man looked to be in his fifties. His face, long and drawn out, was weathered and hard. Slicked-back, almost shiny silver hair—like the follicles hadn't lost their color due to age but instead retained their natural hue. His midnight-black suit appeared to be custom tailored, wrapping his gaunt frame like a second skin. Sam met the arctic, steel-colored eyes boring into him from a wan complexion. A miniature, malignant serpent slithered and coiled between the vertebrae of Sam's neck. The apparition before him looked like Death without the flowing robes and razor-sharp scythe.

A low lump of fear, as cold and merciless as cancer, formed in his gut. His nerves unraveled, and he had an almost overwhelming urge to flee.

"By my 'background,' you mean someone who's been damaged and deemed unworthy to hold a weapon?" Sam put as much sarcasm into the words as possible.

Sam waited for this doppelgänger of the Grim Reaper to back down, like everyone else who had approached him with similar offers. Instead, the piercing steel eyes flared with anger. "Are you through with your little pity party?"

"Look, I don't know what your angle is, but my plan is to be back on the front lines in a few months. I should have recovered enough——"

"We both know that isn't going to happen." The rail-thin man leaned in, his eyes blazing. "You are getting stronger, but you'll never be the man you once were. And once you're cut, that's it. So knock off the bullshit, and give me your attention."

Sam glared at him but refrained from further comment.

"We need good men like you to do jobs no one else is qualified to do. You will be back out in the field, working for your country, still fighting the enemy, just from a different perspective." The man didn't wait for a reply but instead reached into the inside pocket of his suit coat and pulled out a business card. "Give me a call."

Only an embossed phone number blemished the card's pristine, white surface. Sam looked up to ask the stranger's name, but he had vanished. Impossible given the open floor plan of the gym, but as Sam looked around, perplexed, he could find no trace of the odd, steel-eyed man.

The heavy ball of dread deep inside him shifted. After a few troubling minutes, he tucked the card in his pocket and continued working out.

☆☆☆☆

A month later, Sam emptied the storage unit his ex-wife had rented in his name. She had not included any furniture in the little ten-by-ten space with the large roll-up door, having kept all of it along with the house. He went shopping to fill the emptiness of his new apartment. Using the stipend from his injury, he bought a bed, couch, dresser, TV, a simple dining set, essentials such as dishes, and general whatnot from the local big box store. He hadn't realized how much time and energy it took to set up a new place from scratch.

For the next two weeks, he unpacked and washed dishes, wiped down cupboards, ran loads of towels and sheets at the local Laundromat in between workout sessions. By the end of each evening, he collapsed into bed, exhausted, his leg throbbing as if medieval blacksmiths had used it to quench their glowing irons.

His physical therapist pronounced him as "healed as he ever would get." In spite of the grim diagnosis, Sam could run five miles and had regained some of the speed of his former athletic years. He went to see his former commanding officer about reenlisting. But the man Sam respected gave him a pitying look he detested, confirming the truth: Sam would never again follow this, or any other soldier, into combat.

He sank into a deep depression, becoming despondent and listless. Years after joining the military, he had come full circle, arriving at the exact same place he had been when he used to drive his bike aimlessly in the deserted city streets. At least now he didn't have to come home to his ex pushing him to get his life together so they could have a family. The thought of being tied down with the commitments of a father and husband filled Sam's stomach with dread. She'd done him a favor by leaving him. He would only be able to screw up his own life instead of that of his wife and their two-point-five tax deductions.

But, free from domestic responsibility or not, his recent purchases had carved a considerable divot into his checking account. He had been so focused on getting back into the military he hadn't started looking for work. Soon, Sam would be forced into taking some piss-ant job he hated or lose his apartment. But if he remained frugal, the money would last another six weeks.

He had spent another long day at the gym. Physical therapist or no physical therapist, he still worked out like a demon. So instead of searching the want ads, he popped a beer and plopped down on the couch, shoving the whole becoming-a-functioning-member-of-society problem aside as he flipped through TV channels.

His stomach gurgled, and from his lax position on the sofa, he could see into the kitchen. He had stocked it with enough supplies to film one of those celebrity cooking shows featuring an ill-mannered, short-tempered chef and his sorry lot of hopefuls. But thawing, chopping, and sautéing felt like an overwhelming undertaking. Besides, it didn't seem worth the effort for just one person. Instead, he wandered into the unused space, opened his junk drawer, and rummaged through the slew of bright, various-colored take-out menus he had accumulated in the months since he and the military parted company.

Sam selected a blue one featuring happy shrimp and indecipherable Chinese characters on the front. He opened the menu for the dirty little restaurant up the street, and something fell out, flittering and tumbling end-over-end to the floor. He reached down to pick up the mysterious escapee, intending to toss it back into the drawer, then froze. Standing stock-still, hand grasping the drawer's dull brass knob, he could have been a department store mannequin displaying the latest in worn hoodies and aging sweat pants.

Sam stared at the business card the silver-haired reaper had given him, and something substantial and ponderous inside him worked loose.

As if some maniacal puppeteer had taken residence in his skull, throwing switches and pulling levers to manipulate both his body and thoughts, he reached for the small black phone. He'd brought the device with him to place an order for kung pao chicken and fried rice. Instead, he typed in the ten digits from the card and tapped the little image of a handset. A hundred years of innovation and techno-logical evolution designed the intricate circuits and relays that created the link between the phone pressed to his ear and the one carried by the steel-eyed man. Yet for all that advancement, when the call connected, Sam hesitated and fumbled the words like a butterfingered quarterback. "Yeah, this is—"

"Mr. Bradford," the cool, authoritative voice on the other end of the line interrupted him. "I'm glad you called. Yes, the position is still available. When will you be able to pry yourself from your *busy* schedule and come meet with us?"

Weird, Chet said, *it's as if he was expecting you.*

Eeriness filled his stomach, driving away the hunger that had been plaguing him just minutes before. He felt that thing inside him shift again. It—that thing he could neither see nor identify but which felt as black and jagged as a plummeting meteor—sat perched on the edge of a precipice. If it broke free, it would release a furious energy that would tear him and his life apart. When that happened, Sam had no idea what, if anything, would be left. Something more permanent and dire than the accident in college, joining the military, and getting shot in Afghanistan combined awaited him.

Hang up! Chet screamed. *Hang up before it's too late.*

For once, Sam ignored his alter ego. "Tomorrow."

"Fine. Tomorrow at oh eight hundred. Write this down." Sam flipped over the little menu with the happy cartoon shrimp and indecipherable Chinese writing, grabbed a pen, and jotted the address down in the margin.

Sam started to say, "Okay, let me make sure I've got this," but the line had gone dead. The hairs on the back of his neck stood on end. The serpent had returned.

☆☆☆☆

Sam's GPS led him to a small, nondescript office in a strip mall. The sign next to the door read, "International Relations." He went in and gave his name to the receptionist—a young, pretty woman, professional to the point of being cold. The plate on her desk declared her name to be Claudia, and she told him they had been expecting him and to have a seat.

Three chairs and a small coffee table with ancient magazines adorned the tiny waiting area. Uninterested in the five-year-old copies of *Field and Stream*, Sam sat, staring at nothing. A hazy thought of whether he had gone insane drifted through his mind when he sensed someone watching him. Snapping back to reality, he looked up to see the icy steel eyes observing him from the doorway.

"Please follow me," the silver-haired man instructed.

Sam hesitated, a feeling of being at a crossroads grasping him. The man had already disappeared down the hall. Sam glanced at the front door and then to the hallway, going back and forth as though watching a tennis match. He had been trained to evaluate a situation where lives were on the line and make snap judgments. Now, a severe case of indecision racked him, the feeling so intense he could almost hear the gears of his mind grinding, flailing from one choice to another.

Claudia cleared her throat. "He does not like being kept waiting. I suggest you decide."

Sam took one last look at the door, glanced at Claudia who still watched him, and got up. In a daze he took one step, then another, following the path down the darkened hallway and into a future unknown.

Chapter Sixteen

At the end of the corridor, Sam trailed the silver-eyed man into a utilitarian room with stark white walls, a plain, pattern-free tiled floor, and harsh florescent lights. A long, simple table with a single chair sat square in the center of the space, a neat stack of papers the only thing on its plain brown surface.

At military attention against the far wall stood four stern-looking men and one woman. They wore navy and gray, starched wool uniforms, second cousin to the Marine Dress Blues he used for ceremonies and other formal occasions. Sam didn't recognize either the clothes or, save for the small American flags on their shoulders, the insignias that adorned them.

The silent sentinels stared straight ahead yet seemed to be watching him at the same time. He knew how to do that, look without moving his eyes. He'd done it a thousand times.

Like the day he handed Sam the business card, the steel-eyed man wore an impeccably-tailored black suit. In comparison to everyone else, Sam felt slovenly in his jeans and hoodie.

"Please, sit," the man instructed.

Sam paused, reconsidering his decision. "What is this?"

The man arched one silver eyebrow and indicated toward the stiff wooden chair.

Sam sat as a heavy foreboding settled in. The situation seemed foreign yet somehow familiar. As the man handed him a piece of paper and a pen, his apprehension slipped away, replaced with something akin to coming home. The transition from one extreme feeling to the other flowed without so much as a pause. In no way could he articulate or reason how he knew this organization or recognized these people. By signing the document, he would become a mere cog in something much larger and more important than himself.

The document appeared to be a standard non-disclosure agreement. But as his eyes traveled down the tightly scripted page, words like "treason" and "unlawful disclosure" and "federal imprisonment" made him hesitate. This was anything but standard. At the bottom, a bold line waited for his signature. Under it, an ominous sentence demanded his attention. "I understand and agree to the rules, regulations, and penalties outlined in this document and renounce my right to private representation for infractions, voluntary or involuntary, of said rules and regulations."

His eyes widened. *Ummm...holy shit*, Chet said.

No shit, Sam replied. *These guys are serious.* Sam touched the pen to the line.

Are you sure you want to do that? Chet asked, but the words had barely been uttered before Sam scribbled his commitment across the bottom of the page.

Triggered by Sam's compliance, one of the men stepped forward and placed a simple electronic tablet in front of him—the screen illuminated only by a single empty square. "Place your hand here," the soldier said.

Sam laid his hand on the small LED screen, and a bar of light quickly traveled from one end to the other.

The soldier took both the tablet and the signed document and left the room.

No one else moved, but a sudden tension that hadn't been there a minute before filled the air. A feeling identical to the one he'd had before the RPG sailed from a cratered clothing boutique in Afghanistan, ending his military career and leading him to here, gripped him.

Given there were six people in it, the room remained eerie in its silence. The perfect line of soldiers, with the conspicuous, empty slot of the man who'd taken the document, continued to stare straight ahead. He couldn't even see these concrete sentries breathe. The steel-eyed man remained standing at the table, not watching the doorway, not watching anything. After several uncomfortable minutes, the soldier returned and resumed his position in line.

The man in the black suit slid another document in front of Sam, the words "Loyalty Agreement" printed at the top of the page.

"Please sign this."

"I don't even know what I'm agreeing to," Sam objected.

"Come now, Mr. Bradford. Surely you have this figured out."

Sam just stared at him. Two could play at the quiet game.

The man sighed. "We are a branch of the military used to find people deemed a threat to our nation and its people and take appropriate actions to deal with them."

"What branch exactly is this? I don't recognize the uniforms." Sam looked again at the soldiers.

"No, you won't because we don't technically exist. There are no line items for Congress to approve. No oversight committees. No laws governing our actions. We are self-contained, self-funded, and tasked with an impossible job which is far too important for bureaucratic meddling. This is an elite group, and you have been extended a one-time invitation. The question is: Are you smart enough to accept?"

Sam stared into the unwavering cold eyes. He glanced at the soldiers who were not looking at him but watching his every move and then returned his gaze to the document. "Loyalty Agreement" screamed at him from the page.

*I don't think…*Chet began too late. Without reading it, Sam signed his name on the bottom line.

That thing he'd felt shifting toward the precipice since the evening before fell over the edge, plummeting to depths unknown, and Sam went with it.

Signing the document threw the switch on a fantastic but frightening machine. The female and two of the male soldiers turned and marched from the room. The remaining men stepped forward. One of them said, "Mr. Bradford, please come with us."

Confused, Sam looked at the steel-eyed man. "I don't understand. What's happening?"

"Think of it as boot camp. These gentlemen will escort you to your barracks where you will be issued a uniform and standard supplies. Dr. Wilks, our in-house physician, will perform a full medical evaluation. Provided you pass, your training begins at oh six hundred tomorrow."

"I can't just drop everything. I have an apartment, bills to pay, things to wrap up. I have a life."

"Actually you can. All those trivialities are being taken care of as we speak. Your apartment and transportation are being secured; loose ends such as credit cards and utilities are being handled. These things will be turned back over to you in time, but there are procedures we must follow. So, for now, do not concern yourself with them. Please follow these gentlemen. You have a busy schedule."

"I don't even know your name." Everything moved too fast. "How will I contact you if I need you?"

"My job as your recruiter is complete. Since this is the last time we will speak, you do not need to know my name. Our organization is highly compartmentalized, a structure that has helped keep it intact when other such institutions have collapsed. Please do not ask questions. You will be provided with information as it pertains to you but nothing more. Congratulations and good luck, Mr. Bradford." He strode from the room.

Perplexed, Sam allowed himself to be led away.

The next day, he began a regimen that made his days with the physical therapist look like a Sunday morning yoga class. When allowed to leave, his legs quaked, and he dripped with sweat.

After a quick lunch, his real classes began.

First on the agenda: a series of investigative lectures. From the time his physical training ended, he studied the subtleties of finding people who did not want to be found. The lecture topic: Learning to look for details and clues, seeking people out and discovering what new identities they had given themselves. Tools existed, of course—high tech search engines, cameras, and so forth—but his weapons of choice, reasoning and intuition, could not be purchased. In these lessons, he excelled. Sam's methodology allowed him to track his quarry using the scantest of details, following one piece of evidence after the other.

Next, he began the core of the curriculum, a class taught by Dr. Wergent, a short, stubby man who looked like a turn-of-the-century British professor. Heavily bearded but thin up top, Dr. Wergent wore pants too big even for his rotund stature and had a propensity for professor jackets with big patches on the elbows.

The professor's groundbreaking hypothesis on the underlying motivations of human interaction had caused a row in the mental health world as specialists debated his controversial theorems. He had been on the verge of either phenomenal success or absolute career implosion when he had been hired by The Agency.

"We think we are individuals," Dr. Wergent began during Sam's first class, "and in many ways we are, but deep down we are all the same. We have needs, generally react the same way in a given situation, and can be manipulated and controlled if you know what switches to throw and buttons to push. I have spent my life's work trying to understand the elemental components of human interaction and have come up with what I call *The 122 Rules of Psychology*.

"No one is immune to these rules; no one is exempt. But the trick"——he raised a thick finger to emphasize the point——"is knowing how to apply the Rules to get the desired result."

The doctor had half a dozen specialists to assist him, all of them authorities in one part or another of the doctor's edicts. Sam worked hard, memorizing large swaths of information, practicing scenarios, evaluating the results, and trying different courses of action. They taught him objectivity and how to keep his emotions from dictating his actions or affecting his decisions. Then he graduated from the classroom and began actual field training.

The Agency designed these lessons to be realistic and prepare him for life as a solo agent. Others in his class found remaining objective and distant difficult, and as the weeks went by, more and more of his classmates failed and left the program. But Sam breezed through the classes. He already possessed the most important qualities: He could compartmentalize his emotions and keep a huge number of details organized on his mental bookshelf.

His first real-world practice assignment had been to find a married, church-going, middle-school teacher named Lorraine Dexter. She had assumed an alias and created a new life in her early twenties to escape from an abusive man who had, on multiple occasions, almost killed her. She never revealed her past to her new husband and had been selected as the target for Sam to sharpen and hone his new skills.

The instructors gave Sam a few details of the mark's life and a vague description. Sam tracked her down in record time then befriended the family, spending time with both the husband and children and seducing the teacher. As their sexual depravity deepened, they met at different hotels and spent one poignant night in Lorraine's own bed while her husband slept down the hall—the couple's fight a product of Sam's manipulation.

After Sam broke it off, Lorraine might have survived the ordeal with nothing more than a few guilty feelings, but the lesson continued, testing his fortitude. He had next been instructed to send an anonymous email with details of her past life and pictures of her in the act of sexual deviance. The images, sent to both her current and ex-husbands as well as the school board, did not show Sam's face, only hers. Sam performed this act of betrayal with neither the joy malice brings to the deranged nor the feelings of remorse experienced by those whose actions can be controlled by guilt and reason. He observed with clinical detachment the destruction of her life by scandal and divorce.

After passing this test, his next task had been even more complex. He manipulated a gay man, Theodore Madel, who worked at a bank into transferring funds from large customer accounts to a Swiss account provided by Sam. Believing he had a chance at a romantic relationship, Theodore covered the tracks of his theft like a mother wolf guards the location of her den, weaving an intricate trail under brush, doubling back over fallen trees and sinewy streams. Only the most determined could follow the path of his complex deception.

But the camouflage only bought time. The banker, a great numbers manipulator, could not eliminate the paper trail. When the ribbon and wrapping paper fell off via a thorough audit, the betrayal would be exposed. Sam had convinced Theodore to steal a car and meet for a secret rendezvous, after which the two of them would slip out of the country together.

The plan had been brilliantly conceived and executed. Only, someone sent another anonymous email to the lead detective of a high-profile crime unit. When the banker pulled into the small hotel on the edge of a tiny East Coast city in a stolen Pontiac, the police lay waiting for him. After he entered the small hotel room, they burst through the front door, slamming him to the floor and cuffing him under gunpoint. In the ensuing trial, he had been found guilty of all charges and sentenced to ten years in the state penitentiary.

The prison's newest resident would complete but a month of the punishment before bumping a large inmate with a shaved and tattooed head in the meal hall. The convict returned the favor by ramming a shiv into Theodore's neck later that day, severing his spinal cord. The paralyzed ex-banker lay helpless and naked in the shower as the other inmates kicked him to death.

Unfortunately for his family, no witnesses stepped forward to testify to the crime.

These everyday folks had been selected to test Sam's ability to follow orders without question and without regard to the humaneness, or lack thereof, for his actions. His weapons training, sharp from years in the military, had been further honed so he could remove these individuals himself instead of relying on anonymous tips and others to do the job for him. In every facet of his new position, he had surpassed all expectations, including his own.

Having passed the program, Sam once again worked for his country. His purpose—to protect the homeland from anyone, either domestic or abroad, that threatened the freedoms he held dear—drove him to work until exhaustion forced him to stop.

He had no blood on his hands; these people had made their own choices. But Sam left a wave of despair and unhappiness behind him as damning as if he'd pushed that sliver of metal in the man's neck himself.

But what of it? These lessons—just extensions on chapters in a textbook—had trained him to control and manipulate those around him. If a few had to be sacrificed for the greater good of God and Country, the importance of democracy bore that cost.

After training, Sam had been turned over to his handler, Josha, who awarded him his first assignment. Sam completed the objective—to find a tax evader who kept millions of government dollars—in record time.

That first job led to a series of others. Year after year, face after face. The names of those he sought, and the identities he assumed, cascaded together in a soupy blur of images that often left him feeling vague and dazed.

Losing himself in a different identity, becoming someone else, and separating his true feelings from that of his assumed persona made him an excellent agent. But at times, when undercover for months, he had to look at his driver's license to remember his own name.

☆☆☆☆

As Sam continued down the highway, the rumble of the bike's engine reverberating through his bones, he scrolled through the memories of a thousand lives he'd touched but never actually been a part of. The destinies he'd changed and the futures he'd destroyed. He'd done it for the greater good. But, he wondered if somewhere in the last decade the man he'd hoped to be and the man he thought he'd someday become had gotten lost. Or maybe, that person, that man, never really existed at all.

This thought struck a nerve, but he shoved it out of his mind before these seeds of misgiving had a chance to sprout roots.

He really didn't want to think anymore. Sam thumbed up the volume on the helmet's internal speakers. The music blaring in his ears, he bore down on the accelerator, toward the fly-crap-sized town of Walberg and his target.

Chapter Seventeen

Just a touch over eleven hours later, Sam turned off the highway and followed Pocahontas' directions down a series of side streets. He passed a faded, weather-beaten sign announcing he had entered the town of Walberg—*The Sweet Spot of Arizona*, population 1102.

He pulled into one of the slanted spaces in front of a small coffee shop just as the little GPS unit announced he had arrived at his destination. The cracked sidewalks and deserted, heat-baked streets, devoid of any signs of life, hosted but a lone tumbleweed blowing through the nearest intersection on a journey to nowhere.

This is the "sweet spot" of Arizona? Chet, who had been quiet most of the trip, asked. *Seriously, who do they think they're fooling?*

Sam sighed. His alter ego's crude, sarcastic streak sometimes annoyed him, but Chet had a point. The place felt wrong, with its sandblasted, sun-bleached buildings and boarded-up storefronts; it held a poisonous, hopeless vibe that seeped into his bones.

He pushed through a glass door with "A Real Drip" stenciled on its marred and scratched surface. He waded into the small, dimly lit shop where Monica had sent her last email. The smell of coffee, sweet cinnamon rolls, and a faint underlying mold enveloped him as he stepped across the threshold.

Spotlessly clean, the coffee shop had been decorated in what could only be called dilapidated-chic. Most of the bargain-basement, fancy stools sported duct tape over their cracked, vinyl surfaces. In the corner, a florescent light sputtered in the final throes of death, one last dramatic dance as it prepared to join its fallen brothers.

Sam made his way to the front counter where a perky woman of about thirty smiled and asked if she could help him.

"Just plain black coffee, please."

The chubby barista's prematurely gray-streaked, black hair swung back and forth, her ponytail pendulum almost mesmerizing. In a few years her chub would likely bloom into full-fledged fat. She just had that look.

The early arrival of crow's feet said she'd worked hard her entire life. Sam could see her story as though reading her autobiography: she had been born into a lower-middle-class family that had to scrape by for the bare necessities; during her toddler or early elementary-school years, her parents divorced; she worked for minimum wage, cleaning and cooking, in all likelihood, the positive aspects of the little coffee shop were due to her efforts and diligence; she didn't own the place and did the best with what had been handed to her.

As she filled a large white mug, she asked, "Where you headed?"

"Couldn't *this* be my destination?"

She cocked an eye at him. "Is it? Most people who come through this late are on their way someplace else."

Sam checked his watch, half past seven. "This is late?"

"Here it is. Jus' about ever'thing is shut up tight. I was getting ready to close myself."

"Oh well, then I should take this to go. Don't want to keep you."

"No, no it's fine. Sit down and rest a spell. Have to clean up, and that'll take half past a freckle and quarter to a hair. You can keep me comp'ny while I work, Mr…?"

"Morrell. Peter Morrell, but my friends call me Pete." She offered her small, doll-like hand. He felt mammoth as his paw enveloped short stubby fingers jutting out from a hand so plump the knuckles formed concaved indentations. He took a seat on one of the wobbly stools.

"Mary Beth Sanders, though in another month, it'll be Mary Beth Cooper." She held her hand up, showing him her small engagement ring. The tiny stone gave off a meek sparkle in the low light. Her smile glowed far brighter than her cubic zirconium ever would. The hope in her eyes broke his heart. Her life had been disappointing and difficult, and like most brides-to-be, she seemed on the cusp of something better. If this establishment gave any indication, the particular stallion she had hitched her wagon to would only let her down. In the next few years, that lovely light would fade, replaced by the dull, flat reality of her existence.

"Well, congrats!" He smiled with fake enthusiasm. "Is the lucky man from around here?"

"Aa-yep," she said, in an accent misplaced on the western side of the country. "Ralph. Ralph Gerald Cooper is the lucky man. Sounds all proper like, maybe even classy don't you think? He owns the place. Been workin' together for the better part of fou' ye'rs er so. Well, one thing led to another, and soon I'll be Mrs. Cooper. Ain't that just git all? Ya know, they say that ninety percent of all romances start in the workplace? I used to think that was hogwash, jest an excuse for folks to fool around, but brother, now I'm a believer! And my Ralphy, he's got aspirations. He's gonna take the profits from runnin' this place to start other businesses, maybe even a theater for showin' the latest movies. Can you imagine, a theater in a little town like this? It'll be a hit with the teenagers, that's for sho'!"

Chet shook his head, eyes downcast, without anything to say for once.

She bubbled on about this and that as she cleaned the espresso machine and wiped down the counter. He didn't have to say much to keep the wheel of her running monologue spinning. An occasional "You don't say?" and "Really?" and she seemed more than happy to fill him in on everything from who managed the diner to the latest scandal at the Methodist church.

"I don't know much about the goin's-on at the Catholic or Seventh Day 'Ventists whatcha-ma-call-ems. They are all going to Hell anyway, so why bother with what they're up to?" She paused for a moment. A disapproving look crossed her face as if she'd caught him red-handed stealing from the donation plate. "You aren't Catholic or Seventh Day 'Ventist, now are ya, Mr. Morrell?"

Her impending judgment lurked behind her smile, ready to pounce as if she expected him to proclaim he not only belonged to both sects but also washed the feet of the Pope on the weekends. He laughed. "No, I'm neither."

Her face relaxed, and she smiled, the crow's feet at the corners of her eyes crinkling. "Well, thank the good Lord for that. So tell me, Mr. Morrell, what brand of Christian are ya?" Her eyes sparkled. He guessed Mary Beth knew a lot about everyone in town. On the surface, she schlepped coffee and pastries, but she specialized in information as her main stock in trade. Her brown eyes watched him, assessing. It would be a mistake to try and bullshit this woman too much. What she didn't have in book smarts, she clearly made up for in cunning.

Oh, Ralph, you are going to have your hands full, my friend. How the hell did he pull off the fake diamond? The fake life? Sam needed to keep her talking, and to do that, she had to trust him. So, he went with the truth.

"Well, first call me Pete; Mr. Morrell is my father. Second, to be honest ma'am, I don't hold to one particular religion." He had started picking up the dialect.

Sam applied a liberal application of:

Rule #35:
Sound as native as possible.

It is often imperative to sound as though you belong. We trust those that are like us, part of our group, and hold skepticism against those that are perceived as outsiders. Exercise caution when imitating accents or using local dialect and vernacular. Precision and accuracy is essential. If an interloper is detected, mistrust and often outright hostility will be the result.

—*122 Rules of Psychology*

He continued, "I would like to think there is someone up there looking down on us, running the show, but I haven't seen any evidence of it. Did a stint in the military with some time in Afghanistan. Lots of guys prayed every day, but it didn't seem to matter which ones did and which ones didn't. They all died, had their legs blown off, or had to deal with kids killing themselves in the name of Allah."

"Horrible. Just horrible," she conceded. "Them people in the Middle East have such crazy notions of what's right and wrong. Every day I see it on the news, and all that's goin' on, it just breaks my heart. But I think the good Lord will prevail; there's just a lot of evil that's gotta be vanquished. Am I right?"

"So true, Mary Beth."

"So tell me, Mr. Morrell, are you married? You got no ring, an'"—she glanced out the window at his bike—"most ladies I know would never ride around on that thing." And just like that, she shifted gears, from novice preacher to town gossip again.

Unlike you, she doesn't mess around, Chet said. *Maybe we should pass her name onto Josha as your replacement? First your religion, now your marital status. What have you got? Some rumors about the Methodists? Good to see the fine taxpayers of this country are getting their money's worth. Hang up your pipe, Sherlock; there's a new sheriff in town. Face it, this hillbilly is kicking your ass.*

As always, Chet nailed it, but Sam needed to give a little more before he could get any real information from her. "When I came back from the war, my wife decided that she didn't want to be married anymore. Tried talking her into changing her mind, just give it some time, but it didn't make a difference. She didn't want the military life, movin' all over, husband gone for months on end, so she left, takin' just about everything with her. I'm out now, traveling from place to place, trying to find somewhere to settle and figure out what I want to do with the rest of my life."

She stopped scrubbing the counter and put her hands on her hips. "Oh, it's so bad these days how nobody stays together no more. They say more 'n' more people are split-tin', just givin' up without nary a thought, an' pretty soon there just won't be no more married folk. Not me though, no offense, once I say my 'I do's,' that's it." She set her rag down and leaned against the counter. "Mr. Morrell, it's real nice of you to open up like that, with me bein' a stranger and all. But you gots to remember that God has a plan for all of us. He works in mysterious ways. Maybe His plan was for you comin' here tonight and meeting with a little country girl. Our reverend, Mr. Callhoune, is just about the nicest man I know and certainly the most Christian. You should come to church with me 'n' Ralphy and meet him. He'll be able to tell you all about the plan that God has for you."

I'll bet. "Well, that's nice of you ma'am."

"Oh, for heaven's sake, stop calling me ma'am. Call me Mary Beth, seems we should be on a first name basis by now, seein' as how we's talkin' about you comin' to my church an' all. You know," she said, her face impassive though her shifty eyes betrayed her manipulative inten-tions, "you should really think about tryin' the place on. It's a nice little town. Before you know it, we could even be neighbors. Why, a little house just down the street opened up. You should look at it in the mornin'. I know the realtor. Here, let me give you his name and number."

"He isn't a thief?"

She laughed. "Oh, they're all thieves, aren't they? He's Ralphy's cousin and 'bout as honest as they make that breed. B'sides, he's the only one in town. You gotta go through him you want any prop'ty anywhere 'round here."

"So, a lot of new people like me moving to town?"

"Oh, they come and go. Though you know,"—she tapped her teeth like the idea had just occurred to her—"a purty little gal did move here just a little while back. Kinda quiet. She don't mix much socially, but she started workin' at the lawyer's office. She talks real smart, so she's got an education from someplace. Think she's from up north somewhere." Mary Beth appeared to be a little frustrated at the lack of information.

"Really? Well, if a smart girl like that thinks this is a good place to settle, maybe I'll kick its tires and see how it feels."

"So, is yer divorce done, you know, with the courts and all?"

"Yes, it's been final for a while," he replied, already knowing where Mary Beth intended to take the conversation. He let her.

"You seem like a nice enough fella, for bein' out of town and all. You shoul' stop in the lawyer's place and say hello to that little gal. Her name's Susan. She's not all glamorous, like in the movies, but down-to-earth purty."

He chuckled. "And the matchmaker comes out."

"Oh no! I'm just sayin', if you stop in there and talk and maybe ask her out to coffee, who knows where things might lead?"

"Coffee, huh? And just *where* would I take Ms. Susan to coffee?" *I'll tell you where: someplace you can eavesdrop.*

"Well sir, there's only one coffeehouse in town, 'less you count that swill they serve down at the diner, and I do not. 'Sides, the diner ain't the type of place a lady wants to go when you're just gettin' to know her. She already spends a purty good amount of time here."

"Oh?"

"Yep, we's the only place in town that's got free WiFi," Mary Beth said, her eyes sparkling with pride. "She comes in ever' Sunday with her computer."

"She only comes in on Sundays? It's funny how we are creatures of habit." Sam made an effort to make his voice as casual as possible, trying to hide his disappointment. Susan might have been a possible lead, but if she hadn't been there that morning, then she couldn't be Monica. He would have to begin searching elsewhere.

"Well, now that you mention it, she did pop in this mornin'. Surprised me a bit. Little outta character, but you know the young an' all. Don't know what she was do-ing. I think it's some lawyer stuff. Not real interestin'."

Bingo. "So," he said lowering his voice and leaning in as though eavesdroppers abounded, "you say she's pretty?"

"I-yup. Five-five. Dark hair with blonde roots. Hazel eyes. About twenty-five maybe. Real serious. Quiet and polite."

"I see." This Susan girl sounded like Monica—the de-scription fit, as did the timing of using the WiFi, and she worked for a law firm. Check, check, and check. The pos-sibility still existed that it was the wrong person. However if it came to it, Mary Beth seemed like a reliable busybody who could be counted on to match him up with someone else if need be.

He would set up shop, then begin formulating a plan and a reason to stop by the law office. How quickly could he get her identity confirmed and take care of business? Sometimes those that were underground got lonely and wanted someone to talk to, so he got the drop on them within a couple of days. Others, he had to go to more extreme, messier measures, to verify their identity. Easy or hard, it all depended on her. He'd love to get the job done and leave this dusty little shithole as soon as possible.

"First things first," he said, "I've been on the road all day. Anywhere around here I can stay tonight?"

"Ah, yep!" She beamed with pride. "My sister is runnin' the night shift at the fanciest hotel in town. Just tell her I sent you, and she'll give you the best room in the joint."

Chapter Eighteen

In his hotel "suite," Sam studied Monica's picture: blondish-brown hair, intelligent hazel eyes, dark complexion, smattering of freckles, and a distinct Marilyn Monroe mole above her thin lips. A pretty girl, though no one would confuse her with the temptress who had seduced one of the country's favorite presidents.

Mary Beth said Susan looked about twenty-five. That and the rest of her description fell into alignment with the pictures in front of him. The barista had been playing Cupid, trying to pair the two of them up, so she did her best to make Susan sound attractive. The physical part matched, but polite and quiet? From everything he'd read, Monica had been anything but. Insolent and disruptive, disrespectful and incorrigible seemed to be her modus operandi.

I don't like this, Chet informed him.

Sam frowned. *I know. There are some inconsistencies. Maybe Mary Beth talked so much it only seemed like Susan was quiet and polite.*

That's not what I mean. This case, there isn't shit in it that makes a lick of sense.

Sam paused, laying Monica's picture on the desk. *Which parts?*

All of it. Look, I could see these mob guys using her, but somehow she magically became third in command of a billion-dollar operation? Impossible. You work your way up in the business, you know that. If they like you and you don't mess up, maybe you get to keep all your body parts. If they don't, then you wind up in a hole in the ground with your head mounted above someone's mantel between a prize buck and one of those plastic singing fish.

Sam searched through the stack of papers and pulled a report. The informant fingering her as a chief in the mob had only been identified as a "reliable witness" within the organization.

Chet said, *There's nothing other than the one police report that says anything but "college student." Not the murder, not the drug charge. Zilch.*

Her intelligence tests are off the charts; maybe they liked that about her and decided to use her. Maybe she's like some super economic or business strategist?

Chet sneered. *Or maybe she learned to walk through walls and teleport into bank vaults. You're reaching.*

Sam shook his head. *But she went incognito as soon as the shit hit the fan with the mob boss. Of everything, that is easily the most damning piece of evidence. I don't care what else the file says, she's got something to hide.* Sam had finally scored a point. If he could have done the touchdown dance, he would have.

But you don't know what.

Sam turned the page on the police report. *Well, I guess I'll have to find out.*

Maybe you will and maybe you won't. And if this Susan and Monica are the same person, why the hell did she move to this God-forsaken wretched place on the edge of nowhere? Why not simply go dark for a while in the city, move out to a farm, or, if she's really that smart, give herself a new identity someplace else? Someplace where she could have a life. This may as well be prison.

She could be trying to hide, Sam pointed out. *Pissed off the wrong people like you said. Who knows? She's super smart, maybe that's what those sorts do to throw the rest of us off. None of this makes any difference. We aren't doing a documentary, we just need to find her, not learn her life story.*

Uh oh. Look out, everyone. Here comes Prince Uncharming. Since you're on a roll, U.C., maybe you'll be able to dropkick a dwarf and shoot all the forest animals on your way to butcher the damsel in distress.

Sam rolled his eyes at his inner conscience. *I hardly think she's in distress.*

Whatever. Do what you have to do to justify not thinking and blindly following orders. For the record, your song and dance is getting old. It's time for a new routine.

In spite of Chet's disapproving glare, Sam shoved his doubts aside. He had been hired to track and find, not to question. *I'll get the verbal confirm and check in with Josha. Maybe by then new information will have been released.*

Sometimes clients wanted verbal confirmation, which meant Sam had to get his targets to confess their identities. The upside? Virtually no chance of misidentification. On the flip side, verbal confirms took a lot more time and required intimate contact. He had to gain the target's trust, so much so that they felt comfortable enough to reveal their true identity.

Yeah, okay, Chet said. *Carry on, soldier.*

The discordances troubled Sam too, but he had a job to plan. He sighed, flipped the inch-thick folder back to the first page, and started reading again.

Chapter Nineteen

The next morning, Sam set up an appointment to look at the little house Mary Beth had told him about. The real estate agent offered directions, which Sam declined. He doubted he'd have any trouble navigating the four square miles that comprised Walberg.

Itching to get in some exercise, Sam slipped into his running gear and headed down the main avenue. He wanted to get the lay of the land, and hopefully the extra blood flow would knock loose some of the mental rust that kept the blinders on. Chet seemed certain Sam had missed something, but he had no idea what that something could be.

The bleached hands of the town clock had yet to strike the 8:00 a.m. hour, but the asphalt already shimmered with wavy rays of heat from the merciless sun. The harsh, unforgiving desert light did nothing to improve the demeanor of the little city. Half the businesses had boarded-up storefronts, and those that remained open looked like they were on the brink of financial collapse. The suburbs had an even more decrepit, abandoned vibe. The vast majority of the housing consisted of mobile home parks and neglected ranch-style bungalows.

After his depressing run, Sam showered and went to the little diner for breakfast, the only eating establishment besides The Cluck House for forty miles in any direction. He pushed the plate aside halfway through the meal. The daily "special"—watery eggs, greasy bacon, and hash browns—would sit in his stomach undigested for hours. He tried to drink the swill the place passed as coffee, but after a few sips, he simply couldn't add it to the indignities he had already bestowed upon his stomach.

Mary Beth may be a town simpleton, but she had been dead on about the brew. He paid his bill and headed toward the door to meet with the realtor.

Sam parked his bike in front of the ramshackle ranch. A forty-ish, undistinguished-looking man in a cheap plaid suit with a mop of sweaty red hair waited on the crisp front lawn.

He approached the man that had to be Ralph's cousin, Bobby. Sam disliked him on sight, the feeling of repulsion as palpable as though he'd bitten into an apple only to find half a maggot inside. He didn't need much from the realtor. Just a little information, and he could be done with him.

Put on your dancing shoes, and fire up the acting skills. You're going to need them, Chet said.

Bobby stepped forward, holding his hand out for the mandatory shake, and Sam caught a whiff of unpleasant body odor. The real estate agent introduced himself and smiled, displaying a mouth full of bad teeth and emitting the putrid smell of his acrid breath.

He loathed touching the man but, having no choice, returned the greeting. Upon release, Sam's palm was damp with the other man's sweat. He wiped his hand on his jeans, though he wanted to take a bath in hand sanitizer.

If Bobby represented the successful businessmen in Walberg, what the hell did Brother Ralph look like? No one would call Mary Beth a knockout, but seriously, the testosterone pool the women of the town had to choose from must be very shallow indeed.

"So," Bobby began, "Mary Beth tells me you are thinking about moving to our little corner of the world. Well, you couldn't have chosen a nicer patch of earth. And talk about impeccable timing! Right now, we have so many excellent opportunities to buy. Some great houses just came on the market, for a steal too."

I'll bet, Sam thought, but he said, "Really? Good time to buy, huh? Why is that?"

"Oh, lots of reasons folks are selling. With the new pipeline that went in a few years back, folks are buying bigger and better. Putting some smaller lots on the market for a single gent such as yourself to come in and snatch up a good deal. But let me tell you, more and more from out of town been coming here to settle, so these deals are going quick."

"Uh huh." The numerous foreclosure signs around town countered this statement, but Sam let it go. "Well, I'm not looking to buy, I just want to rent."

The smarmy salesman's face faltered for a second, before he pasted a grin over his frown. "That's not a problem. Several pieces of prime real estate, including the one I'm showing you today, are lease with an option to buy."

Sam nodded as though the idea had merit. *Yeah, there's no chance of that happening.* "Okay. Well, I heard you put a new gal that came to town not long ago in a good place. Tell me about that."

Bobby might have been a greasy buffoon, but his businessman's hospitality gave way to old-fashioned suspicion. "Now why would ya want me to tell ya about that?"

"Well, from my experience, people from in town get better deals and get shown the prime pieces of land before us out-of-towners. You just said this house has the option to purchase and I know a fair deal about buying and selling houses, so by knowing what she got, I'll have a baseline of what to expect." Sam, of course, knew little about the housing market, but he wanted to get right to the point with the little man, who likely had all day to pussyfoot around.

"Well I don't know who you've been talking to, but that ain't the case. No sir! It don't matter where you're from, you will always get a good deal with Bobby Cooper. Always. That little gal you mentioned, let's see," he said, tapping his yellow teeth. "Oh yeah! I put her in a nice little green-and-brown bungalow with shutters and fireplace on the south side of town. It's on Sagebrush Lane. We can drive over if you're thinking her place is better than the one I'm showing ya. It ain't, but if you're worried, we can."

"Show me around the place first." So Bobby led him through a tour of the house. Sam, though no expert on building construction, thought the place looked closer to being ready for the wrecking ball than new tenants. Large chunks of concrete were missing in the foundation, and thick peels of faded paint waved in the hot, lazy breeze. When they stepped on the porch, it groaned and creaked. Their combined weight could very well cause it to fail while they stood on it, and Sam breathed a sigh of relief when they stepped onto the weed-infested sidewalk. Bobby, so engrossed in his own spiel, continued to prattle on, failing to notice his customer had stopped paying attention.

At some point, Bobby switched from talking about the house to boasting about the town and surrounding landscape. "You won't find a better place for things to do. Hiking, exploring, ATVs. And the nightlife. Why, there's so much to do, I'm not sure where to start."

Sam couldn't take any more blather, so he interrupted the smarmy little man. "I'll take it."

"I—What? Huh? Come again?"

"Here's what I want you to do. Give me a copy of the lease. I'll read it over and bring it back to you later in the day. After I move in, I'll think over purchasing the place and let you know."

The little man shook his head. "Well, just so you know, I have a couple from Florida coming to look at it this afternoon. They're pretty serious about buying."

Sam stared at him until Bobby started to squirm, caught in the obvious lie.

"Want me to drive you, or are you gonna follow me?" Bobby asked.

"I'll follow you."

They drove the five minutes to Bobby's ramshackle un-air-conditioned office. A lazy ceiling fan, its blades black with dust, stirred the stale air. A half hour later, Sam had the thick stack of documents that, once signed, would make him the proud tenant of a run-down, two-bedroom "bungalow." Bobby reiterated that he could not hold the place and that Sam shouldn't risk not signing right then and there.

Right. Besides, Sam had really only met with the man because he needed the documents. He didn't care two bits about the house.

Sam despised the smarmy real estate agent, and he disliked the town. The citizens had a defeated, slump-shouldered air about them. They had simply given up and accepted the inevitable slide of their dilapidated city into oblivion. The place had no money and no relevant source of income. If not already broke, it would be soon, new pipeline or no new pipeline. In a few years, it would be deserted—just another abandoned ghost town in the middle of the desert.

He asked himself again: Why would a smart girl like Monica move to a hellhole like this?

Chapter Twenty

Relief from the oppressive heat washed over Sam as he entered the air-conditioned law office of Bunder and Associates. Simple, old-fashioned filing cabinets lined one of the dark, paneled walls of the small and efficient space. Other than a modest waiting area, half a dozen second-hand desks, which might have been new in 1955, took up the bulk of the floor. Not big-city prestigious but clean and well organized, the place seemed distinguished for the little town of Walberg.

Only two people occupied the office—both women. One sat behind a desk at the back of the room, sorting through files from a pile of boxes. The haphazard mountain of paperwork stacked around her looked on the verge of collapse. At any minute, the whole precarious slew appeared as though it would crush her in an avalanche of legal briefs, affidavits, and resolutions. Distinct, white chords dangled from her ears, sending tinny music drifting through the cool air.

The other woman sat behind the desk closest to the entrance and read something with such affixed attention, Sam could only surmise the document she held must be a vital and pressing piece of town legislature. He couldn't see her face, and no nameplate adorned her desk, not that there would have been room for one among the random assemblages of papers.

Neither of them glanced his direction when he came in, but the one with the headset waved and told him to have a seat.

After several minutes, the woman at the first desk set the document aside and looked up. "How can I help you?"

Sam studied her face as he approached. Hazel eyes, freckles, dark complexion, Marilyn Monroe mole. Nailed it.

She gave him a once-over as he approached, her eyes stopping on his smile, and she reflected the one he beamed at her. She leaned over her desk as he took the opposite seat.

"I'm thinking about signing a lease on a piece of property, and I wanted someone to review the paperwork for me before I do. The real estate agent seemed a little..." Sam pursed his lips.

"Trustworthy and on the up and up?" the woman offered.

"Ummm, not *exactly* what I was thinking."

"Smarmy?"

He grinned and pointed at her. "Exactly."

She held his gaze. Her pupils had grown since the beginning of their conversation, blotting out a good portion of the hazel irises surrounding them. "Yes, well we only have one real estate agent in town, and as hard as it is to believe, Mr. Cooper has been known to try and take advantage from time to time. Let me see what you've got."

Sam handed her the paperwork Bobby had given him that afternoon. "I'm Peter Morrell." He extended his hand.

She stood, smoothing out her skirt as she did so. "Susan Rosenberg. Nice to meet you."

Give her a little start, then reel her in, Chet said.

I know what I'm doing, Sam bit back. *This isn't my first rodeo.*

I'm just making sure you know not to blow it. The first meeting is the most crucial, and you're not exactly Casanova.

Would you like to take over?

If only I could. Look, just pay attention and don't eff up, and it should be a cakewalk.

"Oh, Susan! You're the other newbie in town."

She went rigid. She stared at him with suspicion, her mouth tightening to a slit while her eyes narrowed. Her entire body tensed as if preparing to run.

Bambi smells fire, Chet said.

"And how exactly do you know this?" she asked. She seemed to be going for an air of nonchalance, but the rigidity of her body told a different story.

Sam pretended he hadn't noticed the changes in her demeanor. Laughing, he said, "The first place I went to when I got to town was the coffee shop, where I met the proprietor's fiancée, Mary Beth. It took Cupid all of about five minutes before she was trying to pair us up. I probably have far more insight about your coffee habits, marital and dating status"—he ticked off the points on his fingers—"your new house, your job, basically your entire life." He coughed gently into his hand and feigned embarrassment. "It's far more than I have any right to know."

Susan visibly relaxed. Her shoulders returned to their office-bound slump, and she laughed too.

Rule # 15:
The quickest way to bond with someone is through a common enemy.

Nothing will give two individuals or groups of people something in common as swiftly as a shared foe. This creates a rich ground in which to plant the seeds of bonds and alliance. It forms a bridge and assists those from differing ilks and backgrounds to almost immediately coalesce into a single, unified team. This adversary can either be real or perceived, their threat great or small. No actual qualities or facts matter, only that both parties believe they may have or could potentially be wronged or manipulated by said enemy.

—122 Rules of Psychology

"My god, that woman is presumptuous, isn't she?" Susan said, shaking her head. "Guess I'm not really surprised. She has been trying to match me with just about every eligible bachelor in town. Now that we have about tapped that pool, she's been hitting up random strangers."

"She is a fountain of information. Though, if my good friend Mr. Cooper is an example of the *eligible* bachelors, it's no wonder you're still single."

"Oh, I know, right?"

"They all that bad?"

"You have no idea. So nasty."

"On behalf of my gender, I apologize."

Though Sam never let his eyes drift from the lady sitting across from him, he saw in his periphery that their conversation had caught the attention of the woman sorting through the files. She had popped out the ear buds and now pretended to not listen as she worked.

Susan snickered. "Well, thank you." She turned back to the business at hand. "Let me review the documents, but you should be just fine. Bobby simply isn't creative enough to do anything funky to the fine print of his contracts."

"That's a relief. When can I come back for them?"

For the first time, she glanced at the papers he'd handed her. She flipped through the first few pages, then her eyes drifted back to his. "I should be able to get to this by late afternoon. Why don't you stop by around five? I'll have an answer for you then."

Sam needed to be in control of both her and the situation. Letting her dictate the time would take away some of his power. So he made a joke about people from Florida coming to want to snatch up the property, mimicking the smarmy sale man's voice. If he could distract her, even make her laugh, she wouldn't see the manipulation tactic. She agreed to have the papers done by three.

Sam flashed his most winning smile and left.

Chapter Twenty-One

S am pushed through the glass door of the law office of
Bunder and Associates at half past four. As he entered,
Susan looked up from the stack of documents, and her
expression changed from one of mild curiosity to one of
disapproval. The other woman from the office no longer
lurked behind the wall of papers. Three's a crowd?

She looked at her watch. "I thought we agreed on
three?"

He had gone back to his hotel and showered, then
sat around waiting for time to pass. He needed her to
anticipate his arrival. The longer she did, and the more
she wanted him to return, the more in control he would
be of their conversation and, if one came about, their
evening. "Sorry, traffic was a bitch."

She stared at him for a heartbeat then grinned. As
he approached her desk, he saw she had applied a little
makeup. He couldn't stand it when women wore heavy
dollops of garish eye shadow and trowels of pink lipstick.
But she looked refreshed and, along with her change of
clothes, had a put-together appeal. And could that be?
Yep, a bit of perfume too.

Lonely girl meets the new boy in town.

"Yeah, well it *is* rush hour, so next time you have an important meeting scheduled, please plan extra travel time."

"Noted. So, I guess I missed my time slot. Can you look at your calendar and see when the next available appointment is?"

"Hmmm. Wow, I'm just not seeing anything. How about next March? Yeah, no, sorry, nothing sooner. Can I put you down for, say, three? Oh, wait. It's you. Best make it four-thirty."

As they continued their banter, Susan not only grinned, but a twinkle also sparked in her hazel eyes. Of all the pictures he'd seen, her high school portrait had been the only one in which she'd smiled. But in that lone photograph, the expression looked forced and placating; here, it seemed both genuine and happy.

She's having fun, maybe for the first time in a very long time, Chet observed.

Being on the run does tend to suck out the joy out of your life.

So does being chased by people who want to kill you.

Well, Sam replied, *perhaps she shouldn't be doing things that make it necessary for her to be removed from society. Then she wouldn't have to live that way.*

Sam leaned in. "Tell you what, how about I make you dinner? I couldn't stand the thought of eating whatever roadkill the diner has on its menu. I picked up some supplies, and there's more than enough for two."

"So, there are some problems with that. The first is that I don't even know you. You could be a lunatic." She tipped her head. "A girl needs to be cautious."

Score one for the legal chick, Chet said. *She says she doesn't know you, but clearly she does.*

Sam chuckled. "Well, I suppose I could be a lunatic. What does your intuition tell you?"

She studied him, and the skepticism in her eyes resolved itself. Finally Susan said, "That you probably *are* crazy... but not dangerous."

Chet sighed. *I take back the point and fine her two more for blatant stupidity and hormonal desperation. Maybe she's not as smart as everyone says?*

"What's the other problem?" Sam asked.

"You're looking for a place to live and thus are probably staying in a hotel. The out-of-towner accommodations in this shitty little burg leave something to be desired. And though I haven't personally stayed at any, I'm pretty certain that none of them have kitchens. I feel quite sure that you have missed out on the rental, so no luck there. And even if you *did* have the new place, did you also pick up pots, pans, plates, and so on? You look like a smart man, so tell me, where exactly were you planning to cook? Really, Mr., ummm, what was your name again?——Morrell——what is your agenda?"

She's on to you, Chet informed him.

I've got this.

Do you? Oh, I can't wait.

"Very well reasoned, Counselor. You've got me. I don't have an agenda, per se. I was just hoping that someone might let me use their kitchen. I really am a good cook, and I clean up after myself. You won't even know I was there."

That's a double entendre, Chet said.

"Really? And so you thought, 'Oh, small town hospitality and all. Surely someone will invite the handsome stranger into her house.' Is that pretty much it?"

"So, handsome, huh?"

"You're avoiding the question, Mr. Morrell," she admonished but blushed all the same.

Bring it home, Chet said. *Not even you could eff it up now.*

When you've been doing this job as long as I have, there is zero possibility of a blowout. "Well, everyone seems so friendly I thought surely someone would show some small-town hospitality. Maybe I'm wrong. Perhaps I should just go down the street, get a cat burger, lie in my hotel room, and listen to the sound of it clogging my arteries. Such is the way of things."

And yet you did... Sam could almost see Chet shaking his head in disappointment and disgust.

"Gross," Susan said.

"Tell me about it. Have you seen the menu at the diner?"

She studied him for a minute. "So, you do the dishes?"

☆☆☆☆

A scream ripped Sam out of his rough slumber. Susan sat up next to him, breathing hard, her face a mask of terror and tears. She had been draped over him when they fell asleep in her bed—her head on his chest with him running his fingers through her hair—and now they were soaked in her sweat.

He placed a hand on her lower back, trying to comfort her. "Are you okay?"

"Nightmare." Her whole body shook in aftershocks of the terrifying experience. Whatever she'd just dreamed about had scared the hell out of her. Her quaking hands dumped half of her cigarettes onto the floor before he took them from her and lit one for her.

If he said that she'd woken him up by screaming, then she might just let the bad dream explanation lie. But if he led her on, like she'd already revealed details about herself, he might get her to tell him more. "It sounded like hell. You were talking in your sleep. I couldn't tell what you were saying, but the longer it went on, the worse it got. I thought you were angry, but then you started crying. I was about to wake you up, but you screamed and about scared the crap out of me."

"I hate that dream. I have it all the time."

"What happens in it?" The moonlight shone through the large window, bathing the little room with a luminescent glow. He studied her profile, half of which remained hidden in the shadows cast by the soft white light. He really wanted to know, but would she tell him?

The night before, she'd surprised him by asking for a ride on his motorcycle, in spite of what Mary Beth had said about *ladies* never riding around on one of those things. He'd started off carefully, not wanting to scare her, minding the speed limits and his manners. But the further from town they'd gone, the faster she'd yelled for him to go. Soon they had been flying down the thin strip of asphalt in the middle of the desert. Even riding harder than he'd ever pushed the big bike, she'd still wanted to go faster.

When they arrived back at her place, they'd chatted over cold beers while he seared crusted salmon and baked homemade fries. They'd taken the food out onto the front porch, where they swapped stories—her about Lisa, the drama queen of the west; him, some of his more amusing military stories—while they laughed, drank more beer, and watched the stars.

At the end of the evening, he'd pulled her into his arms and kissed her. She'd returned the gesture and then took his hand, leading him to her room. As they rolled around in her bed, she had again surprised him by enthusiastically vocalizing her pleasure, and he wondered if it had been loud enough for the neighbors to hear. Something about the performance smelled off, but he couldn't put his finger on what. Almost as if she had been putting on a show. But why?

Then she had laid her head on his chest and fallen asleep until scaring him awake.

Still breathing hard from the nightmare, she looked at him, her skin glistening with sweat in the moonlight. She'd shared her body with him, but some things were even more personal. Would she keep the details of her dream to herself? "I killed a man."

He knew this. Read the grim details in her dossier a thousand times, but still he wasn't prepared for the matter-of-fact way she'd delivered the information. "Ummm, what? Really? What happened?"

"That's what the dream is about. After my dad died, mom decided to drink the county dry and screw every lowlife on the western seaboard. One night she passed out, and the bastard she'd brought home decided to pay me a little visit."

"Oh, shit."

"Yes. I was only twelve, but the perv wanted some more action. I disagreed and sent him to the big bar in the sky."

He knew the story, but it fascinated him to hear her version of the details. Monica's mother had spiraled out of control after her husband had died. The psychiatrist's diagnosis had been that she'd slipped into a deep, manic-like depression. As a result, instead of embracing her sole-remaining family member, the mother shoved the girl away. The situation devolved until one glorious evening the mother had screamed out profanities in a drunken tirade during Monica's middle-school graduation and had to be escorted from the premises. Her mother's invitations to attend any future functions had been permanently revoked by the school board.

Monica had been required to bail her mom out of jail on two separate occasions for possession. By the time the girl had turned fourteen, she lived by herself while her mother stayed with one boyfriend or another.

"She didn't show up when I graduated high school, top of my class I might add."

Probably for the best. "Congrats. That's not easy in the best of circumstances. Sorry about your mom, though."

"Yeah, I wasn't surprised or really disappointed. My best friend, Angel, her mom more or less adopted me. They were the only ones that I cared were there."

"Still, it had to sting."

"Well, that's life isn't it? Things don't always work out the way you want." Susan had begun to trace the deep scars on his thigh with her fingertip. "What about you? Why are you here?"

Rule # 73:
Blend some elements of truth into your background story. It increases believability.

Stories are, by definition, fiction. Trying to formulate a past on the fly while making it sound believable is difficult unless great thought and planning has gone into the structure and background. However, blending elements of truth, no matter how trivial the details, into the tale lend it credence to the ear and can get it past the most honed of bullshit detectors.

—*122 Rules of Psychology*

"Well, since my wife left me, I've been a bit lost." Sam watched her as he continued his well-rehearsed saga. Eye contact, relaxed body language, and a reflective tone would make him appear sincere and earnest. He gauged her reaction, giving her just enough then wrapping up while he still had his audience's attention. "I've only had a few people in my life I truly cared about; the first was my wife..."

"And the second?" she prompted.

"My brother. He was my absolute best friend."

Oh, boo hoo. Going on about your brother again? What the hell? You didn't have to go there. You could have left it. Chet's words rang with indignation.

I'm going where the story leads. That's all. She needs to trust me.

This isn't a therapy session, and you aren't her patient. Don't go overboard. We are information gatherers, not information providers.

"Was? What happened? Can you go stay with him?"

"He's dead." The weight of guilt over his brother's death lingered in the background. Sam sensed the lumbering hulk looming nearby and avoided it, as he always did.

She didn't say anything as he gathered his thoughts.

He continued, "So anyway, after I finished physical therapy, I tried to figure out where I was going and what I wanted to do with my life. I got a little money because of my injury, not a lot, just enough to get by for a while. Started traveling the country—Chicago, D.C., New York, California, all the big exciting places everyone always says they want to see— but so far, no place has struck me as home. So, here I am, trying the opposite of everything else."

"The opposite being small, remote, and decrepit, with no hope of a job or future?"

She'd made references and little jabs about the horrendousness of the town the night before, too. Given that, he asked himself the big question again: Why had she come here? He had hoped that by talking to her, he'd unravel some of these mysteries, but random threads of that tapestry only seemed to be leading to more unknowns.

"Suppose so," he said. "I actually didn't know anything about the town before I got here. I was driving and found this wide patch in the road. My bike took the off ramp, and here I am. My life has been turned upside down so many times I don't know which way is which. So I thought, why the hell not?" She must have run out of questions because she remained silent, so he asked one of his own. "So you graduated top of your high school class, then followed your dreams to be a lawyer?"

Anger flashed hot and white across her face. Had he crossed an imaginary line? But she hadn't been looking at him, staring instead out to space as if deep in thought. Then a small smile played on her lips. "Well, that was the plan."

He had been guiding the conversation most of the evening, but his control had been slipping away. Now he had no idea where she intended to take it. "But it didn't work out? Looks to me like you're living the dream."

Chet snorted.

"Well, looks can be deceiving. I went to NYU on a full scholarship and was all set to be a big shot lawyer. But then I overheard a conversation I wasn't supposed to."

"What kind of conversation? Who was it?"

"It was between a drug lord and his hitman. Maybe you've heard of the Laven Michaels case?"

Sam almost never had time for television, but he tried to remain abreast of current events. So he spent two or three hours a week reviewing articles and reading blogs. The case had made national news. Not since the arrest of

Al Capone had such a significant mobster been on trial. "Oh, yeah. Who hasn't? It's all over the headlines and on every news channel. They have some star witness, though that doesn't seem to be enough because, by all accounts, the case seems to be falling apart."

You know where she's going with this, don't you? Chet asked.

Yeah, I think so.

Go ahead. Ask her, Chet told him. *I'll bet she has a good, though unverifiable, story.*

"Wait. Is that you? You're the witness?" Sam asked.

"One and the same. They wanted to 'protect' me, so here I am in witness protection, though I think witness prison is a better name for it. They locked me away, using me when they want and forgetting about me the rest of the time."

Told ya, Chet said. *The question is: What are you going to do?*

I really have no idea, Sam admitted. *None of what she said is in her file. But if she were the star witness in a major trial, The Agency would know about it.*

Maybe they do, but they kept that information from you?

No. They wouldn't do that.

Chet just shrugged.

As he listened to her talk about the unfulfilled promises of her continued life and education, he tried to relate this to everything else he knew. But the new information looked like the wrong piece of the wrong puzzle.

Not a thing fits together. Sam flipped through the file in his mind, searching for a clue that would tie Monica's story to the intel Josha had provided. The school and the sudden disappearance might connect if he could trust what she'd said. But The Agency would never send him after someone just for testifying... Would they?

Maybe The Agency you now know isn't the same one who hired you. Things change. Have you thought about that?

No. Sam hadn't. And more importantly, he didn't want to. *Yes, things do, but the simplest solution is usually the right one. So we have two choices: either we're talking major corruption and conspiracy, or our mark is lying.*

You have a point, but I'm telling you, something doesn't smell right.

Sam tuned back in to Susan. "So, they stole your identity?"

"Witness protection, baby."

"Wait, so you're saying your name isn't Susan?"

"Nope. Monica Sable, star witness and slave to the system." She held out her hand. "Pleased to re-meet you."

Gotcha, Chet said.

"Wow. I don't know what to say to that," Sam told her, and he didn't. Nothing lined up. Did she know a lot more than she let on? Had she simply been playing him all evening? He didn't think so. Sometimes, those that lived underground created elaborate fabrications to explain away their situation. Monica's intelligence had been a factor all along, and this story could just be another example of it.

Though WITSEC did explain the sudden disappearance in New York and her being here, in this town. It explained a lot of things.

She laughed. "You don't *say* anything," she said and rolled over on top of him. She kissed him, blowing smoke deep into his lungs. She took a deep drag off her cigarette then stamped it out. As they continued to kiss, the smoke drifting in a lazy haze around them, Monica began grinding against him. She then dipped her hip, and he moved inside of her. Like their conversation, she had control now and rotated her pelvis in a steady rhythm.

She moaned loudly, echoes of their night ruminating in his ears. Monica sat up, leaned back, and put her hands on his chest, riding him. Her cries became louder, growing in intensity and urgency. It seemed a bit much even for her. Monica screamed as she slammed her hips onto his. Her wails bounced off the walls in a final long crescendo.

She collapsed on top of him, holding him inside of her. The sweat stuck them together like glue, but she seemed to have fallen asleep, so he didn't try to move.

No other confirm had ever gone like this one, and he had no idea what to make of it. Everything she said could conceivably mesh with the contents in her dossier, but it contradicted the file too. Her breathing against his chest slowed, steady and deep, while he stared at the moon through the bedroom window.

Sam didn't find sleep until the first rays of light broke the eastern horizon.

Chapter Twenty-Two

The next morning, Sam woke alone to brilliant sunshine pouring in through the window. He stared around the small space, vacant of all knickknacks, pictures, and other such paraphernalia.

How odd. Does she actually live here? Chet asked.

Right?

Where's Martha Stewart when you need her?

Did this lend credence to her tale of being in WITSEC, or could the lack of personal touches be a quirk of her personality?

Sam retrieved his phone and typed out an email message. He detailed the relevant parts of conversation they'd had, specifying that he'd gotten a verbal confirm and that he had successfully identified the mark. He had started to attach the pictures he'd taken, when he heard her coming down the hall. He slipped the phone under his pillow and pretended to just be waking up.

Monica entered the room. She had on a thin silk robe with her hair tied back. In her hands, she brandished two large mugs of coffee and a plate of cinnamon rolls.

"Good morning," he said, sitting up.

"Good morning to you. Hungry?"

"Starving."

She handed him a mug and then offered him a pastry and a napkin.

"Thank you," he said, then took a sip.

She nodded. After setting her own breakfast down, she dropped her robe. Did she mean to crawl into bed with him? Maybe continue with a little of the excitement from the night before. Instead she pulled a dress off a hook and slipped it over her head.

He'd been on the sending end of the "It's time for you to go now" morning message many times before and pretended not to notice the hint, hoping to continue their conversation. He'd thought over what Chet had been telling him, and it warranted consideration. But to explore that further, he needed more time with her. "What's on your agenda for the day?"

Come one, come all, tell us why the little lady needs to go, Chet called. *She's got things to do and places to be, we just need the excuse. Gentlemen, place your bets, please. Place your bets.*

An appointment. Hair or doctor or something, Sam said.

Work. She's going to say she needs to go to work.

Come on, Sam replied. *That's too obvious. Besides, it's Saturday. She'll come up with something brilliant. Watch.*

"I need to go to work."

Ha! In your face, Chet mocked. *Who's the brilliant one now? Come on. Say it. Who's your daddy?*

He'd been paying more attention to the conversation with his inner conscience than to the one with the woman standing before him until she asked, "May I give you a little advice?"

She's probably going to tell you the same thing I've been telling you all these years: Get out of the spy business. You suck.

Sam rolled his eyes at his inner-conscience. *Nice, but somehow I doubt it.*

Maybe she's going to give you pointers on your lack of lovemaking skills. Remember the woman from West Virginia? What did she say? Something about raising your hips higher? I thought I'd died and gone to heaven that was so awesome.

Come on, Sam replied. *Did you hear her last night? I thought she was going to wake the dead.*

That was a show. You and I both know it. Besides, the only one that will be dead soon is her.

Chet's remark sent a narrow streak of unhappiness through Sam, and on the trail of that, came a stab of indignity at the unjustness of her situation. Instead of continuing to banter with his inner voice, he simply said, *Touché.*

He took another sip of his coffee. "Sure."

"Leave town."

"Pardon?"

"Leave. This place is a cesspool. The town is dying. The economy's in the toilet. There're no jobs and no prospects. It would be impossible to build a life here. Save your money and save yourself. Get out before it drags you down and sucks out your soul."

"What if one has a romantic prospect?" He shot her a charming smile.

"No. That's not going to happen. I had fun, but this was a one-time deal. I have to stay here, but you shouldn't."

You need to talk to her. Get to the bottom of this. Something smells bad, and it isn't just the economy, Chet said.

I know. I know. I'm trying. I'm not sure what else to do. The lady is asking me to leave, and I can't stay. I've got the confirm and orders. I'm open to suggestions though.

Spill it.

Chet's simple solution startled Sam. *Pardon?*

Tell her that you've been assigned to look for her. Give her a chance to explain everything.

Sam shook his head. *Ummm…no. That sure as shit isn't going to happen.*

Chet had nothing further to add.

Sam nodded. "Okay, I understand. I'll get dressed and get out of your hair." He stood and pulled on his clothes. Finishing his coffee, he headed toward the door.

"Thank you," she said to him as he exited. "I had a nice time."

He didn't understand the horrific knot in his stomach or the sense of betraying someone he should be protecting. She was just another mark, no different than any other. For one awful moment, he had been back with his ex-wife, Tracy, and she stared at him with hurt, sorrow, and loneliness in her eyes. He had wanted to protect her too, yet, like with Monica, had failed. He wanted to apologize, to make things right with Tracy slash Monica, but the desire was impossible and irrational.

Instead he turned on the stoop, touched Monica's chin, and kissed her gently. "Thank you. If I don't see you again, I hope things work out. I really do." He climbed on his bike and drove away under the glaring gaze of his inner conscience.

On the edge of town, Sam parked on a wide patch of road, reviewed the email he had written that morning, and finished attaching the pictures. He scrolled through the images of the law office and Monica's run-down shack of a home, ones of her at work and in bed asleep. He paused on the last, studying the woman's relaxed, trusting face. As he stared, he searched for the answers that had to exist though remained elusive. Unsatisfied but having no reason to delay, he closed the documents and prepared to relay the information.

Before he had a chance to send the message, detailing the sad story of Monica's existence to his boss, Chet piped up. *Are you sure about this, chief? Tell Josha it's the wrong girl, the wrong town. Whatever. It wouldn't be the first time they've given you bad intel. He'd believe it.*

Sam's finger hovered between the *send* and *cancel* buttons. *Last chance.*

Sam pressed his finger to the screen then dialed a number from memory.

"The intel looks great," Josha said by way of greeting. "I wish I had about a dozen more of you. Talk to me."

Under his alter ego's glare, Sam gave a brief synopsis of the same information contained in report he'd just sent.

"You got the confirm?" Josha asked.

"Last night." Sam told him the details.

You're a moron. Chet's disgust coated the chastisement.

I'm a soldier.

Same difference.

Sam heard Josha type on his keyboard then pause before speaking again. "Client confirms. It's her."

"Do I do the drop?"

Pause, more typing, then, "Yes."

"When?"

Josha didn't hesitate this time. "Immediately."

Chapter Twenty-Three

S am lay sweat-soaked beneath a bedraggled bush whose soul had been sapped by the relentless glare of the sun. Darkness had descended, but the hard-packed earth he rested upon radiated heat that rivaled the one he'd been exposed to all afternoon. No other location offered this level of concealment and isolation from the populace, while still providing the access and line of sight he required.

He had scoped out Monica's neighborhood. During regular workdays, most of the residents would be away.

He had assumed his position four hours earlier to be certain he would not miss his opportunity. If he somehow didn't connect, he could use the knife tucked in his boot, but he preferred the quick tidiness of the silenced rifle. He could slip out of town without having to first clean up a mess and worry about trace evidence.

In spite of the copious amount of water he'd drunk, his head hurt from dehydration, and his eyes stung from the biting, wind-blown sand. Damn, he hated this place.

A car drove down the street and parked. The reverberating slam of the vehicle's door echoed from the front of the house. Monica had arrived.

Earlier in the day, Sam had removed the screen of her house to make sighting the trajectory of the bullet easier. Looking through the rifle's night scope, he stared down the hall of the little bungalow. The infrared technology allowed him to see the fuzzy details of the walls and bookshelves but bathed everything in a neon green—the exact same color of the slime ghosts from the second-rate flicks he and his brother had watched as kids. In this case, it looked as though a B-movie ghoul had materialized out of the silver screens of his past and succumbed to an explosive case of diarrhea inside the suburban bungalow.

When Sam detected movement, his mind returned to the present. A glowing image of a woman stepped through the entrance of the house. Fuzzy, luminescent hands closed the front door, and a brilliant demon leaned against the wall. Sam centered the scope's crosshairs on the creature's gleaming head.

His finger, which had already been tense against the trigger, applied subtle pressure. Chet, who'd been quiet all afternoon, chose that instant to voice his opinion. *Dude, for the record, you're a moron.*

What? We've done this a thousand times. She's just another perp.

Sam internally cringed at Chet's disapproving glare. *Are you sure, or are you just saying that to justify your actions? You've had doubts about this case since day one. For once in your life, it's time to stop being a soldier and think. This can't be undone. Neither Josha nor his intel can be perfect all the time. Something is off; maybe you should go in and talk to her? After that, if you're still hell-bent on doing this, there's always the alternative in your boot.*

Sam hesitated. Just a little more pressure from his finger and the decision would be made. Which way? Monica's existence hung in the balance. Sam let out his pent-up breath, deflating. He relaxed his grip and lowered the weapon.

"Shit." He picked up the gun and slammed it to the ground. "Shit. Shit. Shit." He pounded the heavy rifle against the concrete of silicon and rock, then beat the weapon with his fist. Anger and frustration flowed through his veins as he tried to comprehend what had stopped him.

Go talk to her, idiot, and find out, Chet instructed.

Sam finished with his tantrum and sat in the dirt like a belligerent toddler. After a minute, he took a deep breath and calmed himself. Chet had a point, though it still didn't sit well with Sam. He needed to get more information. Once he had all the facts, he could make his decision. He started to stand when his world went black.

☆☆☆☆

Sam woke on his back, his head propped up on a rock. Stars overhead and flashing red lights greeted his eyes. He tried to rise up. The dehydration headache he'd experienced earlier in the day felt like a moth's kiss compared to the vise that now squeezed his temples. He propped himself up on his elbows to get a better look at the chaos surrounding him.

Where Monica's modest house once stood, a raging inferno consumed the space. Staring at the cratered, burning house, understanding dawned, and he slinked away to where the motorcycle sat hidden. His head screamed in protest as he righted then pushed the big bike down the road. He wanted to climb on and drive away, but he had to keep the noisy engine from attracting unwanted attention.

After he had gotten a safe distance away, he started the bike and rode off. Stopping at the same wide patch in the road where he had sent the email, he turned off the engine. Instead of helping, the silence only seemed to exacerbate the hornets, armed with ball peen hammers, pounding in the inside of his skull.

Pulling out his cell phone, he dialed Josha's number.

"Done?"

Sam wondered if his boss even knew how to say the word *hello*. "Well, in a manner of speaking. Someone got to her first."

"What happened?"

Sam fought through the daze that still plagued him from the explosion and relayed the details of his evening, leaving out the part where he failed to pull the trigger.

Josha remained silent, and Sam gave him time to process the turn of events. After a minute his superior asked, "So, you're sure she's dead."

"I saw her in the scope right before the place went up. No one could live through that."

"All right. Consider the case closed."

Though unsatisfied, Sam had no choice but to let it go. Whether by his hand or someone else's, Monica had died, and nothing further could be accomplished by continuing the investigation. The injustice of her demise tried to assert itself, and he shoved it away. "So what's next?"

"What's next is a little R and R."

"What?" Sam recoiled as if he'd been slapped. "Where are you sending me?"

"Nowhere. That's the point."

"I don't need a vacation. Just tell me what my next assignment is."

"Look, Sam, I just checked the records, and you haven't taken any time off in almost four years. I'm not giving you anything for three weeks. I can't; it's policy."

Sam started to protest, "I don't——"

"And," Josha interrupted, "if you fight me, I'll make it a month."

"Okay, I'm not arguing, just telling you how it is."

"Go on."

Sam pursed his lips. He didn't want, nor did he need, to lie around doing nothing when so much had to be fixed in the world. He had been born to protect his country from the threats that bombarded it, and he couldn't do that from the sidelines. "I don't need any time off. Really. I have plenty of down time on assignment. Besides, I like to keep busy."

"Sam, have you ever thought about having a life? When was the last time you spent the night in your own apartment?"

"I was there three months ago."

"Only because you were tracking Monica and one of the leads was in L.A."

"Still…"

"Look, you are one of the best, but regulations are regulations. Go do something besides work. Meet a girl. Get laid. Go surfing. According to your file you used to do that, remember? But whatever you do, don't call me."

Sam punched his bike. "Fine. Three weeks."

"Good man. Have fun," Josha said and disconnected the call.

Sam opened the music streaming service on his phone and chose one of his traveling blues channels. Though it killed his head, he turned up the volume to drown out the voice of his conscience who wanted to continue to ponder, question, and work through his unresolved feelings for his mother or whatever. *Kiss my ass, Chet.*

He took one last look around the arid wasteland, started the Triumph, and dropped it into gear. A minute later, he crossed the city limits of the thriving metropolis of Walberg to the soulful melancholy guitar riffs of Stevie Ray as the talented prophet sang about the crying sky.

You tell 'em, Stevie. Poor bastards sure as shit could use a few tears or something from Heaven. Sam gunned the engine and headed toward home.

PART 3

Chapter Twenty-Four

Monica drove out of Walberg on the back streets to keep off the main thoroughfare. Not many roads crossed the desert, so she took the first highway she came to, teeth rattling. Her hands shook so hard she could barely keep the Audi in its lane. But as full-on darkness descended and the miles spun out, the shaking subsided.

A sign flashed in her high beams, indicating the town of Sinalta lay just ahead. The fuzzy map in her head pinned her at about seventy miles east of Walberg. As she passed through the decrepit little city on the edge of nowhere, a pair of headlights snapped to life in her review mirror. Monica's breath caught in her throat. Her knuckles turned white as she bore down on the steering wheel and pressed down on the accelerator. The Audi responded, sailing over the blacktop with a smooth grace. But no matter how fast she moved, the lights grew larger as the other car closed the gap. She needed to go faster, but it took all of her effort just to keep from veering off the road.

Monica cursed. It hadn't taken the homicidal bomber long to find her. He must have waited just in case he missed, and now he chased her with a raging intensity so great only her complete annihilation could soothe his fanatical desire for carnage. No chances this time. No mistakes. She wouldn't be able to elude him and couldn't hide in the desert, but she'd be damned if she wouldn't make him work for it. Monica pressed harder on the gas pedal. The engine growled in response, and the wind howled like a demon.

As the pursuing vehicle caught up, the glare of its lights—level with the Audi's back window—shone through with a blinding intensity that scorched her eyes. At any second the deranged killer would bump her, sending her car careening into a cactus or flying into a culvert. Suddenly, the tailgating car swept out into the oncoming lane and moved up beside her. Terror shrieked through her veins as Monica dared to look over, certain she would see the madman with a gun aimed in her direction.

A pickup full of teenage boys, laughing and hollering on the lonesome highway, met her gaze. One of the hooligans in the back of the truck took a long pull off his beer, then tossed the empty and stood. Wrapping his arm around the roll bar, he turned and dropped his pants, mooning her. The boy's friends howled with approval. Monica rolled her eyes then flipped them the bird, which only made them hoot and holler louder.

Ahead, a cross street intersected with the highway. At the last second, she slammed on the brakes and spun the wheel. The Audi chewed gravel, its tires squealing in anger, but as the rubber grabbed hold of the asphalt, she floored the accelerator around the corner.

She watched in her review mirror, but the truck did not give chase. Fear gave way to the anger that surged in her blood. This should never have happened. The FBI should have been watching out for her. Crew Cut's only job had been to keep her safe, and with her on such a tight leash, he should have been able to do so with ease. It's not like she'd gone anywhere or told anyone…

Her eyes widened as an image of the man on the motorcycle flashed through her mind. Peter. It couldn't be a coincidence that he'd appeared on the same day she'd gotten her tracking device off. Or that he'd left town, and then her house had been blown to smithereens.

But had Crew Cut been under orders to remove her tracking device? If so, and the FBI agent proved to be innocent, who in the organization had told him to do so? Jon? If not, then Crew had been bribed or otherwise finagled, and the FBI had a corrupt agent in their ranks.

Peter had been hired to kill her, but why hadn't he just done so? Why seduce her first? Maybe using the victim one last time for his own pleasure had become part of the assassin's creed?

Of course, she'd been using him too. She'd wanted to strike back and screw with the FBI in any way she could. A smug expression crossed her lips at the idea of Crew Cut and his hoard frantically making phone calls as she spilled all to Peter.

But then her smile faltered. Could she be as much to blame for Peter getting at her as the people in charge of keeping her safe? Why did she always fight the system so hard? Maybe if she'd just gone with the flow, things would have worked out. Laven would have died or something, and she could have gone back to her regular life. Unlikely, but not impossible. He had to have enemies. And really, what had possessed her to open her damned mouth and tell Peter her name in the first place? And shouldn't the FBI have come barreling in the second she'd revealed herself?

These questions circled her mind like vultures targeting an injured deer.

This wasn't the life she'd envisioned when she started at NYU. She'd hated her life in Walberg—the city was shit and most of its citizens assholes.

Until the incident at the library, Monica had always been in control of her own destiny. She had given that up for a while, but now the time had come to take the reins back. Somehow.

She could hypothesize scientific principles, calculate derivatives, and pontificate on the philosophers of the Renaissance, but evading the FBI and hitmen? Phantom ideas barraged her at such a dizzying pace, each of them vying for her undivided attention, that she could not maintain focus on any one of them. Just as she attempted to grasp one of these roaming specters, it dissolved.

Monica took a deep breath and quelled the stymieing thoughts. What did she know? From the mystery novels she consumed by the barrelful, she knew not to use her credit cards or cell phone. In fact...Monica fumbled in her purse and shut the FBI-issued phone off. She opened the Audi's window and threw the little marvel of technology into the gutter, watching in the mirror as it hit the side of the road and broke into a dozen pieces.

In the fictitious renditions of life as portrayed on the silver screen, the police often snared their quarry by triangulating signals or whatever. The task, so trivial and commonplace, had become part of the standard curriculum in Law Enforcement 101. Inexperienced as she was, she nevertheless wanted to make it as difficult as possible for Jon and his goons to apprehend her. Picturing the smug expression on the bastard's face when they captured her due to some rookie mistake only doubled her resolve.

So she did the only thing she could think of: put as much distance between herself and Walberg as possible.

The all-night truck stop where Monica stopped to fill up the little Audi had an attached convenience store that carried everything from auto parts to cheeseburgers. She bought some food and basic supplies for life on the lam, including a pre-paid cell. As she loaded her purchases into the trunk, she noticed the pump jockey leaning against the wall smoking a cigarette, eyeing the flashy little red sports car.

Shit. She sighed, and her shoulders drooped. Could she drive anything more conspicuous? She needed to maintain as low a profile as possible, an infeasible task as long as her wheels looked like they belonged parked at an A-list celebrity auction.

Maybe she could find someone willing to trade their Buick or Chevy for the Audi? But that seemed messy and time consuming; besides, she didn't have the title, and the registration would be in Lisa's name. What if the person she tried to sell it to thought she'd stolen it and called the police?

She closed the trunk, went back into the store, and returned a few minutes later lugging several bags, which she added to the ones already in the small trunk. Apprehensive relief filled her when she saw the jockey no longer lounged against the wall, but prudence told her to put this place behind her as quickly as possible.

Walberg had receded in her rearview mirror but so too had the adrenaline rush that had propelled her, and she found herself yawning as exhaustion filled the chasm left in its wake.

But before finding somewhere to spend the night, she had more to do. She started the car, and steered it out of the lot and back onto the road. After another hour of driving the headlights flashed on a sign for the Kofa National Wildlife Refuge. Monica guided the car into the deserted parking and surveyed her surroundings.

No cars lingered in the deep pockets of shadow that lay like seas of inky darkness outside the sparse pools of eerie yellow light cast by the overhead fluorescents. She paused, listening, but could hear nothing save for the crickets and the occasional truck as it downshifted on the lonesome highway.

Satisfied no one would bear witness, she opened the car's little trunk and removed the large tire iron she'd purchased at the truck stop. The Audi's creators had built the car for those screaming for attention. Fire-engine red, compact, and sleek, the design fell woefully short of satisfying her current needs.

Monica intended to spray paint the car and be done with it. But the shiny metal gleamed under the artificial light, beckoning. She walked around Lisa's little indulgence, looking for just the right place. She found a spot that seemed particularly tempting and raised the heavy iron over her head, then brought it around in an arc—not dissimilar to the one she'd used to bash the brains in of the man who tried to rape her all those years ago—and smashed it into the passenger door.

It made a deep *whomp* as metal met metal and teeth-rattling vibrations reverberated through her arms and shoulders. She raised the iron and brought it down again, the dent evolving into a divot. She moved a few inches to the rear and gave the divot a twin, then another.

As she continued, pain spewed out of the ragged holes in her soul. It fed the anger, which came alive, erupting out of both new and ancient scars.

"Bastards! Who do you think you are you can just lock me away?" She brought the iron down on the hood. She cursed at her father for dying and leaving her with a drunken whore of a mother. She screamed at Peter for killing her friend. While yelling at Laven for being such an idiot as to not check his surroundings before meeting with his murdering friend, she pulverized the Audi's little four-circle symbol, putting a satisfying hole in the grill.

She climbed up and hulked out on the front of the car like a 1950s movie monster, sending paint flakes and chips of metal flying as she brought the bar down on the roof while shouting at the top of her lungs, screaming her throat raw.

Over and over, she slammed the iron down until the muscles in her arms and back throbbed, rendering her tormented hands numb from the violent vibrations. At last, she fell into a sobbing heap on the asphalt. The battered iron bar, flicks of red paint embedded in its surface, clattered on blacktop as she tossed it aside.

The hellish pain and rage of her life flowed out of her, streaking down her cheeks. As the last of her sobbing subsided, a calm settled over her.

Weariness weighed down her body as if it had been infused with lead, but she forced herself to climb to her feet and retrieve the newspapers and duct tape she'd purchased. She covered the windows, mirrors, and lights of the now bashed-to-shit Audi. Even in her frenzy, she'd been careful to leave these undamaged.

Then she pulled out the final purchase: five cans of flat black spray paint. She covered every square inch of shiny red metal that had survived the bludgeoning.

With a silent apology to whatever species she endangered by placing her leftovers in the landfill, she stuffed everything into a nearby dumpster, then stood back and admired her handiwork.

Well, she'd wanted something that wouldn't be tempting or eye-catching, and now she had it.

The parking lot was still deserted. She could just spend the night here—find a corner spot and curl up on one of the Audi's seats—but then she'd be visible and vulnerable to anyone that happened by. Plus, in the sun, the car would turn into a pressure cooker in about five minutes.

Monica rummaged around in the trunk and pulled out a can of diet soda, then she rolled down all the windows and turned on the radio. Not many channels broadcast in the middle of nowhere, so she tried the *CD* button. A French rock band blared through the speakers.

She didn't speak the language, but the bass thumped and the guitars shrieked. Monica instantly fell in love and cranked up the stereo to wineglass-shattering decibels. She took a long pull off the cola, crumpled up the empty can, and belched long, loud, and deep as she powered her way out of the parking lot toward parts—and a future—unknown.

Chapter Twenty-Five

At just before two in the morning, Monica pulled into the dirty parking lot of a motel. Weeds grew from cracks in the asphalt, and aged pages of sun-bleached newspapers adhered to the brick siding, glued in place by ancient rain showers. She picked the establishment with the flickering neon sign that boasted rooms by the hour, day, or month, passing up nicer major chain accommodations because this place would probably accept cash and ask no questions.

The gaze of the greasy man behind the counter crawled over her as she approached the window, the sensation of being groped as palpable as though he had been using his hands to explore the contours of her body.

In the old Superman movies, the hero had the ability to see through barriers by simply wishing to do so. Unlike the man of steel, who perpetuated the advancement of humankind through the pursuit of truth, justice, and the American way, this man's superpower—visual molestation—would have been used only to satisfy his unquenchable lust for leering.

Monica pried his gaze off her breasts when she handed over the night's rent plus an extra forty dollars. The money disappeared in a neat sleight of hand that would have impressed David Copperfield. The pervert's kryptonite was greed.

When he handed her a key, attached via a chain to a ridiculously large plate with *199* printed on its surface, his hand unnecessarily fondled her fingers. His lips and eyes formed a slow jack-o-lantern smile as he wished her good night, making the hairs on the nape of her neck stand on end. Monica left the counter as fast as she could without actually running, pulling out a small bottle of hand sanitizer and hoping the miracle of the disinfectant would wipe away the unclean feeling.

She followed the cracked sidewalk until she reached unit 199, inserted the key—the too-large paddle obnoxiously banging against the metal of the door—and, glancing around to make sure no one observed her, pushed inside.

She wrinkled her nose in disgust. The room had the musty, depressed aroma of desolation and cheap, mildewed carpet. Thinking of the slimy hotel attendant, the FBI, the mob, and, of course, Peter, she set the deadbolt on the thin door then jimmied the room's only chair under the handle. The hazardous conditions warranted more Fort Knox-like security, but under the circumstances, she could do no better. She looked one last time at her pathetic precaution then shrugged and turned to the bed.

Questionable stains whose origins she preferred not to think about darkened the bedspread, giving it a patchwork appearance. Ordinarily, the place would have sent her packing, but the events of the day hadn't even been in the same universe as ordinary.

She dumped her meager belongings and lay down fully clothed, falling asleep the moment her head hit the pillow.

Chapter Twenty-Six

Monica woke from a dreamless slumber to harsh sunshine bleeding through the thin, cheap drapes of the hotel room. When she sat up on the edge of the bed, her foggy memories from the night before played through her mind like scenes from a Quentin Tarantino movie rather than images from her own life. The only thing lacking in this saga was a white knight. Her flick required someone dashing with large muscles, extensive experience living outside the law, and a knowing aw-shucks smile to arrive on the brink of disaster and save the damsel in distress.

She waited.

When neither Matt Damon nor Daniel Craig burst through her door, she sighed and picked up the remote to the battered TV set and clicked the power button.

She hadn't expected the television to even work, and she almost jumped when she heard a low electrical hum as it buzzed to life. She flipped through the channels, but only a kid's program playing a *Sesame Street* knockoff and a news station worked in this remote corner of the globe. The idiocy of the singing animals only slightly outweighed the idiocy of the news anchors, so she chose the latter.

They transitioned from fluff story to fluff story, so she left the box on for background noise and padded into the tiny bathroom. She stripped and stood under the hot spray of the shower for what felt like hours. The grime-coated tub looked like it contained enough botulism bacteria to wipe out a small village, but the wonderfully strong water pressure massaged the exhaustion from her body, washing away the worst of the brain fog. Her arms and back ached, and she discovered a huge, source-unknown-but-shaped-vaguely-like-Texas bruise on her thigh. The deep purple looked sick and malignant in the jaundiced light filtering through the shower's stiff plastic curtain.

As her mind wandered, a momentary flash of panic tore through her at the possibility that the perp who'd blown up her house had waited around to watch it explode. He could have seen her drive off. Undoubtedly the assassin would have been amused by the antics of the pickup truck full of teenage boys that had chased her just outside of Sinalta. He might be disappointed they hadn't finished the job for him…

She nearly jumped out of the water to hide under the bed, naked and wet——the monsters under the mattress had to be more friendly and accommodating than the ones that dogged her in real life.

But if she had been followed, she'd be dead already. He wouldn't have waited around until she'd had a good night's sleep before putting a bullet in her brain. So, following that logic, neither the would-be assassin nor the FBI knew where she hid.

Calming her racing heart, she shut off the water. She dried herself off with a towel as soft and plush as dirty burlap then wandered back into the front room, taking stock of what she had. In summary: almost nothing. No clean clothes or toiletries, and everything else she owned had either been taken by Special Agent Jon and his henchmen or burned in the fire.

"In other news, a Walberg woman was killed when her house exploded…"

Monica spun around and froze as she came face-to-face with her Arizona driver's license photo—hair bunned, eyes staring, expression somber. The picture had a dour, depressed tone no professional photographer could hope to replicate. Only the Department of Motor Vehicles had the ability to capture that sort of soul-wrenching unhappiness. She fumbled with the remote and turned up the volume.

The clip changed to the "At The Desk" anchor, and Monica's picture got relegated to the left corner as she received her five minutes of fame. "Susan Rosenberg, local paralegal from Walberg, was killed last night when her home exploded. Authorities report that a gas line under her house had been leaking methane and was ignited by a spark from an electric source, most likely a light switch."

The segment shifted to the burned hole that had at one time been listed by Bobby as a "Classic bungalow in the heart of suburbia." How would the smarmy salesman spin the sale now? Perhaps, "Airy and open to nature, with great fixer-upper potential."

The camera panned to the scorched metal hulk that had been her car then a quick "eye witness" interview. The interviewee, her neighbor Todd or Trey or something, said he saw the house on fire. He then added for emphasis, "It was hot." Those were his final words before switching back to the news anchor.

Way to be descriptive there.

"The explosion has been ruled an accident." The news anchor completed the segment by reminding her audience that if they smelled anything unusual when entering their home, they should leave immediately and call the gas company from a neighbor's house. The camera angle changed, and the newscaster's expression transformed to one of happiness as she announced, "Imagine being a kitten in a basket full of yarn…"

Monica clicked the power button, the scene of the cute and playful fur ball wrestling with red and green yarn shrinking to a pinpoint of light before winking out.

Dead. Everyone thought she had died. Really? She had expected to live on the run, having to watch over her shoulder. But being dead… What exactly did that mean?

All she knew was that she needed both coffee and a plan. But first, she wandered back to the bathroom to get dressed.

She picked up her blouse and sniffed the pits. It didn't smell too rank, but then again, she had grown accustomed to the dank odor of the hotel, so who really knew for sure? She stared at the sink, considering washing everything in the little basin, but then she'd have to wait for her clothes to dry or be forced to put them on wet. She could handle wearing day-old pants and shirt but hadn't sunk so low she would wear soiled underwear.

Monica winced as she slid, commando, into the slacks, her back protesting at the stretch and pull of bending over to thread her feet into the pant legs.

Lisa would have undoubtedly had an entire armada of hair and makeup supplies in her ample purse, paired with the skills of a starlet's—say JLo's or Madonna's—dressing team to go with them. But Monica's modest shoulder bag carried no such provisions. So she ran her fingers through her hair, trying to straighten and untangle the worst of the knots, then splashed cold water on her face.

She took a deep, cleansing breath. For the first time in memory, she had gained her freedom. As a dead girl, she had been released from the oppressive weight of the FBI pawing through her life and tracking her every movement. Free from living in a place she hated. Free to be under her own control for the first time since that day at the library about a million years ago.

The bomb hadn't so much wiped the slate clean as blown it to bits, sending the shards of her old life to all corners of the globe.

She wiped the steam from the mirror, and her eyes widened in surprise. Braless, in a loose blouse, with a new, relaxed demeanor—she could have been a Feng Shui consultant or even a street musician. Donning her Audrey Hepburn sunglasses, Monica smiled at herself in the mirror, then shouldered her purse and headed out to the car.

The Stardust motel lay on the outskirts of a small town Monica didn't know. She drove up the main strip, slipping the Audi next to the curb in front of a small coffee shop. The few citizens strolling the sidewalks didn't give the battered car a second glance, and she pushed through the glass door of the Happy Lizard Bistro.

The clean and well-kept shop contained just a smattering of patrons seated at small round tables next to the big windows facing the street. On a television hanging from a ceiling corner, the same news station she'd watched in her room dished out snippets of drama in bite-sized, thirty-second segments. These tiny soap operas intermixed with promises of more of the same. The recent trend of networks playing cute and hilarious videos swiped from the Internet—nothing more than cheap gimmicks—screamed of desperation.

These guys have even less idea of what they're doing than I do.

Monica turned her attention to the counter attendant. The girl behind the cash register, with braces and a deeply pocked face, rang up her order for a giant chocolate mocha and the biggest cinnamon roll in the display case. She was already dead; screw the calories.

"Oh, that poor thing," the girl said.

Monica followed Pock Face's gaze, and her blood ran cold as the TV network recycled the news segment she had seen earlier. As the clip ended and her dour photo faded from the screen, she thought, *This is it. The jig is up. This coffee girl is going to scream, "Oh my god! You're her, the one in the news."*

Instead, acne girl said, "I hope she didn't have kids or anything," then handed Monica her food.

In a daze, Monica carried her purchases to an empty table where she picked at the cinnamon roll. The authorities thought her dead—the victim, not of the mob hit trying to tie up a loose end, but of faulty workmanship and a rogue possum with a taste for gas lines.

Pock Face, though probably not an Ivy League scholar, had looked at the image on TV and directly at "Susan" standing right in front of her. Yet the cashier hadn't recognized her as the person from the news segment. If *she* didn't make the connection, maybe others wouldn't either. Maybe Monica had a chance.

She finished her food and wandered down the street, becoming more confident with each step as her anonymity remained secure. She found an open thrift store where she picked out several outfits and a pair of half-worn running shoes. For less than a hundred dollars, she had the semblance of a wardrobe again.

Three doors down in the Laundromat, she read old magazines and watched TV while her clothes spun and rinsed then tumble dried through the industrial-sized machines. She folded her clothes and drove the beat-to-shit Audi back to the motel.

She'd escaped—disappeared like Houdini and fooled the police, the FBI, everyone. She flexed her arms, kissed her tiny biceps, and roared. *I am a self-assured woman. I am Xena the warrior princess. I am Joan of Arc.*

I am...deluding myself. What I am is lucky and in need of help.

Since both Mr. Damon and Mr. Craig seemed otherwise occupied, she turned to the same person she always did.

Lisa's laptop had been amongst the files in the trunk of the car. Monica started it up and logged onto her email. The screen did a weird pause and flash thing, similar to what her own had done last week when she'd opened the email app. The odd hiccup only occurred once, and then the computer seemed to be fine.

She disregarded the PC's behavior and clicked *New Message*. But then she paused. Did she really feel like typing all of this out? So much had happened. Maybe she could just say, "Call me." The room had a phone. Then she remembered one of the other things she bought at the truck stop and set the computer aside.

Rummaging through the packages of nuts, protein bars, and bottles of water, she pulled out what she sought and plopped down on the bed. She removed the packaging containing the pre-paid cell phone, powered it up, worked through the little welcome menu, and then dialed a number she knew by heart.

"Hello," Angel's voice came through the little receiver, and relief flooded through her.

"Ang, it's me."

"Mon! Oh my god! How are you?" Angel sounded pleased to hear from her. After a heartbeat, she said, "Wait, what's the matter? You said you weren't supposed to call me, and I don't recognize this number. What happened?"

"Jesus, Ang, how do you do that?"

213

"It's a gift. Now spill."

"I need your help." Monica began to pace the room.

They talked for a few minutes before Monica disconnected. Her angel had taken flight, on the way to rescue her. Again.

Chapter Twenty-Seven

Sam rode east on a lonely patch of highway toward his empty apartment. As the blacktop slipped under the bike's wheels, he puzzled through the mess he'd left back in Walberg.

What mess? Chet asked. *You did exactly what you always do. Put everything aside and did your job. Didn't consider what you were doing, didn't listen to me, just handed that girl over to Josha without really thinking it through.*

But I did listen to you. Sam shook his head. *I didn't pull the trigger, and I was going to go in and talk to her.*

Yes, but she's still dead. Maybe you should have thought it through sooner. You might have been able to save her.

Sam shrugged. *What's to think through? She's obviously involved in the drug trade, or Josha wouldn't have had me looking for her.*

Jesus, okay, maybe. But maybe not. What about what she told you? Chet's indignation turned the question into an accusation.

What about it? Sam snapped back.

Witness Protection. The trial. Don't you think you could have at least followed up? Run a couple of web searches? Done a little digging for more information? That's your stock-in-trade, right? Finding out the dirt on people? Or do you only do that when you want to manipulate them? And once you have what you need, it's sayonara baby.

Sam had no response. Chet wasn't wrong.

His subconscience continued, *So why didn't you? Is it because Monica reminded you of Tracy? You remember Tracy? Your ex?*

Screw you. No.

Dude, I live in your mind. I have access to everything. You can't hide anything from me.

Okay, so maybe she did…a little. So what?

So, I'm just sayin', maybe you didn't want to dig deeper because you didn't want to think about her.

Dr. Freud, I presume.

Whatever, you need to reevaluate this.

It was true. For a minute, Sam had been back—back with Tracy and that whole mess. But he couldn't place the connection between the two women.

Sam had once led the charmed life of a popular, full-ride college athlete. Academically mediocre—though all the right people had predicted a promising, prominent future as a pro soccer star—he hadn't worried about his grades. Only a sophomore at UCLA, he had already been meeting with recruiters who were more than willing to help him lay out his career.

He and his fraternal twin brother, Jake, had attended yet another college frat party. Usually these impromptu bashes proved fun, but an hour in, the party lagged. He had considered walking back to their apartment when a sandy-haired girl strolled into the room arm-in-arm with a man built roughly like a Kenmore refrigerator, only bigger. In that instant, everything else around him stopped; his whole being transfixed. Never taking his eyes off her, he leaned over to his brother and said, "Hey, see that girl over there?"

Jake followed his gaze and found the tall blonde. "Yeah, what about her?"

"I'm going to marry her."

Jake rolled his eyes and sighed. "Little Bro, first of all, you also said you were going to marry the brunette you saw at the coffee shop last week, and before that, the chick in the bookstore was *the one*. Remember? What happened there? Crash 'n' burn, baby. Neither wanted anything to do with you. Face it, when they were handing out charm, I got a double helping, and you got the crumbs. Second, do you see the three-hundred-pound meat locker she came with? The one that looks like he grinds skinny-ass shrimps, like you for instance, in his morning, steroid-laden protein shakes? Before you go sending out the invitations, Romeo, maybe you should run your plan by *him* first?"

"Come on, all I need is for *someone* to distract the walrus so I can talk to her."

"There are just so many ways this could go wrong."

He punched his brother in the arm. "You're supposed to be my wingman; are you saying you're not up to the challenge? Besides, isn't it worth it for true love?"

"You are absolutely *so* full of shit it's oozing out of your pores."

Sam grinned and fluttered his lashes at Jake, knowing his brother had already climbed on board.

Jake sighed. "Fine. Give me a couple minutes." He set his beer down and, as a way of parting advice, thumped his finger against Sam's chest. "Don't. Mess. Up." He waded into the crowd toward the couple.

Sam watched as his twin strolled up to the big man and smiled his charming Jake smile. They started talking. A couple of minutes later, they headed outside. Sam followed in his brother's wake.

The sandy-haired beauty stood talking with a couple of other girls. Sam caught a bit of the conversation, something about school and finals. He walked right up to her, looked into her bright blue eyes, and hit her with his best opener.

"Hi," he said.

"Hi, yourself." Sam's heart quickened as she flashed a shy smile.

Her friends looked at them, sized up the situation, and vanished into the crowd. God bless women's intuition.

Something inside him melted, and he knew the end of his bachelor years had arrived. "So, I ummm, was standing over there and thinking it was time to go when I saw you. Something made me come over and talk to you. I'm not particularly good at this actually." The words stumbled and bumbled their way out of him.

She blushed. "Well, you're doing pretty good so far. I'm Tracy." She offered her hand.

Heat rose in his cheeks. "Sam." He gathered her fingers into his own.

They didn't drop hands when she asked, "So, my boyfriend has disappeared. Don't suppose you had anything to do with that?"

"Maybe. My brother..." He didn't finish because someone built roughly the size of a Kenmore refrigerator, only bigger and a lot angrier, spun him around.

Jake said, "Sorry, Little Bro. He figured it out." A fist, about the same size and density of a block of ice, made high-velocity contact with his face. *Makes sense*, Sam thought as he passed out. *The dude's a fridge.*

A year and half later, Sam and Tracy had plans to be married right after he graduated. She still had a year more, but, for the time being, would drop out. They discussed the matter thoroughly and came to the conclusion that she had her entire life to finish school. For their first few years, they would move around the country together as he traveled with whatever soccer team he chose. She wanted to travel, and what better way than with a new husband on someone else's dime?

Everything changed on the night of the accident. A few insignificant seconds that meant nothing and everything.

Each click of the clock's racing hands seared into Sam's brain like the frames of the worst home movie ever—high-def and 3D, crystal-clear images recounting his failure. He had always been powerless to prevent the demon in his mind from playing this horrid piece of footage over and over.

The beast fed the film into the projector's spinning wheels and cogs. Sam could hear their *click click click* and the underlying hum of current driving the machine's mechanisms. Each time, the same dread and hopelessness filled him. Sam, an audience of one, viewed the most pivotal time in his life, reflected on the silver screen of his mind. The inevitable emotions it dredged with it felt as fresh and alive as the night it happened.

The incredible, ever-charming Jake had convinced a buddy to let them borrow a fully restored 1963 Cobra. While cruising the streets—Jake behind the wheel—Sam popped open the glove box to discover a small baggie hidden among the maps, insurance card, and car registration.

"Hey, hey, check this out," Sam said, holding the small bag of white powder for Jake to see.

"Oh, man, we don't need that. If you want an adrenaline rush, I'll give you one." He revved the engine for emphasis.

"Oh, come on. You can't tell me you've never wanted to try it."

"No, I haven't." Jake looked at him for far too long while guiding the vehicle along a row of parked cars. "Yeah, okay. Maybe I have."

"See." Sam smacked his brother's shoulder. "I knew it." He opened the bag and scooped a little of the powder onto his finger. He held it to his nose, hesitated, then snorted. He did it again with the other nostril.

"All right. All right. Don't hold out on me."

Sam repeated the process, offering his brother his powder-laden fingertip. Jake looked at it, dipped his head, and snorted.

At first nothing happened, then fireworks went off in Sam's brain. "Bam!" he yelled. "Wooooooo!"

"Bam is right! Oh my gawd, that's awesome!"

"Right?"

"Hey. Want to have some real fun?" Jake asked. He turned up the radio and floored the accelerator.

Every time, the movie ran through the old reel-to-reel: his brother missing the curve and the Cobra flying over the embankment; the roof breaking off and Sam being thrown clear just before the vehicle landed, tumbling end over end with his brother still in it.

Sam tried to will a new ending to the sequence. But he couldn't re-write that script, and every damned time, it ended with him kneeling in the muddy grass as Jake, bloody and broken, screamed in agony. Driving rain, sleek and gray in the artificial light of the halogens, poured over them as the brothers' lives changed forever.

That one incident became the catalyst for a series of events that seemed hell-bent on destroying his life. It started with the loss of Sam's college scholarship, and on the heels of that, Jake began his dance with the drug demon. The death tango consumed not just his brother but also Sam's life with its voracious, insatiable appetite. Just after Jake made his final spin around the dance floor, Sam had to face the devastating loss of his parents, both of whom passed within a few days of each other. Sometimes he felt like the subject of a country western song, where good lives go bad and good people go dead.

With his scholarship revoked, Sam had to drop out, just two short terms from finishing college, but he and Tracy went through with the wedding anyway. He planned to get a job and save enough to finish at the expensive school, but neither had any idea just how much their lives would change. Two years later, having built up so much anger and rage at what had been lost, Sam drifted from dead-end job to dead-end job.

He and Tracy had no backup, no plan B. Their free ride through life had been lost, and Sam had no idea where to go or what he wanted to do. He got into the habit of rising early and riding his bike without a destination on the quiet morning streets—not looking for anything, just taking comfort in the solitude of the deserted city.

One morning, he passed a small office with a big banner hanging outside that read *First to Fight*. He had driven by it a hundred times without notice, just another hollow venture in a soulless city. But this time, something clicked. He slammed on the brakes of his bike, skidding to a stop in the middle of a normally busy intersection. If anyone had been behind him, he would have been killed.

The thought of being part of something bigger, giving his life order and structure, had appealed to him so much he parked the black motorcycle and went into the small recruiting office.

Like the night of the accident, Sam would remember every detail about this pivotal moment for the rest of his life. The smell of polish and floor cleaner. The gunmetal desk. Small filing cabinet with the dent in the side. Dark, tiled floor. Posters of courageous-looking soldiers next to gold plaques for bravery on the wall. All of it meticulous, dust-free, and in perfect order.

The man standing behind the desk looked just as disciplined as the office surrounding him. His body hard and lean; his crisp uniform covered in patches and badges, all of which, though completely unfamiliar to Sam, seemed to be in perfect order too. The slim gold name badge pinned on the soldier's starched, blue shirt read *Burdett*. Square-jawed with a hard-edged face, the man appraised Sam as he entered the small office. After this day, he would never see soldier Burdett again, but he would never forget that name and the way their eyes locked.

No one in his family had ever been in the military, but Sam walked right up to the desk and told the soldier he wanted to sign up. The recruiter didn't move or say anything for an entire minute, just evaluated the disheveled, out-of-shape derelict standing before him. The man's eyes never left Sam's face, and his expression did not change when he asked, "What can you offer your country, son?"

Sam had assumed he would tell them he wanted to sign up and that would be that. He didn't know what he had to offer his country. "I want to get my life put back together. I am tired of wandering without a purpose. Don't know exactly what I can offer other than my devotion and hard work, but I'm willing to figure it out if the Marines are willing to help."

The man regarded him with piercing intensity. Sam, never one to back down, returned the gaze, unflinching. Soldier Burdett said, "All right, son, let's see if you've got what it takes."

When Sam got home, he told Tracy what he had done and that he shipped off to boot camp in two weeks.

His wife went ballistic.

"What the hell? You made this decision on your own without even talking to me first? This affects both of us, you know. Now suddenly I'm supposed to just drop everything and follow you around as they send you all over the goddamned place?"

"The plan was for you to follow me. We were going to see the world together, remember?" he shot back.

She hit him in the chest. "That was different, and you know it. I was going to be a soccer star's wife; going from base to base is not the same thing. What if they send you to fight the war? That's what the military does, you know. People die in wars! You've been having a rough time of it with your family and all, I get that. But you don't just make this kind of decision without thinking it through. This will completely change everything." She stopped in her rant for a second then looked hopeful. "Maybe it isn't too late to back out? Like when you buy a car, they give you a couple days to change your mind?" She stared at him, her eyes pleading, and a huge, plump tear ran down her cheek.

He should have cared more, been more understanding, but he felt...nothing. The tears didn't make him want to hold her. The desperate look in her eyes didn't tug the strings of his heart into changing the path he had chosen.

Tracy had tried talking to him over the last few months, complaining he had become more and more difficult to reach. He'd pulled into himself and shut her out. He could see that. The problem was he had become powerless to do anything about it.

"Look," he said, searching for the feelings that seemed to have vacated the premises and left no forwarding address, "I haven't been myself, haven't been a good husband. We can't have kids right now because I can't be a good father until I get past this...this blockage or whatever it is. I think the military will give me structure and put my life—our life—back on track."

They had been talking about getting pregnant. Well, really it had mostly been her. She had always wanted kids, and in the last six months, she had been trying to convince him the time had come to start their family. He thought she wanted to fill the emptiness she felt as he pulled away, but it was the wrong reason to bring children into the world.

"We can get through this without doing something so drastic. There are people you can talk to. What you went through was pure hell, but we can find help, Sam." This moment, like the one at the recruiter's office, and the look in her eyes—one of despair and longing—scorched his memory. He wished he could take it back, a million times over, but he couldn't.

She had been trying to comfort him, but, as had become the norm, he emotionally shoved her away. "You have no idea what it was like. The calls at three in the morning to come get Jake out of jail, or later, when I found him in the alley..." He choked up and struggled to get himself under control. "Found him lying there like that. Then all that happened with mom and dad. Your family is still alive. You can go there and have happy little reunions in your perfect little nuclear world. I can't. Mine are gone, and I have nothing. If you understood that, if you understood me, you would know that just talking to someone will never be enough. That is such a weak way to deal with shit. I don't get why people think you can talk your way through your problems. Everyone I love is gone, and all the words in the world will never bring them back."

He ignored the pain in her eyes that screamed he couldn't have hurt her more if he'd punched her. She had been with him, stood by him as he dealt with Jake. Been there when the call came from his hysterical mother when she couldn't wake his dad up. Been there when they lowered him into the ground and cried with him as he wept after finding his mother's lifeless body a week later. An empty bottle of sleeping pills on her nightstand. The note she left simply read:

Take care of yourself. I am sorry. It isn't your fault, I just can't deal with this and don't want to be alone. Know that I have always loved you and always will. Mom.

The note had been written on their family stationary—*Greetings From the Bradfords!* superimposed over a picture of their last Fourth of July while the boys still lived at home. Teardrops, shed while she wrote, smudged the ink his mom had used to compose her final farewell.

When Sam put the order in for the double headstone, he'd assumed it would be years before they carved his mom's final information. But the slab of granite, still untouched, waited at the engravers when he called and added to the work order.

He learned stoicism to survive. It became his closest and, in time, only friend. He compartmentalized his feelings and learned he had the unique ability to examine them from

226

the outside. Sam could view his emotions with the same clinical detachment as a scientist examining a rare and unusual species of insect. He could then lock those feelings away, never having to experience anything.

Impassive detachment gave him the ability to block out the pain, but it prevented him from feeling the good too. He could pretend, and do a convincing job of it, which made it possible to do the work that would become his career but left him cold to those that cared about him.

Yes, Sam had been brutally unfair to his wife, but he just hadn't cared anymore. He'd turned his back on her and walked out the front door.

Chapter Twenty-Eight

D^{ear Sam,}

This is the hardest thing I have ever had to do...

The first time Sam finished reading the letter, he had to wipe away a tear running down his cheek. He stared in surprise, disconcerted by his wet fingers. Taking a deep breath, he reread it. After the third time through, he folded the letter, closed his eyes, and centered himself.

He envisioned a small glass cube on the floor before him. He stood and walked around it, examining it from all sides. In its clear depths, he could see all the pain, anger, love, and happiness he had experienced with Tracy, like an archaeologist studying a fascinating artifact pulled from some deep, ancient, and forgotten tomb. It was interesting how such experiences could make people, including himself at one time, euphoric but also drive them insane. He watched the twisting deluge of Chroma and images of their life as they played out on the glass surfaces.

At first, bright, happy pictures rolled on the tiny silver screens: him seeing her for the first time; them laughing until late into the night; their courtship, how hard he worked to impress her; how happy they had been in the shitty little apartment on Brookhaven, talking and making love; their intertwined bodies; waking together on weekends with nothing on the schedule.

Then the swirls and eddies started getting darker as events in his life grew out of control. The prism had become so dark, the planes that formed its sides turned black with sinuous foreboding. One last fleeting image of Tracy's anguished face trying to reach out to him and his own angry rebuttal flicked across the six-sided shape. It then grew dark and still.

His chest cramped as a pang of intense loss struck him like a hammer, and he wondered if he needed to see the medic for treatment of a heart attack. He reached down and picked up the little cube, unlocked his mental closet, and put it in its designated place amongst its brothers. He closed the door of the little room, sealing it and all the other colorless objects in total darkness.

As he *snicked* the lock shut, the pang in his chest intensified, giving him pause. Would he experience the full breadth of the pain after all? He waited. The feeling passed, and he gave an internal shrug.

As Sam left the sleeping quarters, he tossed Tracy's letter into the trash.

Chapter Twenty-Nine

A couple of weeks after Sam received Tracy's letter, his crewmate, Armon, picked him up for patrol. On the Jeep's seat, a thick manila envelope lay like an omen. Without reading any of it, Sam worked through the stack of marriage-dissolving legalese, following the trail of yellow sticky notes to sign here and initial there, while Armon bounced and jounced them down the road toward the motor pool.

His friend remained quiet as Sam dropped the envelope in the mail. The click of the flap reverberated in his ears, like a door slamming shut on his past.

In the settlement summary letter, Tracy informed him she kept the house, the car—everything except for his clothes, some mementos, and his bike, which she put into a storage unit. The key had been included in the envelope. A week earlier, he'd heard she and the man she'd been sleeping with, Chuck, got engaged and, by all accounts, seemed happy.

When Sam returned to the States, he never bothered to let her know.

"Look out, ladies," Armon called when they met up with the half dozen men in the squad, "we gots ourselves a free boy here, and he's lookin' to get laid. And man, oh man, looks like he just hit the mother lode. I ain't seen so many ugly old pussies in one place since the nineteen fifty-five Hooters reunion."

"Asshole," someone said.

"That true? You a free man now?"

"That's right, Collins," Armon replied, "an' he's looking to get some. So you better be watching your purty little behind, or he'll be slipping it to you in the shower."

"All right, enough. Let's go," Sam ordered.

They headed out of the base toward the south side of the city, the banter among his men ending as they switched into professional mode. Their assignment, to patrol one of the many deserted suburbs, felt like more than just busy work, and he thought his men sensed it too.

The loud Humvees required them to wear headsets to communicate, but no one said anything as they trudged down the dusty road.

Sam focused on the terrain, looking for threats and inconsistencies among the desolate, crumbling buildings, burned car skeletons, and holed-out businesses. These had, at one time, been restaurants and clothing boutiques, but now they only served the lingering ghost patrons unable to move on from this world.

The farther they travelled past the decimated debris that littered the streets and decorated the landscape in a morose tableau of genocide, the more tense he became, like an electric wire forced to carry a larger and larger current.

Something's not right, Chet said. His alter ego hesitated, as though unsure what conclusions to draw based on the facts laid out before him.

What is it? Sam questioned. He could see no signs of life, and none of his men raised an alarm as they continued down the quiet streets.

I don't know…something. Wait.

"Halt." Sam's voice interrupted the static on the intercom. The small group, traveling no more than a couple miles an hour, did not delay as they followed his order, and with a soft squeak of brakes, the Humvees came to a stop. Already on full alert, his men prepared to move, trusting their CO's instincts.

"Did you see something?" Armon, his assistant squad leader, asked as he scanned the area around them, searching for threats.

"No." But the hair on the back of Sam's neck stood on edge. Chet didn't say anything for a minute, but something felt wrong. Off somehow. Sam didn't know what threat they faced, but he followed his instinct.

Back! Chet yelled in his head.

"Back! Back! Back! Now!" Sam shouted.

In unison, the drivers of the Humvees threw the vehicles into reverse and hit the accelerators. Their training and complete faith in their CO prevented any hesitation. That simple, vital trust saved their lives. The large vehicles hadn't travelled more than ten feet and were still speeding up when everything went to hell.

An RPG sailed through the air, launched from inside one of the abandoned buildings. The missile soared past the empty space where the lead Humvee had been just seconds before and exploded into a rusted car skeleton on the far side of the street. The big vehicles stopped, and the Marines piled out. Through the cloud of smoke created by the explosion, Sam glimpsed armed men running out of the building. Bullets from automatic weapons pinged off the Hummers and pulverized the ground around them.

The crew took up the 50 caliber machine guns mounted on the Humvees while other soldiers fell to defensive positions. But the thick smoke prevented the men from being able to see, forcing them to fire blind.

Sam radioed for backup and ordered his men to the outside flank positions.

As his soldiers fought, the militants started falling. The smoke began to clear, giving them better visibility. Ten, maybe twelve men advanced on Sam's position, while others fought crouched in doorways. The men raining bullets down on them from the windows on the third and fourth stories of the building proved to be the worst threat.

Sam could see two. He lined up his rifle on the first, held his breath, and took the shot. The man slumped, half hanging out the building, his gun falling to the dirt below. He sighted in on the second gunman and had been about to pull the trigger when he heard the call through his headset, "Man down! Man down!"

Sam steeled his concentration, centering himself. Nothing could be done without removing the threat from above. Again, he held his breath, aware that every passing second could mean the difference between his man living or bleeding out. He pulled the trigger.

Through the rifle's site, he saw the enemy's head explode like a watermelon as the projectile tore through the man's face.

Sam looked around, evaluating the situation that had begun to turn in their favor. He cursed under his breath when he spotted Armon lying in the dirt, bullets ripping the bloody ground around him. He needed to get his man out of the line of fire.

Next to him, Collins crouched behind the hood of the Humvee. A precise, methodical shooter, the other man pulled the trigger with a calm, practiced ease. With each report of his gun, another bad guy fell.

Sam got Collins' attention. "I'm going to go get him." He indicated toward the fallen soldier. "Ready?"

Collins nodded.

Sam threw a smoke grenade, letting it billow for a few seconds. He relayed his intentions through the intercom and charged in.

The enemy gunfire turned toward the new target, and Sam responded with his own. He dodged and weaved, working toward the unprotected soldier lying vulnerable in the dirty city street.

Sam reached the big man and rolled him over. The lower back of Armon's uniform had soaked through with blood.

"What the hell, boss?" the injured man croaked. "You are the dumbest cracker I ever met in my life." Drops of dirty blood clung to his dry lips, and his breathing was labored.

"Shut up, I'm here to save your stupid ass. Let's go." Sam cupped his elbows under Armon's armpits and dragged the 250-pound man back toward cover. "Ever think about skipping a meal or two?" Sam grunted.

When Armon didn't answer, Sam knew that if he didn't hurry, he might as well not do anything at all. He dragged the big man to the periphery of the fighting when a slug tore through his thigh. Collins, still covering him, found the target and put a bullet in the gunman's forehead. As Sam went down, two of his men grabbed him and Armon, hauling them to safety.

A MEDEVAC chopper left the base as soon as the first man went down, and while they waited for its arrival, the medic tried to slow Armon's bleeding. Someone else wrapped a tourniquet around Sam's shredded leg. As the last of the militants fell, the men loaded the injured soldiers into the helicopter and flew back to base.

The doctors removed the bullet that had slipped past Armon's armor and lodged itself in his lower back. He would be in recovery for weeks but would otherwise be all right. Sam had more extensive injuries.

The slug split when it hit his femur, leaving fragments of lead behind, and the doctors had to search for them among the splinters of bone. The bullet had created a hole about the size of a nickel when it entered the back of his leg. But when it exited, it left a saucer-sized crater in its wake. Because of the extensive damage, the doctors didn't know if they would be able to save his leg.

In the end, they patched him up and put him on strong antibiotics. Both he and Armon went home to recover. After three months, Armon headed back to the front lines. Sam underwent another surgery, and weeks after the final operation, he started physical therapy.

His doctor admonished him to go easy, but he pushed hard, not accepting the verdict and sentencing of his injury. Weight training, walking, yoga; he became a machine with a single purpose: to get back into the field. His physical therapist lectured him if he didn't go easier he would set himself back. The first time he tried to run, something in his knee snapped, and he lay on the edge of the dirty street writhing in pain.

Sam got to keep his leg, but he couldn't fight for his country any more. The angry, mocking scar tissue and scattered memories remained the only remnants of his life as a soldier. Walking without a crutch took over a year, and several months after that, he could do so without a limp. He eventually recovered enough to run again, but he'd lost the speed and nimbleness that had once made him a star athlete. The Marines labeled him a hero but also unfit for duty, so he finished the duration of his military career behind a desk shuffling papers.

Sam slipped out of his military life unnoticed, much like he had slipped in. Half a dozen of his buddies greeted him as he packed out his duffel one last time. Tracy had not been with them.

☆☆☆☆

Two hundred miles outside of Walberg, Sam stood in a little copy store, using their shredding services to dispose of the Peter Morrell identity as he had done with a thousand others. But as he pulled out of the parking lot toward the highway that led to L.A., something kept nagging him. Events of the case felt askew, or perhaps something within The Agency itself had changed.

He tried to put it out of his mind. But as he shifted gears on the big bike, working it up to cruising speed, he wondered if maybe he needed to do a little more research on an otherwise closed case.

Then again, maybe I'm just going crazy. He gunned the throttle heading toward home.

Chapter Thirty

Monica glanced out the window every couple of minutes, waiting. Tires crunched on gravel, and Angel pulled into the Stardust Motel parking her dilapidated Beetle next to Monica's beat-to-shit piece of crap on wheels.

As Angel raised her hand to knock, Monica cracked open the door. "Get in here." She slinked her arm out, grabbed her friend, and pulled her through. She had Angel in an embrace before the door had finished slamming shut.

She held her childhood friend, taking comfort in her smell and familiar embrace. "Thank you for coming," Monica said in her ear.

"Oh honey, anything for you."

"Everything's such a mess."

"Knowing you, this doesn't surprise me." Angel stepped back and looked her up and down. "Nice clothes."

Monica gave her a half smile. "I only shop at the finest boutique thrift stores."

"Okay, so what happened?"

"I'm not sure where to even start," Monica said as they sat on the bed.

238

"Yes, actually, you do. There's no one else here, no FBI, no police, so start at the beginning. This time, don't hold anything back."

"If you know what I know, you'll be in danger too. You need to be aware of the risks."

Angel lifted an eyebrow. "Seriously? First, if someone started interrogating me, or whatever they call it, do you think they'd believe me if I said I didn't know anything?"

Monica shook her head. "Suppose not."

"Second, I should never have let you leave without me, and I'm not making that mistake again." She took Monica's hands in hers. "Like it or not, you're stuck with me. Got it?"

"I love you," Monica said.

Angel cocked her head. "Aww. I love you too. Now quit stalling and start at the beginning."

Monica took a deep breath. "Well, after we left the diner, shit really started going downhill…"

She talked for over an hour before she got to the part about the man on the motorcycle. "So, this guy, Peter, asked me to look over some documents for him. But really, now that I've thought about it, I think he just used that as an excuse to finagle a date out of me."

"You went out with him?" Angel's surprised expression matched Monica's own feelings.

"Yes." She told Angel about the evening and subsequent night they'd spent together.

"You told him your real name?"

Monica stood to pace. "I was so pissed at the FBI. I really wanted to screw with Crew Cut. The bastard had been eavesdropping on everything I've said for the last six months. I wanted to give him something to listen to. You know, verbally give him the finger."

"Well, you did that."

"Yeah."

Angel stood and faced her. "I've tried to tell you before, Mon. You fight the system like a demon and that's admirable, but at the same time, it causes all kinds of hell in your life."

"I was really tired of taking shit from those guys."

"You don't take shit from anyone, and it's one of the things I love about you. But perhaps just this once it would have been better to go with the flow." Angel sighed.

Monica had been on the receiving end of this argument a thousand times before. Her friend might have a point. It was possible that things worked better when you went with the flow. Maybe.

"So anyway." Angel got into the bed and lounged against the headboard. "After you kicked him out, he just left town, and that was that?" She waved Monica to continue.

"Maybe."

"What do you mean?"

She told her about Lisa wanting to stay the night and throwing the keys, then the subsequent explosion.

"Christ! Lisa saved your life by being a self-centered bitch."

Monica forced a laugh at the dark irony. "Suppose she did. Anyway, I had the keys, so I 'borrowed' her car, and, well, here I am." She held up her hands.

"So you think it was Peter who tried to kill you?"

"I'm positive. The only thing is he went through a lot of effort to make it look like an accident. We spent the night together. He had ample opportunity to quietly take care of things, if that was his goal, and just slip away. But he didn't." Monica shook her head. "Yet…"

Angel sat up straight, her face pale.

"What?" Monica sat down next to her. "What's wrong?"

"I have something to tell you."

"You look like you've seen a ghost. What is it?"

"Maybe I have." Angel took her hand again. "Mon, honey, you know I love you, right?"

She nodded. "Yes, but right now you're scaring me."

"You should be scared. It's my fault." Angel dropped her eyes.

"What? What's your fault?"

"The man on the motorcycle, and maybe even the explosion. What did you say his name was?"

"Peter. Peter Morrell. How is any of this *your* fault?"

"I think… Oh, Mon."

Monica lifted Angel's chin so they stared eye-to-eye. "Spill it, girl."

"I think he called me."

"What? When?"

"About a week ago. I don't remember exactly." Then in a rush, she said, "He told me his name was Tom and he went to school with you and that you lived with him and that he'd fallen in love with you. But you disappeared, and he never got a chance to tell you. He knew so much about your history, it seemed like the real thing. He seemed so legit that I thought…oh…I thought… Shit, I led him right to you."

"Tom? Yeah, he let me use his apartment. He called you? How did he get your number?"

"Yes, and I don't know. He said you told him about your childhood and that you two talked all the time. He knew about your past, with the baseball bat and your mom and all that. Did you tell him any of it?"

Monica shook her head. "Tom said that? I never breathed a word. You know me. But you didn't know where I was. You didn't even have my phone number. If Peter was posing as Tom and called you, how could you have led him to me?"

Angel looked back down at her hands. "I gave him your email."

"You mean the one I told you to never, never, never give out?"

Angel nodded.

Monica remained quiet for a minute.

"I'm so sorry, Mon. It's all my fault. You almost got killed because of me." Unshed tears shimmered in Angel's eyes.

"No, Ang, I almost got killed because that's what these mob bastards do. It was inevitable they'd eventually figure out a way to find me. I don't know how he did it with an email, but it seems logical."

"You don't hate me then? I'm so sorry." A tear burst through the dam and spilled down her cheek.

"I know. Hon, I could never hate you. You're my angel, and you came all this way to save me...again. These guys are really smart and will do anything to get rid of me. Just ask Lisa."

Angel nodded. "Have you made a plan?"

"Yes. My 'plan' was to call you."

Angel laughed. "Good plan. Anything beyond that?"

Monica shook her head. "That's all I've got. I'm so out of my element, I don't even know where to begin."

Angel scratched her head. "These guys are really resourceful. We need someone like that on our team."

"Okay, but who?"

"I know you don't want to hear this, but we need to find this Jon person."

Monica stood. "No. No way. I'm done with the FBI."

Angel held up her hand. "Look. Peter was hired to get rid of you, either for revenge or whatever. We both agree on this, right?"

Monica nodded.

"So he found you by tracking your email somehow. The only question remaining is who, if anyone, is in bed with him? The only one that fits is Crew Cut, but even that doesn't seem very likely to me. If he'd wanted to kill you, he's had a lot of chances. All he had to do was let you escape from the safe house and then put a bullet in you as you ran down the road. But he didn't; he took you back inside and put a tracking device on you. It's a sucky thing to do, but that behavior seems like the opposite of someone who means to do you harm."

"I don't trust that bastard."

"I know, but the FBI seems like the best option. The only option really. Can you get in touch with any of the agents?"

She shook her head. "Communication was strictly a one-way street."

"Okay. Well, I don't think it's safe to go back to Walberg. Peter may be waiting for you. It's unlikely, but it isn't worth the risk."

Monica asked, "Okay, how do we find them?"

"Simple. Twenty-six Federal Plaza."

Monica sat back. "Huh?"

Angel shrugged and smiled. "FBI headquarters. Anyone who's watched TV knows that."

"Really?"

"Really. Come on, get your stuff together. We'll drive."

Monica hesitated. It felt like jumping back into the viper's nest, but she couldn't argue with Angel's reasoning. Finally she nodded. "I hope you're right."

"I am."

"Then let's go."

They gathered Monica's newly purchased wardrobe and headed out to the parking lot. Angel pulled out her keys and said, "It's gonna take a while in old Betsy, but she should make it."

"No, we'll take my car." Monica opened the trunk of the beat-to-shit Audi.

"Ummm, what the hell? *This* was Lisa's car? She owned her own practice, and this is what she drove? Things in that town were worse than I imagined."

"Well, yes and no. The car might have had a little… accident." Monica told her about stopping at the park and working the Audi over.

"Wow. Don't mess with you."

"Sometimes a girl needs to blow off a little steam."

Chapter Thirty-One

The scent of pine cleaner and soap assaulted Sam as he walked through the apartment he hadn't seen in months. The maid service supplied by The Agency came by once every week or so to dust and clear out the cobwebs made by industrious little arachnids hoping to catch a meal in the vacant flat.

The refrigerator brimmed with fresh fruits and vegetables, cold cuts, bread, even a pint of milk. Sam knew without having to check the expiration dates that everything would be safe to eat. The clean, spotless icebox looked as though it had been filled that morning. A neat stack of mail and the early edition of the *L.A. Times* sat on the counter.

The Agency wanted him to feel like a regular person—just another Joe kicking back after a difficult week on the job. But to Sam, this life felt staged, and he was a two-bit actor in a way-off-Broadway one-man production nobody cared to see. In his absence, *they* handled his mail, paid his bills, and even falsified his phone records so it appeared like someone spent time in this empty dwelling. On paper, he looked like a regular, functioning member of society. But in reality, nothing actually existed, only the façade perpetuated by an agency that technically didn't exist.

He had the appearance of a life without getting to live one.

The apartment matched the address on his driver's license, but the 1200 square foot "townhouse with a view," as it had been marketed so long ago, didn't feel like his home. No place did. Sam had long ago forgotten who supplied his utilities or who to give the rent to at the end of the month. The grocery store he used to shop at had been torn down and a strip mall erected in its place. He had been gone so long he'd missed the transition. He didn't know any of the neighbors or the neighborhood. Sam had become an intruder, another stranger in a foreign land.

Maybe he had become a little too reliant on The Agency.

Sighing, he wandered down the hall to his room where he tossed his few belongings onto the bed. His body ached from getting caught in the explosion. His back throbbed, his head still hurt, and every time he moved, he found something new on him that had been injured. The mattress beckoned, but first he wanted to wash off the grime of the road. In the master bath, he started the shower, and soon the little room filled with thick steam. Sam got in and stood in the heavy spray, the scalding water pouring over his head in cascading sheets as he tried not to think. If he let his mind wander on anything other than a case, it went places he'd rather it not. Except now he had no case to ponder.

He stepped out of the shower thirty minutes later, dried himself off, and climbed under the sheets. Exhausted, he thought he'd sleep for a week. Three hours later, his eyes popped open, and he found himself staring at the dark ceiling.

It seemed his mind had been hard at work while his body rested. For the next couple of hours, he tried to temper the mental stream while throwing a random curse at the digital clock on the nightstand—its red eyes mocked him as it doled out minutes he *should* be sleeping.

The sun had just touched the sky through the bedroom window when Sam gave up. He got out of bed and slipped into an old pair of jeans and a worn UCLA sweatshirt, pleased that they still fit, and padded to the kitchen. He didn't bother to check the coffee maker, just clicked the "brew" button, knowing The Agency had set that up for him too.

A few minutes later, he carried a steaming mug into the living room. Sam retrieved his laptop from the leather travel bag he'd dropped next to the door and plopped onto the couch. Pulling a small remote from the drawer, he started the sound system, filling the room with lyrics from Eric Clapton's melodious and soulful guitar.

He took a sip of the dark coffee, which helped to break down the early morning cobwebs, while he waited for the Mac to boot. When it finished, he double-clicked the icon for the client half of the tracker app installed on Monica's computer. If anyone logged on, the program would notify him. He minimized the window, opened a web browser, and started searching.

☆☆☆☆

Monica and Angel left the Stardust Motel and drove all day across the Arizona desert.

Angel seemed to be enjoying the power of Lisa's little indulgence and didn't spare the ponies. Cacti and tumbleweeds blurred past in a haze, reminding Monica of the night she'd gone for a ride on the back of Peter's motorcycle.

They flew over the state border midafternoon, and as the land grew dark, Angel guided the car off the main strip and up an old gravel road. She parked on a high bluff overlooking the Colorado flatlands.

When she got out, Monica wandered over to the precipice, where just enough light remained to see the merciless molars that lay in the maw of the chasm below. She stared for what felt like an eternity then raised her eyes to the vast landscape spread out before her.

In full daylight, the plants of the inhospitable barrens seemed flat and muted, but at night, many of them blushed with a faint, phosphorescent luminance, reflecting the glowing moon. The view was similar to the nights in Alabaster Cove when she walked the beaches alone. The occasional school of florescent jellyfish would lounge on the surface of the sea, dotting the murky blackness like underwater paper lanterns. The vastness of the desert looked similar, but instead of an isolated patch of light, the dots of illumination went on for hundreds of miles, disappearing with the curvature of the Earth.

The harsh land, scorched during the day, cooled as soon as the sun fell behind the mountains to the west. A refreshing breeze tousled her hair and tickled her neck as she inhaled its arid crispness.

Monica stretched her back and legs, marveling at how much better she felt freed from the shackles of the depressing little town. The oppressive hand of the FBI, however brief the hiatus, no longer encircled her throat, asphyxiating the life out of her.

She was free.

A thought struck her, and she turned to Angel. "Maybe we should just keep driving? Screw the FBI, screw the mob, screw everyone. We'll just travel from place to place. There's so much to see, and neither of us have any obligations. I'm dead and you…well you were already planning to give up the grocery job. Come on; it'll be fun."

Semi-serious, she longed to remain unconfined. She hadn't fought so hard to survive her childhood only to become a pawn of the FBI and an enemy of the mob.

Angel cocked her head. "So we'll just become professional nomads, the crappy little car our proverbial camel?"

"Something like that."

"What about the dream of fighting for the rights of abused and neglected children?" Angel assumed her best Monica impression. "'I've decided to be a lawyer, Angel. I want to represent those who have no voice.'"

"Guess they need to find someone who's up to the task. The person who had that dream died in an explosion a couple of days ago." Monica reflected for a moment, her gaze not focused on anything. When she came back, her eyes found Angel's in the deepening twilight. "I can't believe how badly I've messed up my life. Everyone tells me how smart I am, but I had to call you because I couldn't figure out what to do on my own. I can't even take care of myself. How am I supposed to help the kids of the world who need it? I'd probably make things worse."

Angel came up and stood next to her on the edge of the bluff. She took Monica's hand and said in a quiet voice, "Why don't we just Thelma and Louise it then?"

"Huh?" Monica stared at her friend.

"You're a complete and utter loser. A failure. A pimple on the donkey's ass of society. What's the point in going on?" Angel took a step closer to the ledge. "Right now. Couple of steps and we're flying, at least for a few seconds, then it's all over. No more Peter, Jon, Crew Cut, your mom, the mob, the dream, any of it. A quick, neat end and all your little problems are solved. Come on, let's do it!" She pulled Monica's hand. "Right here. Right now. I'm not screwing around. Ready? On the count of three. One…"

Monica gaped at her, looked over the edge of the cliff, and then back at Angel.

"Two…" Angel took a step back, tensing to run.

"Ang, I don't know."

"What?" Angel snapped, turning to her. "What don't you know? It sounds like you've got it all worked out. It's been kinda tough, so let's just fold up and let those bastards win. Oh, poor me. I've been so abused. My dad died, and my mom's a whore. Sure, I've had a friend that always, *always* has my back and a surrogate family. Sure I got straight A's in high school, a full ride to NYU, and had plans to be a big shot lawyer."

Angel threw her arms up in the air. "But shit got a little rough for a while 'cause I was helping take down some low-life scumbags. Life hasn't been ideal lately, and there's simply no way to get back to the dream. I can't do that with another identity, which is what my friend is going to insist on when we get to the effing FBI headquarters. Oh, poor me."

Angel turned back to the cliff and took another step back, tensing her body for the final leap. "Come on! You're right. There's no turning this boat around. Let's do it! Let's end this thing! Ready?"

Monica's mouth still hung open. Her jaw bobbed up and down, but no words came out, making her feel like a guppy. As hard as she tried to stop them, the edges of her lips curled up, and she giggled. She tried to stop, but the giggles were relentless and attacked her. She laughed harder than she had in years as she mimicked her friend. "Right here. Right now. I'm not screwing around."

"I'm not. Come on, let's go."

Angel's serious demeanor only made Monica laugh harder. "Let's Thelma and Louise it." She fell on her butt in a cloud of dust, not caring about the dirt. Tears streamed down her cheeks.

Angel's face cracked, and a smile played across her lips. A groan turned to snickers, growing until the full belly roll took her. Their combined laughter echoed, amplified by the canyon walls until it sounded like an auditorium full of spectators at a Jack Benny premiere. They lay on the flat rock, the dust clinging to their sweat and tears.

As they regained control, Monica looked at her. "I love you, you know that."

"Of course you do. I'm awesome."

Monica started laughing again, and they lay on the ground holding hands as the sun finished its decent to the west, and darkness claimed the desert.

☆☆☆☆

"I need to get my shit together. My life's a disaster," Angel told Monica as they drank warm beer and smoked. They lay on the hood of the car, their backs propped up on the windshield, the night's unblemished sky a kaleidoscope of brilliant stars.

Monica regarded her friend. "I've been telling you that for years." She took a pull from her bottle.

Angel raised her middle finger in response.

Monica smiled. "What I mean is, you've got so much potential. You just need a direction. What do you want to do?"

"That's the problem, I don't know. I feel like I've been stuck in neutral forever."

"You need to leave The Cove, at least for a while. Go see the world."

Angel indicated toward the desert with a half-full Michelob.

"Yes, I suppose this is a start. But you've had your foot to the floor since we left Arizona. We haven't exactly been sightseeing."

"Well." Angel traced the label on the beer bottle with her thumb. "I wouldn't mind going to Nashville."

"For real?"

"Why not?" Angel replied. "We have money, and no one's going to mind if the dead girl calls in sick a couple of days."

Monica shook her head. "I'm pretty sure that I'm fired. Getting the boss killed and all."

"See? You're free and I've got zero obligations because I don't have a life. What's to stop us?"

Monica regarded her friend, who continued to surprise her. Did anything hold them back? In the eyes of the law, she had stolen the money from the Bunder safe, but so what? Neither of them would fess up to taking it. "Yeah, okay, let's do it."

The women clicked bottles.

Chapter Thirty-Two

Chum in an ocean full of great whites stood a better chance of survival than Barry Yamalki. Laven Michaels, his single most important client, stared at him from across the marred wooden table. Laven's unsavory mood radiated from him in waves of dark energy. The heat of it scorched Barry's skin, and he often wondered how he didn't come away from these meetings blistered and sunburned. He, the head of the team that did all of the mob boss' legal work, couldn't remember a time, not a single one, when the stocky man had been in a good mood.

Laven's entire emotional repertoire seemed to consist only of various flavors of unpleasantness that ranged from displeasure to seething.

"We are working on getting your trial thrown out. I think the odds are well in our favor," Barry informed his client. If the good news pleased the little man, Barry couldn't see it. "If you're unable to face your accuser, everything they have is circumstantial. If that happens, then I think we can get almost all of it dismissed, so we should have you out by the end of the week."

The mob boss stared at him, dark eyes boring in as if he could read the lawyer's thoughts.

Don't ask. Don't ask.

The mantra circled in Barry's head like an out-of-tune carousel. He tried to give Laven a reassuring smile. He knew how people viewed him—cadaverously gaunt, stooped-shouldered, six foot seven with huge, watery gray eyes that swam behind Coke-bottle glasses—but Barry had stood with complete confidence before juries, judges, congressmen, and, on a memorable occasion, the Vice President. In the professional arena, no one intimidated him. But no matter how much he steeled himself, he could never overcome the sensation of being a seal in open waters while this relentless hammerhead circled. With a word or nod, Barry could befall an "accident" or simply disappear if he displeased this man.

And Laven appeared displeased now. "So..." Laven leaned forward, his eyes startling in their blackness and intensity. "What *aren't* you telling me? I don't like being jerked around. It makes me unhappy."

Barry's skin prickled, and he had to focus on keeping the club sandwich he'd had for lunch from escaping. The meeting should have been routine, but Laven must have sensed something. Not deception, Barry never lied, but the withholding of information. Laven always seemed to know. He had the honed instincts of a predator—this innate yet sharpened ability that separated successful businessmen from those doing twenty to life.

Trepidation squeezed Barry's heart as he hesitated.

Laven did not move other than to raise one trim eyebrow. His client would not ask again.

"The unfortunate accident in Arizona…"

"It was only unfortunate for the prosecution, it works in our favor. It ties up a loose end that should make your job child's play. What about it?"

"The locator app that told us where the girl was, well… One of our techs was wrapping things up, and just before he closed it down, it pinged."

If possible, the mob boss' eyes grew darker. A trickle of sweat ran down the back of Barry's neck. He charged an exorbitant fee for his services, but the world did not contain enough antacids to cure the ulcer his doctor warned him had begun to develop in his stomach.

"Are you under a lot of stress?" the man with the stethoscope had asked.

You have no idea, Barry had thought but did not say. Maybe the time had arrived to retire? Having money did no good if he didn't live long enough to enjoy it. Whether the end came via a heart attack or through a midnight trip in the trunk of a dark sedan seemed irrelevant.

"It's possible," the lawyer continued, "that she had checked her email on multiple computers and…"

"No," Laven interrupted.

Barry stopped talking, mouth hanging open, the word frozen mid-syllable.

"When?"

"Yesterday afternoon."

"Where?"

"The IP address was traced back to a hotel in Arizona. The connection cut off before we had a chance to get any images from the camera though, so we don't know who it was."

"What about the MAC address?" The question referenced the *media access control address*, or MAC, a unique identifier for every computer accessing the Internet.

Barry fished through his briefcase and pulled out the report the tech had given him, comparing that with the previous logs of access. *Shit.* "It's different. That was the first time the email had been accessed on that machine. But it doesn't mean it's her. She could have given the username and password to someone else, her friend for instance."

"And you think maybe her *friend* drove from California to Arizona just to check her email?"

Barry didn't have an answer to the question.

"What about her phone?"

"We found it broken on Highway Thirty, about ten miles outside of Walberg. Looks like someone threw it out the window. Again, that could be explained."

Laven's eyes flashed, and Barry knew the glowing, animal-like eyes had been the last thing many people saw before drawing their final breath. "No. The prosecution believes Monica is dead, and it's up to you to make sure she stays that way. This will not interfere with my case. You will take care of the problem. This time, there will not be any slip-ups."

"I understand."

"I hope so. I've been more than patient with your incompetence. The risk you have put me in makes me uncomfortable. When I start feeling uncomfortable, I look for *alternatives* to my problems."

Laven's mood seemed to shift, and he smiled. The shark about to dine. The expression felt worse than the simmering anger. Much worse. Laven continued, "But I shouldn't have to worry, that's what I pay you barrels of money for. Your job is to take care of the details." He paused then stood, fixing Barry with a gaze blacker and deeper than any abyss. "Take care of it, Barry."

Laven walked to the back of the room and banged on the wall. When the door opened, the mob boss exited.

Just before it closed, a guard looked at the pale lawyer, and their eyes locked for a moment as total understanding passed between them. Even on the other side of the bars, the little man scared this enforcer of the law.

The door closed, leaving Barry alone with his indigestion.

Spending twenty minutes with someone who made the fourth horseman of the Apocalypse look like Captain Kangaroo took something from him—his essence or lifeblood or a piece of his soul. Barry didn't know what, only that each time he met with this man, he left wasted—the depleted, empty sensation not dissimilar to having given too many pints of blood. Barry pulled out a small flask and drained the contents in three long, shaky gulps, wincing as the alcohol barbed through his degenerating digestive system. He took a deep breath and closed his briefcase.

He had some work to do, and very little of it had to do with the law.

Chapter Thirty-Three

*L*ocal Woman Killed In Gas Explosion. The headline of the news article Sam had printed from the *Phoenix Sun* screamed at him. Under the damning words, the paper included a picture of firefighters sorting through ash between burnt wall supports that stood like a blackened skeleton of some prehistoric dinosaur.

The article provided the scantest of details about the explosion itself. Using a hacker program provided by The Agency, Sam accessed the fire department's computer system. The formal report and dispatch records held nothing of interest.

Another article, written a few hours after the one published by the *Sun*, gave a few more details, including the victim's name, Susan Rosenberg, Walberg paralegal. None of this helped.

Next to him stood a stack of printouts on the New York City trial. The disintegrating case had made national news, and rumors circulated of it collapsing altogether since the prosecution had lost its star witness. For either dramatic or strategic reasons, they had waited until the last minute to put Monica on the stand. Unfortunately, they'd waited a little too long.

Sam accessed the city's court system, which had everything. The defendant, Laven Seth Michaels, had been charged with, among other things, murder and drug trafficking. Circumstantial evidence abounded, but it had been the testimony and the recording of a conversation by Monica Sable that would have brought the various details together to create a prosecutor's dream.

Brow furrowed, Sam continued researching. Based on all the corroborating information, Monica had spoken the truth. Witness Protection. Drug lords. Evil henchmen. The tale played out like a made-for-TV cop docudrama. He kept searching, trying to find something that countered what the mounting evidence told him. Sam dug, without a break, into the early afternoon. His training instructed him to exercise patience, one step at a time, and he would uncover the trail. This time, though, the path led him somewhere he had not expected.

He had printed information on the defendant, the structure of his organization, his family, everything. Even more interesting, Sam found Laven had a strong rival who had been thrilled when Laven had been put behind bars.

For years, the Michaels family, the largest player in New York, raked in massive profits. As with any successful business, competition popped up trying to get a slice of this money. But unlike other businesses, turf wars abounded, sometimes lasting for years, resulting in massive civilian casualties—nothing more than collateral damage. Laven headed up the family on the east side while a man named Alphonso Delphini ran the family in the west. The two clashed somewhere in the middle. Turf changed hands—taken, taken back, and taken yet again in a perpetual cycle.

Delphini had been quoted as saying that his only wish is that justice be served. The Michaels family was "a menace and a threat to society."

Sam took a long pull on the beer he'd been nursing and sat back staring at the article. *Local Woman Killed…*

Responsibility for her death weighed on him. Sure, Josha had given him the assignment, but he'd had his doubts and could have done this research after Monica told him about her secret life. He hadn't though; he'd just turned her over to his handler then put her in the crosshairs of his rifle, justifying his choices by labeling her a liar.

Told ya, Chief, Chet said from somewhere deep in his cerebellum.

Yes, I know.

She's dead, and now you are going to have to live with that. The bad guys won; isn't it your job to stop the bad guys?

Yes. But why? Why was I looking for her? Was I working for these bastards, or was it a coincidence?

Why don't you find out?

Sam picked up his smartphone and hesitated. The very act of calling Josha—way out of standard operating procedures and going against everything in his training both in the military and with The Agency—would be impossible to justify.

You've already gone beyond S.O.P just by doing this research.

Yeah, point taken. Sam pressed the *send* button.

As usual, Josha picked up the call on the first ring. "How's vacation?"

"Hi, Josha. So far I haven't had much time to do anything."

"What can I do for you?" Josha had always been reluctant to engage in any sort of small talk.

Sam took a breath, preparing to cross a line that could never be uncrossed. "So, the Monica Sable case…"

"Yep, all wrapped up. The customer is pleased. Nice work."

"See the customer, that's what I wanted to ask you about."

Silence greeted him from the other end of the line before Josha said, "You know that's confidential. Even I don't know who it is, the assignment came from up high. I think we're done here. Have a nice vacation."

"No." Sam's voice left no room for argument.

"Sam. You need to drop this."

"This case has bothered me from day one."

"Your place isn't to think about the merits of an assignment. Your job is—"

For the first time ever, Sam cut his handler off, interrupting Josha mid-sentence. "Just shut up and listen to me."

To his great relief, the other man did, though out of respect or out of shock Sam didn't know.

"When I got the confirmation, Monica told me about her situation. I didn't believe her at the time. I figured it was the usual ramblings from someone trying to get away with shit, but something about it rang true. So when I got home, I researched the case, and everything she told me checks out. Did you know she was a star witness in the trial of a drug lord? That without her testimony, the guy will walk."

"No. But what has——"

Sam stood and started pacing around the room. "How is it that we have access to information no one else does, yet somehow it slipped past our radar that she was to stand as a witness? Also, you are aware that someone killed her before I had a chance and the FBI and the police ruled the explosion an accident. They said it was a gas leak."

Josha fell silent again. "Why would the FBI be involved in a domestic house fire?"

"Because she was in Witness Protection. They were working with the U.S. Marshals to keep her safe. I think your 'customer' was the goddamned mob, Josha. That's not who we're supposed to be working with. 'Enemies of the state' are who we're supposed to be finding, remember?"

"Sam, maybe you're just misunderstanding the information."

"Seriously? I've been working for you for almost a decade. How many times have I gotten it wrong?"

"Okay, point taken. But…"

Sam made a fist, clenching his fingers until the knuckles turned white. "There is no 'but,' Josha. We fucked up, and this innocent girl died because of it."

"Shit. All right, let me look into it. For now, do what I told you to do: Stop. Go on vacation. This isn't your problem anymore. I'll take care of it. Send me your research, and I'll be in touch." Josha disconnected the call.

Sam sent his handler everything then went to the fridge and got another beer. Popping the top, he leaned against the counter and stared off into nothingness as he tried to force his mind to think about something else. But the damning headline dogged him, and he couldn't escape its accusatory condemnation. He swore under his breath as he sat back down at the desk and began to go through the information again.

Chapter Thirty-Four

Lisa had never been one to spare herself the electronic amenities and thus had no paper maps in her car, so Angel drove with gusto in what Monica hoped to be the right direction.

"Do you know where you're going?" Monica asked her at one point.

Angel pointed out the front window. "That way."

Monica shrugged. "Okay, good enough for me."

By mid-afternoon, they needed to stop, fill the Audi, and get some coffee. They'd survived okay on the rations Monica had bought at the all-night truck stop on her pell-mell escape from Walberg, but nothing else replaced the caffeine-infused elixir. Angel guided the nondescript car into the parking lot of Nan's Little Big Diner and Gas.

They got out, and Monica stopped just before she pushed through the glass door. "Hey, I'll be right back."

"I'll get us a table."

"Booth," Monica said over her shoulder. When she slid in across from Angel a couple minutes later, she held Lisa's laptop.

"Online dating?" Angel asked her.

"No, smarts. Google Maps. We need to figure out where we are."

When the waitress stopped for their order, Angel asked her, "Where are we?"

If the middle-aged woman with the name badge Coral pinned to her ample bosom thought the question odd, she showed no sign of it as she smiled. "You're about twenty miles east of Burlington."

"Is that in Tennessee?"

"What? No." Monica admonished. "You never did study in school did you? Tennessee and Arizona aren't exactly neighbors."

"Whatever. *Some* of us didn't graduate top of our class and go to NYU."

Monica stuck her tongue out at her.

"Is that where you're headed, darlin'? Well you still gotta ways to go then. No, dear, you're in Colorado. Where are you from?"

"Phoenix," Monica answered.

"Well sugar, I think you're going a bit out of your way. There's a more direct route than coming through this neck of the woods. But generally speaking, you're headed in the right direction. Let's see." She squinched up her pleasant face. She indicated to the highway through the big, tinted windows at the front of the restaurant. "This here is the Seventy. Take that to St. Louis." She arched an eyebrow at Angel. "That's in Missouri."

266

Angel rolled her eyes.

"Then," the waitress continued, "turn right on…on… Hmmm, the Fifty-Five, I think. Then…well then you'd better stop and ask for directions. That's about as far as my mental map goes." She smiled. "So, what can I get you?"

They placed their order, and Monica started up the computer.

☆☆☆☆

Sam lay on the couch. A brigade of empty beer bottles littered the floor and coffee table, and he considered adding another to their fallen ranks when his computer pinged. He had gone through Monica's case for the thousandth time and lain down to rest his eyes. The machine sat across the room, and in spite of having just been thinking about getting up for something else to drink, he decided against trekking across the chasm between his comfortable couch and the desk. When his phone started buzzing from beside him on the floor, he groped for the little device, never taking his arm from across his eyes.

He used both the Mac and the smartphone only for work, not that he had any semblance of a personal life——hence being at home while on vacation, drowning his sorrows in Budweiser. Finally, his hand happened upon the phone, and he lifted it, looking at the little screen. His heart stopped at the message. Someone had started up the laptop with his tracker app installed. He'd never bothered to turn off the alert.

He got up, stumbling over fallen glass soldiers, and made his way to the desk, sobering with each step.

☆☆☆☆

"So, I think we are about here," Monica said, looking at the screen. Angel's attention seemed to have wandered, the history of the little diner in the place card on the table capturing her interest instead.

"Ang?"

"Hmmm?" she said.

"Got a minute?"

"Oh, ah sure." She put down the small bit of trivia and came around the booth, sliding in. She bumped hips with her friend. "Oops."

Monica tried to convey her disgust with a look.

Evidently oblivious, Angel stared at the little screen.

Monica turned back to the task at hand. "So, like I was saying, we are about here." She pointed to the screen. "The waitress was right. If we continue down the Seventy, we could go to St. Louis, maybe check out the Gateway Arch, then on down here." She started tracing another highway then stopped. "You know what the Gateway Arch is, right?"

"You keep this up, and I'll turn you over to the mob myself."

Monica grinned and turned back to the computer screen.

Sam double-clicked the flashing icon in the task bar. The tracker app contained four separate sections: *Monitor, Root, Camera, and Control.* He chose *Monitor* then clicked *Locate.* The machine thought for a minute, then a map of the United States appeared. A bubble indicator pointed to a spot in eastern Colorado.

Why would someone take Monica's laptop to Colorado?

He minimized the window and clicked *Camera.* Within a minute, he connected to the laptop and an image materialized. Two women, cheek-to-cheek, peered back at him in rapt concentration.

Sam's eyes widened with disbelief. Despite the poor picture quality, he recognized the face he remembered from Walberg. Marilyn Monroe mole, a smattering of freckles, dark hair with blonde roots. Monica. She had survived.

The other girl looked familiar as well. He pulled out his folder, rifled through the images and information it had taken him six months to gather, and found it: Angel Humbolt, childhood friend and apparent co-conspirator.

Sam clicked the plus next to the speaker icon, turning up the volume.

He caught Monica mid-sentence. "So, then we take the Forty into…"

"Here you go ladies," someone interrupted. Both women looked up, and he watched Monica's hand reach over and close the laptop, disconnecting the app.

"Shit!" Sam switched back to the maps screen, found their approximate location, and traced until he found Highway Forty. Following that, they could be headed to Nashville or on to North Carolina, or who knew where else?

Relief flooded him; Monica had somehow survived the explosion in Arizona. He didn't know how, but he would figure it out. First, he needed to know where they were going.

☆☆☆☆

Barry stared at the *Connection Terminated* message on the screen in front of him. After his meeting with Laven, Barry had re-enabled the app's alert feature. While he worked through the legal issues, the alarm went off. He had stared at the image of the two women—one he knew and the other he did not—on his laptop. He caught their conversation mid-sentence and thought he'd been poised to hear where they intended to go when one of them closed the computer, severing the connection. He backed up the video feed, took a screen shot, pasted it into an email, typed up the information provided by the little program, and clicked send.

A minute later, his screen flashed the reply. "On it."

He didn't know who had been killed in Arizona—in the end, it didn't really matter—but there would be no mistakes this time. He would not allow this loose end to destroy all he had risked his life to build.

Chapter Thirty-Five

Sam threw some clothes in a bag. He hadn't even been home twenty-four hours yet. He opened a bottom drawer and pulled out a small wooden box. The familiar scent of gun oil took him back to his days in the military, when he'd spent hours cleaning and maintaining his weapons. Someone else had already tried to kill Monica. He wasn't going in unprepared.

He pulled back the slide on the Sig Sauer P229, verified the chamber contained a round, and grabbed several extra magazines. He put the lot in a side pocket of his bag designed to holster the weapon.

This is totally unsanctioned; you don't even know what you're going to do, Chet piped up. *You have no plan. Action without purpose is worse than no action at all, Rule Eighty-Eight, remember? You can't do this on your own. You have to call the boss.*

I don't get it. First you tell me to not send the confirm to Josha, that I need to spend more time thinking for myself, and you berate me because I follow the Rules. Now you're not only quoting them at me like they're the gospel, but all you want me to do is follow the chain of command?

You can't just go half-cocked on some wild mission. You've got nowhere to go, no idea where she's at now, and you don't even know who's chasing her. You can't go into this blind or everyone, maybe even you, will get killed. Not to be selfish or anything, but I have a vested interest in your well-being.

Without the support of The Agency, Sam would only have his skills and wits to rely on. Josha had told him to drop it, that the case had been closed. If he went against his boss' order, he'd be in direct violation of agency protocol and could lose his job, or worse.

But his boss may have already known that Monica had been targeted by someone else. And if that were the case, why send a second party to do a job he'd already been hired to do? Did that mean that Josha, for once, didn't have all the information? Maybe someone above him had leaked it?

It boiled down to either corruption in The Agency or Monica being such a big threat that they double-booked her and the other agent had simply gotten to her first. He'd been over her case a thousand times; no way had they sanctioned two agents. That meant someone had sold information. But to whom?

Then it hit him. Who had the reason above all else to see Monica dead? If she had told Sam the truth that night they'd slept together, then he knew exactly who had hired the hit.

Sam picked up his phone.

What are you doing? Chet asked.

Thinking outside The Agency.

The call connected on the second ring. "Armon." The deep rich baritone sounded more like an opera singer than a former-Marine-turned-NYPD-police-detective.

"Armon, it's Bradford."

"Sam, you old bastard. How you doin'?"

He smiled at the butterscotch smoothness of his old friend's voice. "About the same. How are Jenny and the girls?"

"Man, I wish you was here, I'm seriously outnumbered and out-flanked. I got princesses and pink up to my ass bones." The man's smile resonated through his words.

"And you love every minute of it."

"Just don't tell Jenny. She feels bad so lets me get off to poker on Mondays and b-ball on Thursdays."

"She already knows it, Armon."

"Yeah, 'spose she does. So, what can I do for you?"

He sobered. "I need a favor."

"Didn't figure you called for any other reason.

"The Laven Michaels case, what do you know about it?"

"Not a lot other than what's been on TV and word around the office. What do you need?"

"Everything."

"Can you narrow it down a bit? This is one of the hottest cases in the city. My chief will give me the stink eye if he finds out I'm poking around in it. What's the angle?"

Sam filled him on the specifics of what he needed then hung up and resumed packing.

A half hour later Sam's phone rang. "Bradford."

"Hey, cracker," the rich baritone voice replied. "You don't mess around, there are a lot of folks with their panties in a wad over this. I couldn't get everything, but I did find something that will help you out a bit."

Sam knew his old buddy would come through. "What have you got?"

"You said you've researched everything in the news, right?"

"Yeah," Sam replied, "I've been pounding all the public channels."

"Well, here's something you don't know. We've got a mole in the office of the man who handles all of Mr. Michaels' legal matters, Barry Yamalki. Seems Mr. Yamalki went to see our Crossbars Hotel guest a few days ago. In addition to the regular lawyer mumbo-jumbo, he was told to handle the 'loose end' problem. I'm thinking that 'loose end' would be your girl. Following said meeting, Mr. Yamalki called a local bad boy by the name of Tyron Erebus. Check your inbox; I just sent you the guy's dossier."

Sam sat at his computer and opened the email. He double-clicked on the first attachment, an image file. A scarred face with a large, misshapen nose bent to the right stared back at him. The man might have been in his mid-thirties, but the scarring obscured his actual age.

His eyes disturbed Sam. Their cold lifelessness resembled the deepest pits of a rock floating through the frozen blackness of space. Sam had seen eyes like those before in Afghanistan. They belonged to a man who had walked into a crowded shopping square and detonated a bomb strapped to his chest.

Sam clicked on the second file to find a chronology of terrible things the scarred man had done over the course of his life. At age five, he'd moved into a foster home after watching his parents die in a drive-by shooting. A state-run facility took over his care at age seven when he killed his foster family's poodle by jamming a corkscrew into its chest. When asked why he would do such a thing, he replied, "The dog wouldn't shut up no matter how much I yelled at it. I figured I was going to show the mutt who's boss."

As Tyron made his way through school, he bounced from facility to facility, leaving a path of pain and misery behind him. He received his first conviction as an adult at age seventeen, when he repeatedly raped the mother of one of the families he lived with. The woman suffered the abuse for months before he hurt her to the point she ended up in the hospital.

He spent eighteen months in the Pennsylvania State Penitentiary before a lawyer—as coincidences go, Barry Yamalki—got him out on a technicality. Tyron had been accused of aggregated assault no less than a dozen times, but in each instance, the accuser dropped the charges. He had been under suspicion of multiple homicides, but like his boss, Mr. Michaels, enough evidence never existed for a conviction.

"Cracker, this guy is ruthless. He doesn't have official training other than what he's learned on the streets, but anyone that's tried to stop him has wound up in a hole in the ground. You take my meaning?"

"We've dealt with worse."

"Yeah, I 'spose we have, but we did it as a team. I'm guessing, since you're calling me instead of going through your czar or whoever you work for, this job is off the books."

"Something like that. Can you also get me information on Mr. Michaels' operation? Who he does business with, who he's pissed off, his organizational structure, all of it."

"Let's take a step back here. This guy is one of the biggest kingpins in New York. You will not be able to negotiate with him, blackmail him, or probably even talk to him. There's no way you're even getting close to this guy."

"I don't need to."

"What are you planning?"

Sam smiled. "Just a little creative law enforcement."

"You make my nipples hard when you talk all dirty like that."

His smiled widened. He missed working with this man. "Do you think you can get that stuff for me?"

"Yeah, yeah. Give me a few hours, just be careful."

"Thanks, Armon." Sam disconnected the call.

He had the who, now he just needed to know the where. He clicked back over to the tracker app. The blinking pin showed the place that Monica had last logged on. He examined all the menu options and clicked on *Show All Traces*. The computer thought for a moment, then two more blips registered on the screen.

One pointed to Sam's apartment in L.A. They'd said something in class about the program triangulating on anyone logged onto it. Something about it not knowing the difference between friend and foe. He right-clicked his bubble and chose *Incognito.* Hopefully that hid him from all prying eyes, including Josha's.

He studied the screen. The second bubble seemed to be moving at a steady pace and had almost arrived at the diner. He must have logged on to the app through his phone, but never signed out.

I'll bet that's not the cavalry, Chet said.

Oh shit. Erebus? But how?

With all that's going on, you really need to ask that question? Someone high up has given the opposing team our playbook.

But why?

Does it matter? The question is: What do you plan to do about it?

Time to go ghost. Sam shut down the PC, grabbed his bag, loaded it onto his bike, and headed out. He had a job to do.

Chapter Thirty-Six

He stood in the bank of old growth pine trees observing the little house, the darkness of the night and the shadows of the timbers more than adequate to conceal him. The modest structure sat on a flag lot, several hundred feet from the street and nestled against a woodland backyard. Neighboring structures could be seen in the distance through the trees, but they had been built far enough away for him to conduct his business without the inconvenience of witnesses. One by one, the other homes' lights had been extinguished as the late hour put the world to sleep.

When the glow from the woman's window went dim, he slinked forward, the soft soles of his Converse sneakers making no more than a light rustle in the blanket of cones and needles covering the yard. He'd followed her after her shift at the restaurant, verifying via observation and perusing her mail that she resided alone. The location couldn't have been more ideal. Had she lived in an apartment with units above, below, and on either side, he would have had to adjust his plans. Here, in the middle of nothingness, he had free rein.

He picked the simple lock of the back door and let himself into Coral's humble kitchen. Remaining still, he studied the small space as he absorbed the traces of lavender and floor cleaner that rode on the back of the heavy scent of musty wood. Tyron touched the single chair tucked under a simple dining table, his fingers trailing the smooth, cool surface of the back and sliding down to the bottom where she would have sat. His thumbs traced a rough crack in the cheap vinyl while his fingers splayed over the concave surface. He could feel her essence, her heat, buried within its molecules, absorbed by the cheap piece of furniture after hour upon hour of contact.

He continued his tour of the kitchen, fondling the surfaces of the table, the refrigerator, stovetop, and cupboards, but none of them contained as much of the waitress as that small plane of vinyl, cardboard, and cotton.

Having gotten all that he could from the kitchen, he went into the tiny living room. It felt void of her, a forgotten chamber. Coral never spent much time here. He suspected the batteries of the remote didn't work because she never watched television. The lamps wouldn't work, their bulbs having long ago burned out, and the couch would be devoid of her aura.

Drawn by an elusive magnetism, he moved to the far wall, a large portion of its surface covered by a bookshelf. Coral, the simple waitress from a diner along a lone highway, loved these tomes. He traced the outlines of the books where hands, her hands, had done so a thousand times before, leaving her impression behind.

Tyron could see her imprint as clearly as if she'd written her name in the fog of a mirror and feel her warmth like she'd handed him the jacket off of her back. He allowed her vitality and affection to permeate his skin. The energy flowed into his bloodstream, the two of them becoming more intimate than the most forlorn lovers of any romance novel dared to dream.

He pulled the zipper of his bodysuit, the disengaging teeth no more than a sigh in the still night, removed his shoes and suit, and stood naked in Coral's unused living space. He closed his eyes and held out his arms, clearing his mind of all worldly thoughts and desires, beckoning the gods to join him in this night of celebration and transformation.

Something that he could neither see nor hear, but detected with a sense that defied definition, descended into the room. It circled his unmoving form, touching his face, his shoulders, his thighs, his buttocks, and then came to rest before him. Its hot breath brushed his cheek, and he relished the underlying metallic odor as a child might savor the sweet aroma of fresh-baked chocolate chip cookies on a snowy afternoon. The entity caressed his face, and gooseflesh pricked every inch of his body.

The creature moved closer, and Tyron welcomed it to enter him, absorbing it as though slurping it through his pores. It settled in, taking up residence within him, solidifying his substance, its essence mingling with his cells and interweaving with his fibers. Together they formed a mass more substantial than the two individuals.

Though it felt what he felt and saw what he saw, the other could not directly control him. It had joined him for the ride and the eventual rising. He would help it experience the joys of the flesh which, without a body, it could not do alone.

Their mingling complete, Tyron turned to the task with which he had been both blessed and burdened. A small silk sack clicked softly as a doe's hoof step as he retrieved it from a zippered pocket on his suit. His fingers caressed the slippery softness of the humble tool bag. The contents were alive and ready.

As he moved down the short hall toward her sleeping quarters, the air chilled his skin while the thick carpet massaged his toes and nuzzled the soles of his feet.

He stopped just after crossing the precipice. Coral's beauty, as with all women, lay within. One of the few the gods had seen fit to bless, he had the ability to unleash that beauty, revealing it for the world to gaze upon in wonder. She would show him that which remained elusive and hidden to others.

The softness of her breathing caressed his ear, and he inhaled the wonderful scent of her skin and hair. The lub-dub pulse of her heart beckoned, as poignant as the ping of a radar, and in the total blackness, he knew exactly where she lay.

Tyron loosened the ties of the small silk sack and retrieved a prophylactic. He slipped it on, his body eager and ready. He pulled out a steel blade, pressing its cool, flat surface against his leg. It needed to be as warm as his and Coral's combined love, for it would serve as the key to the conduit in the dance of their intimacy.

Before they could begin though, he needed to conduct a little business. Only then could he explain the rules to her. Women respected a man that laid down a distinct set of guidelines and used both his superior strength and his wisdom to enforce them in whatever way he deemed fit.

He pressed the warmed blade against her neck, careful not to touch her any more than necessary. When they first connected, it had to be while he established the hierarchy. This would assist in her understanding of her place within it.

"Hello, bitch," he whispered in her ear.

Coral's body stiffened, and the black sheen of her eyes shone as they flew open. But she didn't reply.

"I've got some questions for you. If you answer them willingly and truthfully, this will go a lot easier for both of us. If not…" He pressed the knife harder against the soft flesh of her neck. "Do you understand?"

"Yes."

"Good girl." He reached over with his free hand and snapped on the small nightstand lamp. She blinked against the sudden brightness, and her gaze settled on his. He trailed the knife down her stomach, stopped at the top of her femoral artery, high on the inside of her exposed thigh, and pressed firmly. New terror grew in her eyes as she accepted his position of control. Tyron placed the small silk sack on the bed next to her. "Please remove the contents," he instructed.

She hesitated only a second, then with trembling fingers she reached inside and pulled out a two-headed pick, not unlike what a dentist uses to remove plaque, and stared at it.

A pivotal point for him and his lover had been reached. Fear would either cause her to strike at him, or she would give in and accept his leadership. He understood her instinct to fight, saw the sharpening of her gaze. He pressed the knife harder against her leg, stared deep into her soul, and said simply, "Don't."

She paused, and he saw her consider trying even though it meant her immediate death. Then the hardness in her expression lessened, and she set the tool on the nightstand. She continued to remove the remaining tools, each more wicked-looking than the previous.

Years before, he'd started with a complete taxidermist kit, but carrying such a bundle with him had been burdensome. After hundreds of experiments, he'd honed the set to a half-dozen essentials.

She placed the last of the implements on the little table and pulled out four sets of cuffs. He'd modified these himself so the lengths of the chains could be adjusted.

"Now," he said in his most soothing voice, "please fasten these around your wrists."

"No. I can't do that." She swallowed. "You'll…you'll just kill me."

"That is not an inevitability that has yet been decided." He moved the knife back to her throat. "The ebb and flow of the evening's events are based on your cooperation. You do as I say, and there is a very good chance you will see the sun rise in the morning and will once again have the opportunity to ask a customer if they want wheat or white toast with their eggs and bacon."

She needed the lie. Without it, fear would push her into to doing something that could cut their evening short and hinder her transformation.

He motioned toward one of the restraints. "Please fasten this around your wrist."

Coral's hands shook as she attached the cuff. She almost dropped it but managed to click it into place.

Tyron looped the long chain through the headboard, then secured her other wrist with the second cuff.

A huge tear rolled down Coral's cheek as he adjusted the length of steel, stretching her arms and snugging her wrists tight.

He fastened her ankles to the bedframe and resumed his position, placing the tip of the knife, once again, at the base of her throat.

"Thank you for your help. It will make things go much more smoothly. Now, I need a little information. You had two customers, a pair of women, come in during lunch. Where were they going?"

A look of confusion crossed her face. "I have a lot of customers; you need to be more specific."

Even in her defenseless position, he knew she would resist him. He both expected and longed for it. That nugget of resolve would fade to utter submissiveness as he continued to establish his place as her mentor and owner. In return for her servitude, she would receive the joy and comfort of her new position, but more importantly, the salvation only he could offer her.

"Two women, mid-twenties, one with dark hair and blonde roots and a mole on her lip, the other with short hair. They had a laptop and were looking for directions."

She didn't answer right away, and he knew her next words would be a lie. "I don't know who you mean."

He shook his head. "I understand the reasoning behind the falseness of your words, but you need to understand the futility and ramifications of defying me."

The cadence of her lifeblood beat strong and steady just a fraction of an inch below the edge of the razor. He longed for her blazing heat, red as an apple at the peak of season, to pour over his skin. Tyron moved the razor from her jugular and sliced away her t-shirt. The fabric parted as though it had no more substance than cobweb, and he ran the edge of the blade gently along her breasts. He traced the knife down to her ribcage, past her belly, and smoothly slit the cotton of her panties, which also fell away. As he stroked the blade over her exposed flesh, his fingers graced the delicate skin of her chest. Coral's heart raced like a caged jackrabbit.

He ran the blade down the contours of her body. Hip to pubis. Pubis to thigh. Thigh to calf. Steel on steel, he circled her ankle just above where the restraint chaffed her skin. Moving lower, he noticed a blemish, a thick callus, most likely caused from long days of waitressing in cheap shoes, on the sole of her foot.

He *tsked*. "No. This won't do. Not at all."

"I…"

Tyron slid the blade through her skin.

A scream, piercing as a shard of glass, tore from her. She tried to pull away, but Tyron had left very little play in her bindings.

Careful not to mar the muscle, bone, and tendon under the surface, he worked slowly, making his way around the circumference of the bottom of her foot. Once completed, he set the knife on the nightstand next to his other tools and, starting at her heel, peeled away the epidermis, pulling it—and her blemish—free. He examined the raw flesh beneath, sighing. He still had a lot of work to do. It took so much effort to clean up God's mistakes.

When Coral had removed the handcuffs, she'd stopped emptying the silk bag, but treasures and necessities still waited in its depths. Tyron retrieved a clear container of thumbtacks. He removed one and used it to attach Coral's imperfection to the wall. Together they would create a mural unlike those by any other artist in history.

When Coral's voice finally cracked and rang hoarse, he, and the other inside him, smiled. Tyron would not disappoint. He never did.

"Nashville." She said through her sobbing. "They are going to Nashville through St. Louis. That's all I know, I swear."

"Good girl. Did you see the car they were driving?"

"No. No. It was during the lunch rush, and I was too busy to pay attention. I promise I don't know anything else."

"Thank you." He smiled. "Now, shall we begin?"

In Greek mythology, the living passed through Erebus at the moment of death. After making his first kill, Tyron had changed his last name to that of the primordial deity, who in many texts personified a darkness so deep no light could escape it. But he knew this to be false. The god that had granted and honored him with his considerable talents used his hands like gloves to transform that which was flawed to that which was free of defects. Working together in harmonized perfection, they could unleash a soul's splendor and true sanctity.

As the night turned to a phantom, the dawn replacing the specter's gray substance with its orange light, he and Coral worked diligently to release her true inner beauty. As her final transformation commenced, she begged him to release her from this world. Together they had removed all of her flaws, attaching each blemish to the wall as a testament to her rise above all other women.

This undeserving vessel that had contained a lifetime of human imperfections had finally been made worthy of housing the gift of him. As he bestowed this present upon her, the other moved from his body to hers. As they made their climactic connection with her, Tyron released her tether to this world. She cried out in exaltation as the other possessed her, filling the vacancy left behind as the hot red of her essence flowed over Tyron's skin, the mattress, the floor. He too gave of himself, helping the other propel her spirit on its journey from this world to the glories of the one beyond.

In that moment, Tyron longed to leave with them. They, the three of them, could travel the path as one, their souls mingling as they sought enlightenment and peace.

But his time for such a journey had not yet arrived. His work on Earth was not yet complete. So he would trudge on, the ever-faithful servant doing his duty to bring perfection to an imperfect world until finally beckoned into the afterlife to receive his hard-earned reward.

As Erebus stood under the hot spray of the shower, hollow and empty after the quick departure of the other, rinsing off the last of Coral's transformation, his thoughts turned to the snitch and the mongrel she traveled with. The night's events, though sacred and worthy of his time, had taken longer than he'd expected. He would have to move quickly to catch up to them.

He would, though. Of that he felt certain.

Chapter Thirty-Seven

After their change in plans, Angel seemed to have let up on the accelerator, though just a little. She'd kept the little car cruising down the road at 90-plus as they made their way through the Kansas flats. Monica found a wallet of CDs under her seat. Lisa'd had eclectic taste in music, and as the miles slid past, Monica fed one disk after another into the car's stereo. No matter what she tried, though, she kept returning to the same French rock band, listening to their CD time and again.

"What do you think they're singing about?" Monica asked. She propped her bare feet up on the car's dashboard, cotton between her toes, while she painted her nails with a cheap polish picked up at the last truck stop.

Angel looked over at her as the car sailed along the highway. "Well, they're French. Probably pimps and whores."

"Really? Pimps and whores? Is that big over there?"

"Of course. It's totally different in European countries. Naked beaches, nude news, common showers. We're so scared of seeing each other without clothes on here. I don't even know what the big deal is. Tell me, who wouldn't want to see *us* naked?"

"Right? We're totally hot."

"Did you know," Professor Angel continued, "they don't even have walls between the toilet stalls, and everyone shares the bathrooms? No men's and no women's."

"What? I've never heard that before. How do you know all of this?"

"Girl Scouts."

Monica laughed. "What? I was in Girl Scouts with you. I don't remember earning a European Whores merit badge. I think I would have remembered that."

"Well, while you brainiac types are making up new kinds of math and shit, those of us with less-than-perfect SAT scores are learning 'practical' knowledge."

"What 'practical' knowledge?" Monica asked laughing again. "You have no idea what you're talking about."

"You've heard of the Red Light District, right?"

Monica nodded. "Yes, but…"

"Well, where do you think it is? Europe. Pimping and whoring is not only legal over there, it's a studied profession. A respectable occupation." Angel pivoted her head between the road and her friend. "Why, if you were born in France instead of The Cove, you might have aspired to be full-time slut instead of a lawyer."

Monica's eyes widened. "What? No! You're making that shit up. They don't have slut school… Do they?"

Either Angel had developed one hell of a poker face or she believed everything she'd said. "Prove me wrong."

"Okay. How?"

"Take me there, and I'll show you."

As much fun as traveling the world with her friend would be, practicality prevented Monica from jumping online and booking the next plane to Europe. "Ummm, the 'good' guys took my passport, and 'Susan' never got one. Besides, I'm dead, remember? I don't have a job, and anyway, you didn't happen to bring yours along, did you?"

"No, but as I recall, you got a little loan from your last employer. Anything can be had with the right amount of scratch."

"Hmmm, true. So two unemployed chicks traveling the world together. One a dead thief, the other an accessory to robbery. Both fugitives from the law."

"I love it. Sounds like a really bad movie. Now crank up *Pimps and Whores!*"

Monica grinned and spun the dial until the stereo rattled the windows. They sang the incomprehensible lyrics at the top of their lungs.

An hour later, Monica glanced up as she felt the car slow suddenly.

Angel flipped on the headlights as she peered up through a darkened windshield. "What the hell?"

Monica followed her gaze to a sky that had turned from blue to rolling black. The sudden shift in weather had come out of nowhere.

Heavy, dark clouds rolled toward them, flat on the bottom, immeasurable and jagged on the top. The sun perched, as though waiting to be consumed, while the nimbus digested the sky and established its sovereignty in the thin layer between the solidity of Earth and the vacuum of space. Following the ominous precursor, a fortress wall as dense and gray as slate pressed forward, blotting out hope and forming a new, despondent rule over the land.

"What is that?" Monica asked, fear gripping her heart.

"I think it's rain."

"What? No way."

The clouds marched in from the side like a thousand knights on horseback, extending across the flat land and announcing the arrival of the Apocalypse. As though in answer to Monica's denial, bright light flashed and flared within the blackness. A rumble surged through Monica's chest, so low it registered in her heart instead of her ears, and she envisioned the clashing of Neptune's trident against Satan's pitchfork.

The wheat fields lining the highway on both sides rippled and swayed as the wind scurried away from the impending storm, reminding her of the movement of the unhappy ocean from back home.

Angel said, "Maybe that's what they mean by waves of grain?"

"It could be. You'd better pull over." Monica pointed. Ahead, several cars had already pulled off to the side of the road.

"Is that a good idea?"

"Well, these people live here, and that's what they're doing. Besides, in a minute I don't think you're going to be able to see." The car rocked as a strong gust of wind nudged it like a grim deity brushing the vehicle with the back of his hand.

"Jesus," Angel said. "I think you're right."

From the side of the road, they stared out the window as the first few heavy drops of rain pattered on the roof, the sound fat and thick. Monica had already turned down *Pimps and Whores* and now snapped off the stereo. They watched the wall of water make its way across the fields, turning the goldenrods gray before devouring them. The storm, less rain and more river from the sky, pummeled the car. Monica gaped. How could so much water be contained within the clouds?

Like a thousand blacksmiths wielding the tools of their trade, the rain hammered the windshield and hood and roof. Bright spider webs of light lit up the air as the day became night. In the distance, great arches of electricity, furious and merciless, punished the earth, striking it again and again. The sound permeated the car. Would the vehicle even survive? Or would it just fall apart—screws and rivets snapping as the fury of the storm peeled the sheet metal from its iron hide.

Monica focused on the raging with such intensity that she didn't register the car driving past them until the two sat side by side. For an instant, she could make out the blurry driver leaning against the front window. The car's wipers tried in vain to make glass transparent. The stranger, braving the storm, passed, and her attention turned once again to the goings-on outside.

The two women wrapped their arms around each other, eyes wide with wonder as Mother Nature displayed her bitchy side. Monica didn't know how long they stayed like that—at least thirty minutes, maybe longer—but at some point, the pounding changed from a relentless thud to a hard knock. The deluge lessened, and the sky softened as the angry gods moved on to punish the denizens of adjacent lands. Like turning off a spigot, it just stopped—not trickling to a slow, but a sudden cessation. Just like when it began, a trail of flat gray clouds slid past and behind that, blue sky resumed.

The storm continued its march across the land and away from them, leaving Monica with the impression of having survived an angry mob or a stampede of scared cattle.

The women untangled themselves from each other and sat, stunned.

"Huh," Angel said.

Monica peered through the front window. "I looked but didn't see it."

Angel craned forward, following Monica's line of sight. "What?"

"A flying house."

"Oh, you missed it? I saw it. Kinda overrated, actually. Hard to believe they made an entire movie about it, but it *was* a long time ago. Guess they didn't have much else to write about."

Angel's hand shook as she released the parking break and dropped the transmission into drive. Pulling back on the road, she drove slower than before, evidently humbled by the brief appearance of the true master of the land.

Tyron Erebus picked up speed as the storm relented. *What is it with this place?* A little foul weather couldn't deter him, and he drove past farm trucks, cars, and semis that had all pulled over when the rain started. *Pansies. The road is straight.* He'd never driven on anything so uninteresting as this endless highway. At least New York had the crazy taxis, insane bicyclists, and wave upon wave of pedestrians and car traffic to keep him occupied. Here, nothingness stretched for hours. Without the waitress as a distraction—no, an appetizer—he'd have gone insane days ago.

The picture of the bitch and her friend that Barry had sent left him longing to sample the sweet main course and dessert. Oh, the waitress had tasted good, the way she'd screamed and begged, but he had much bigger plans for the other two women. They would be his compensation for spending so much time in this damned wasteland.

In the beginning, Laven had wanted this job taken care of with little fanfare. The mob boss demanded Tyron make it look like an accident, so he'd set the bitch's house to blow up from a "gas leak." Only somehow, he'd missed. He cursed himself for not staying around to witness the carnage, to make sure the job had been completed. But he had wanted out of that dreary place. Besides, the small town left him no place to hide. If he had stayed, he *would* have been noticed.

Barry, the little weasel, lacked the appropriate level of caution. Tyron detested the man and wanted to cut his balls off, sauté them in butter and garlic as the slimy lawyer watched, and then force-feed them to him. But as he picked up speed through the soggy Kansas countryside, he had to admit his gratitude for being released to take care of the situation however he wanted.

Tyron's mind wandered to the endless possibilities and his sweet, sweet reward.

Chapter Thirty-Eight

Sam trailed Tyron and came close to catching up when the day transformed into night. Clouds barreled in from the east. He made a U-turn on the highway and flew to a barn he had passed a few miles back. Just as he guided the bike through the big sliding door, the skies opened up, drowning the land in a torrent of water so thick, if he had been standing in it he wouldn't have been able to see his hand in front of his face. Sam had been all over, exposed to just about every weather condition imaginable, but nothing rivaled the sudden storms in the central part of the country.

Rows of empty horse stalls filled the barn, and a large combine parked against the opposite wall. The machine looked old but still serviceable. While Sam sat on a pile of hay, the storm pounded as if a thrash metal band had decided to hold an impromptu concert within the barn.

Sam opened a map on his phone. The blip representing Tyron continued to move. When everyone else stopped, parking next to the road to wait for the storm to pass, the killer continued in spite of the deluge—driven by a blind, incomprehensible hatred.

To gather any information on the girls' plans, Sam had stopped at Nan's Little Big Diner and Gas. When he pulled into the eatery, a black-and-white cruiser sat out front.

Instead of coming to partake of a burger or the lemon meringue pie, the house specialty, the police officers clustered around a small group of employees in the back corner of the restaurant.

As Sam stood by the door near the *Please wait to be seated* sign, he observed the group huddled together, talking in earnest. One of the women saw him and came over.

"Good afternoon," she said without really meaning it, her eyes puffy and face red. "Just one?"

"Yes, please."

"This way." She headed off into the depths of the restaurant. In the awkward period of time between the breakfast and lunch rush, only a smattering of patrons lined the seats here and there. "Will this do?" she asked, indicating a booth.

"This is fine." He slid in.

She set a menu in front of him, told him someone would be around to take his order in a bit, and turned to leave.

He touched her arm, stopping her. "What's going on?" He glanced toward the group talking to the police. Sam recognized her type—the sort of person that, when asked the right question, would open up, pouring forth a wealth of information. She didn't disappoint.

She peeked back over her shoulder then returned her attention to Sam with a conspiratorial spark glinting in her otherwise tired eyes. "The police are investigating a murder. Someone killed Coral, one of the waitresses here."

"What? Are you serious? What happened?" Sam did not question her sincerity, nor did he doubt who murdered the waitress.

"As a heart attack. Someone broke into her house last night, and they…they…" A fat tear lolled down her swollen cheek. "They killed her in the most disgusting way. Tortured her and raped her. Who would do that? Coral was the sweetest person. What kind of vile filth would do that? Why? Why for God's sake?"

"Are there any suspects?"

"Maybe. A man came in asking about her yesterday afternoon. That's why the police are here. I hope they nail the sonofabitch." She glanced toward the officers and waitstaff. "I need to get back."

"Sure. Thanks."

She left, rejoining the little group in the corner. Sam pulled out his phone and began typing. A few minutes later, he reviewed the police report for the murdered waitress. Each section of the document contained the usual, matter-of-fact, clipped language of "cop-speak." Killers became "perpetrators" and "suspects." Family homes became "crime scenes," and those killed became "the Victim," or, in the case of multiple murders, "Victim A," "Victim B," and so forth.

He'd read hundreds, probably thousands, of these narrations about man's dark brutality, but the gruesome nature of this one surprised even him.

The waitress—the report labeled her "female victim"—had been raped while also being sliced apart. Based on the cut patterns, Sam deduced "the perp" wanted her alive, avoiding lethal incisions to prolong his twisted sense of fun. She must have passed out from pain several times, for her wet pillow and mattress suggested he'd dumped water over her face to revive her. When he either finished or grew bored, he cut her wrists, leaving or watching her bleed to death. The lacerated piece of meat on the mattress bore little resemblance to a human.

For centuries, psychologists have debated how the human spirit could plummet to such depths. What exactly could render a person capable of committing horrific, violent atrocities against the innocent? Some believed nature ran amuck—a perverse code deep in human DNA designed to destroy the weak and purify the species. Others theorized sickness altered the brain, brought on by a physical ailment or defect, such as a tumor or a virus, the perpetrator contracted as a child during some fundamental development stage. A third school of thought blamed mental illnesses, such as schizophrenia or anosognosia, which drove the individual to unload automatic weapons in crowded shopping malls and classrooms full of school children. In these cases, perpetrators taken alive often reported voices within the confines of their own mind telling them—commanding them, often screaming at them—to destroy the pure and innocent.

All of these diagnoses suffered from the same fundamental problem: the removal of responsibility from the deranged, turning butchers and slaughterers into victims themselves. The unhinged blamed their atrocious actions on whatever excuses the people with the wall plaques and alphabets of acronyms after their names formulated to defend them. This same pool of people didn't view these destroyers of humanity as the depraved lunatics they were but as patients, the term itself implying the possibility of a cure. In this twisted perspective, everyone held the victim title.

Some believed that the cowards capable of such reprehensible acts of violence could be cured with the right ministrations of counseling and the correct balance of medications, rehabilitated and someday integrated back into society.

Sam's stomach roiled as he viewed the pictures of the crime scene and thought about a day, years in the future, when someone pronounced this butcher "well" and released him into the world again.

Sam too believed in a cure for such people. After witnessing the atrocities committed by those bent on the destruction of civilization, he had a more direct way to integrate them back into society, and it didn't involve singing *Kumbaya* and talking through their feelings.

He'd gotten up from the booth, never having even ordered, and pushed through the glass door of the diner.

Chapter Thirty-Nine

Monica's back ached, and her legs had started to cramp from the long hours spent on the road. She needed to get out of the car and stretch. "Let's stop someplace and see something," she said as Angel drove them into St. Louis.

"Way ahead of you," her friend replied, a slight smile playing on her lips. Angel made another turn, and the Gateway Arch came into view.

From a distance, it didn't seem very big, but the closer they got, the more it loomed in Monica's vision. Craning her neck to look up, she said, "That's pretty cool, I guess. But I don't really see the point."

Angel cocked her head to the side. "Huh? What do you mean?"

Monica's anger seemed to come from nowhere, but she felt powerless to stop it as she waved a hand toward the structure. "Well, it just seems like a tremendous waste of effort. It doesn't really do anything. You can't have a business in it or go to lunch at the top. I get that it's the city's 'thing' to draw people here. But it takes a tremendous amount of resources to maintain and run, money that could be better spent. Do an ad for McDonald's—it *is* an arch after all—and get it productive."

Angel rolled her eyes. "Gawd, you sound like such a lawyer."

"Whatever. Part of the problem, besides shitty parents, for abused and neglected children is the complete lack of resources allocated by the city, state, and federal governments. There are always other priorities for those institutions, and they usually have nothing to do with the bettering of things for our smallest, most defenseless citizens."

Angel stared at her for a heartbeat. "So, you think they should tear this thing down, just knock it over with a wrecking ball, and use the money to fund orphanages?"

Monica frowned. "I know you're making fun of me, but basically, yes."

"I'm not making fun of you. I've spent a lot of time talking to 'Practical Monica.' She's a smart girl, but sometimes she doesn't see the big picture."

"Practical Monica" placed her hands on her hips and turned to her friend. "No, she sees the big picture just fine. It's everyone else that doesn't seem to understand."

"Come on," Angel said, taking Monica by the hand and pulling her toward the entrance.

"Where are we going?"

"To see why they built this thing. To understand how it benefits society and why we shouldn't just bulldoze it."

Monica sighed. She wanted to pull away, to argue, but Angel seemed to have her mind set, so Monica followed her inside.

They waited in the underground line at the crowded entrance for tickets to the elevator. "Well, I guess if we are going to do this, at least we don't have to walk." Monica huffed in resignation.

They boarded the tiny car, which seemed more like a spaceship escape pod than an elevator, their knees almost touching the mom and two young children on the opposite seats. The youngest child, a girl of about four, held her mother's hand and stared at them with wide eyes. On the other end of the spectrum, the son, a willowy boy of about seven, asked a never-ending litany of questions. "Who built it?" "Why?" "How tall it is it?" "What happens if it falls over?" His poor mother struggled to draw a breath in between answering the relentless barrage. At one point, the haggard woman, pretty in her light summer dress despite the deep-purple lines under her blue eyes, smiled at Monica, exuding a bone-weary tiredness reserved for parents of the very young.

She watched through the small window as steel girders and other building infrastructure scrolled past on their ride up. When the doors opened at last, Monica and Angel let the family exit first. The excited boy tugged his mom's hand, dragging her behind him. Monica stepped out of the pod and stopped short, astonished.

People, a great majority of them children, packed the long, arching room. Dozens of excited little voices chattered as kids peered out the small rectangular view ports. The family they'd rode up with disappeared in the throng. School kids in uniforms, families, and other patrons marveled at the view and technological wonder together.

Monica and Angel wove through the crowd, making their way to one of the windows, and stared out at the landscape below. The clear sky gave an unobstructed view of the river. They switched sides and peered out over the city. After wandering the hall for a little while, they left. Monica didn't say anything on the ride to the bottom.

"So?" Angel asked. "Do we still need to call the wrecking ball people? Mr. Kadafi, tear down this arch!" she said in a decent Ronald Reagan impression.

Monica laughed. "You goob. First of all, it's Mr. Gorbachev. Second of all, it was a wall in Berlin, not an arch in Missouri."

"Yes, Counselor. The distinctions you've observed have been noted and entered into the record."

Monica nodded. "I guess you're right. There is something here. I never thought there'd be any benefit to something so extravagant, but the kids were very excited. It gave the children and the parents something in common to bond over." She thought about it for a minute. "Okay. It can stay."

Angel burst out laughing. "So glad you approve. It would have sucked to have to walk into city hall and tell the mayor, 'Mr. Mayor, I'm afraid I have some bad news for you. You know your arch? Yeah, the one that brings in a zillion tourists a year. Well, Mr. Mayor, it's crap, and I'm afraid it needs to come down.'"

The two women strolled the circular walkway around the arch to a nearby canopy of trees. In the distance, a paddleboat languished its way up the river. Several families, with kids running around, dotted the landscape of the shared grounds. Exhausted parents remained on constant vigil as their children played hide and seek and chased one another along the grassy knolls.

Monica turned her face to the sun, breathing in the Mississippi river air. Her friend had, once again, taught her a lesson about life. She looked over at Angel as they strolled the trail.

Perhaps, just perhaps, a chance existed that they would pull through this thing.

Chapter Forty

Barry Yamalki sat in his office going through news articles and the police reports from the Walberg explosion, hoping to find something that would assist Tyron. Another meeting with Laven loomed in the near future, and if he didn't have good news, Barry's life expectancy might plummet by several years. He'd seen time and again what happened to those that displeased Laven. Being behind bars hadn't slowed him down any. Though his second-in-charge ran the basic day-to-day operation, Laven retained command of the troops.

Tyron had not yet caught and tied up the loose end. Somehow the witness continued to elude him. Barry had been sorting through the dozen or so news articles when something stopped him. With nothing new to report, a resourceful Phoenix reporter, desperate to blather on about something—anything new—started interviewing locals who didn't seem to know any more than the flailing journalist.

Except, in this patchwork of pathetic attempts to rouse a story from the literal and figurative ashes, the correspondent entered the local coffee shop and talked to the woman running the place, Mary Beth Sanders. He got his news quote for the night when he asked her if she had any theories about the explosion and death of the local girl, Susan Rosenberg.

"...*I knew somethin' was goin' on. This town is little, and pretty much ever'one knows all the goin's on of ever'one else. But that girl was so secretive. She didn't want to date no one and never talked about her background or nothin'. You want to know the truth? I think somethin' was going on with her, like she was hidin' maybe. Then after her house exploded, there was the thing with the law office. At first folks was sayin' that Lisa Bunder got fed up with her husband—— Lord knows they's fighten all the time——but usually someone like Lisa'll come 'round after they cool off. Only she didn't. S'posedly, she went to her office, took out all the money from the safe, and drove off. Don't think so. That girl was flighty, but she was real responsible about her business. She'd never just leave it to rot like that. I ain't no detective. Our sheriff is a good man, and I tried to tell him something happened to her. Somehow, that Susan girl is 'volved. See what I'm sayin' there? But he's not thinking so...*"

The police disregarded the woman's wild theories, but Barry started searching. He traced the car and credit cards with ease. He didn't have the card numbers, but he found the car as a matter of public record. He could ascertain their connection from the senator who had connected him with the Agency. The same Agency who refused to continue helping, insisting they completed the project. A misunderstanding, Barry decided. When he first started working for Laven, the mob boss explained that everything was connected.

"See," Laven said from behind his big desk after hiring Barry to handle all his legal needs, "there are threads between everything. They are invisible to most people, which is why the masses have to work so hard. They are busy spinning their own threads because they can't see the ones that already exist. Everything, and I do mean everything, is connected.

"If you know how to see them, and even more importantly how to use them, life becomes your playground. Let's take you, for instance."

Barry stiffened, and his stomach gurgled.

"Your mother," Laven continued, "is in a nursing home in Pennsylvania."

Barry tried to keep his face impassive and hide his shock, but he knew Laven had seen it. Laven saw everything.

"The man who runs it,"—he paused for a second as if thinking—"Greg Hutton, he's got a problem."

"I don't understand how—" Barry began, but Laven ignored him.

"See, he likes the ponies. Every other Friday is pay-day at the nursing home. Greg has Saturdays off, and by Sunday he's broke. Doesn't matter how far up he gets, he doesn't stop until his check is gone. He's lost his apartment. He has no car. Nothing. Everything is gone. So Greg has been living in one of the rooms at the home—eating their food, using their laundry, you get the picture. But it doesn't stop there. He's maxed out his credit cards, and the hounds have been search-ing for him."

"Mr. Michaels, I don't—"

"No, of course you don't because you can't see the threads. You don't see how everything is connected, so let me shed light on it for you. I know all of this because I make it my business to know things. Greg can hear those hounds baying for him in the distance, but they haven't caught him...yet. He's on the cusp of collapse. If the owner finds out his employee is living on his dime, Greg is out. No one will hire a serial gambler that lives on the back of the man who gave him a job."

Laven tilted his head ever so slightly. Cold eyes appraised Barry's face; the mob boss seemed to be able to read the lawyer's thoughts as easily as a highway billboard. "So what? They'll just hire someone else. It's just another bum on the street. In fact, we should tell the owner, right? Get him out of there. Don't deny it. You're thinking it; I can see it on your face."

Barry didn't deny it.

The situation angered him. A man like Greg Hutton used the system Barry paid for. He loved his mother and allocated money to afford her the best care in the best facility the state had to offer. He went every two weeks, without fail, and spent the afternoon with her. She didn't recognize him anymore. He hadn't heard her call him by his name in two years and faced the immeasurable grief of introducing himself to her every time he saw her. Despite the expense, he didn't mind writing those checks every month, but he loathed the thought of someone mooching off of his money.

"But you only think that because you don't see the threads. See, there is a senator in Pennsylvania by the name of Silvia Goldwater."

Barry's forehead crinkled in bafflement. He had no idea where his new boss headed with this tale.

"Silvia is an independent, strong-willed, die-hard feminist, so when she married her four-star general husband, Drake Pinkle Hutton, she kept her maiden name. Are you starting to see the threads now? Greg Hutton is Drake's disowned brother, though the two men haven't talked in years, decades actually."

Barry shook his head. He didn't like the picture his boss painted yet he had no power to stop it.

Laven continued, "So someone with a charitable heart, my organization, let's say, offers to help. We can keep the dogs off and relieve a little of the pressure. A man as desperate as that will grasp any branch extended to him. So now I own Mr. Hutton. His life is mine to do with as I please. Both Drake and Silvia, as career politicians, recognize the potential for scandal if it came out that his brother, disowned or not, had fallen from grace. Once the dogs were done with Greg, a mere appetizer, they would turn to the couple. The hounds, having a taste of blood, would be thirsty for the main course, and nothing would be tastier than a rich general and his senator wife."

A spark flashed in the mob boss' eyes. "I now own the general and his wife too. Talk about a valuable resource. But that isn't where it ends. Do you see?"

Barry did, and his bowels turned to slush.

"Mr. Hutton takes a small sum of cash from us every month, a pittance, really, though it's a king's ransom to him. He lives for these small investments in his pledge to become a fulltime gambler, and from time to time, I've asked him to do small tasks for us. The people that come through this facility are from influential families with deep pockets. Some would make Ms. Goldwater and General Hutton look positively like paupers; you'd be surprised."

Barry couldn't fathom the exact nature of those "small tasks," but he believed them to be significant—very much so.

"You think you applied for this position. You think you beat out the competition because of your charisma in court, your deep understanding and experience with the law. Well, I'll let you in on a little secret. There are hundreds, thousands of lawyers slithering around this city who are better than you. More qualified. More charismatic. They could talk you into the ground. But I don't want any of them. Do you know why?"

Barry did, but he just stared at the little man who, by some miracle, grew bigger by the minute until he towered over Barry like a giant in huge black shoes, poised to crush him like a cockroach. His breath left his body, and he struggled to draw it back in. The air thickened, gelatinous and dirty like used motor oil.

"Because, Mr. Yamalki, I see the threads that connect everything together at a fundamental level. It's what binds us all. Once you see the threads, all you have to do is tug the right one, and you can make anything happen. I don't want a lawyer who's only working for money. I wanted someone who was motivated by more than just greed, which is why you are sitting in that chair and none of them are. I wanted someone connected to me."

When the bitch turned up as the star witness in the case the D.A. built against the mob boss, Barry found the appropriate threads and utilized them, tapping into the resources Laven needed to help destroy the prosecution's case.

Laven didn't use his connections often. Threads, by their nature, exhibit fragility—yank too hard, they stretch and break. Since the FBI held the girl in Witness Protection, Barry had no trouble locating her after placing the right people on the task. The country's own government, the same one trying to put Laven in jail, located her. But the man they'd sent botched the job, and now she ran free.

Barry retrieved the information on Lisa's car, a shiny red Audi. He put in a query to a private detective, a fat old gumshoe Laven kept on staff, and the man found the records of the car as it crossed tollbooths, making its way across the country. The latest hit came just two hours before in Missouri. Barry sent the information to Tyron.

During this research, he found the news item about the murdered waitress in Kansas. Fury flooded his veins, replacing the momentary victory that had just flowed there a minute before, and Barry picked up his cell.

☆☆☆☆

Frustration tore through Tyron. At some point, he must have passed the women. Since he had no idea when he had done so, he spent several fruitless hours searching for them in St. Louis. Other than their descriptions, he had little to go on. They hadn't used the laptop since Kansas, leaving the trail cold. Just when he started to think about burning off some of his pent up frustration with a little "extracurricular activity," like he had done with the cunt of a waitress from the diner, his phone beeped with an email. The small red Audi the women drove, once belonging to the bitch he charred, had passed through a toll-booth less than two hours before.

He climbed into his car and began to pull into traffic when his phone rang. The caller ID read *Barry Yamalki*. Tyron detested the smarmy little man—though in truth he hated almost everyone—and coveted an hour alone with the pompous little shit. Why would Yamalki be calling now?

"What?" Tyron answered by way of greeting.

"What do you think you're doing?"

"You should know; you're the one who gave me the assignment."

"I'm talking about the waitress."

Tyron paused. How the hell did Yamalki find out about that? Tyron did his hobby with extreme care—vigilant not to leave evidence behind. He understood enough about police procedure to know the big things never tripped a man up. The little things did—trace evidence, DNA, bodily fluids, and the like. So, he shaved every inch of skin to ensure he never left hair behind. He'd burned off his fingerprints years before and wore a condom during the wet work.

Yalmaki had taken a dangerous gamble fishing without any proof. Tyron sneered. "I don't know what you're talking about."

"Yes, you do!" The sound crackled and blasted through the tiny little speaker, and Tyron jerked the phone away from his ear.

"You don't need to shout."

"Really? Because I don't think you understand what's at stake here. You were told to eliminate a loose end, but instead you're out there fulfilling some sick fantasy. Quiet—that's the rule of the game here. We're trying to get our boss out of prison, but if you get your ass caught that's not going to happen. There's enough to deal with without you creating a trail for the police to follow. You might *think* you're the best, but even the best can fall. There's a direct link between you and Laven. If the connection to that waitress' murder is made to you, it's going to be pretty much impossible to get him out. Perhaps you'd like to be the one to explain to him why he's doing twenty to life?"

Tyron did not want to do that. Laven, a genius, ran things like the right hand of God—or Beelzebub, depending on the point of view—controlling everyone and everything around him. But he had about as much soul and mercy as flesh-eating bacteria. The mobster made a bipolar madman look tame, but Tyron liked crazy. He related to that spark of insanity, yet Laven also scared him. The man radiated darkness, cold as a black hole, leaving Tyron with the impression that, if the idea struck him, Laven would gut him and eat his liver while sipping a cold beer and watching a Mavericks' game. "No."

"Good. Glad to hear that you can be reasoned with. Now, there will be no more playing. You're done with your sick little fantasies. Find these women, do your job, and make sure it's untraceable. I don't care how you do it, but be nice and neat. I do *not* want to read about it in the paper. Do I make myself understood?"

"Yes."

The call disconnected. Tyron sat in the idling car. He hated the thought of that sniveling piss-ant lawyer calling the shots, but the images of what his boss would do to him should the man spend even one extra day in jail made him shudder. Tyron dropped the car into drive and pulled out into traffic, headed toward the Gateway Arch.

Erebus received his hard-won victory when the snitch and her companion disappeared into the shiny silver structure. He sat on a bench, watching the entrance. Little rodent children ran around playing tag, shouting, and screaming, absorbing him into their chaos. Why anyone would have the blood-sucking leeches baffled him.

When the two women left the landmark and headed his way, Tyron pretended to be involved in a newspaper, pulling the baseball cap low to help hide the telltale scar on his face.

When they rounded the corner, almost out of sight, he got up and followed.

Chapter Forty-One

Monica sat cross-legged in the grass, watching as a paddleboat meandered up the river. Scattered, fat clouds reflected in the surface of the water. From the bank of the Mississippi, she could envision her problems floating away, faint and wispy as cotton. The FBI should be able to help her get a real identity. Perhaps they could even keep the mob thug behind bars for good or, better yet, issue him a one-way ticket to the electric chair. She was sick of looking over her shoulder. She longed to take control of her own destiny, to rid herself of the mob guys, then spend an inordinate amount of time relaxing on some tropical island.

Monica lit a cigarette and, blowing a lungful of smoke, said, "So, I'm thinking—"

"Sounds dangerous." Angel lay on the grass, her hands behind her head, eyes closed. The sun made its lazy descent in the west, and once it dipped below the distant mountains, the light nip in the air would turn to a chill. Already, only a smattering of people remained on the grassy fields, and those that stayed kept their distance, busying themselves with children and blankets.

Monica frowned. "Funny, Ang. In all seriousness, I'm thinking about Paris."

"What about it."

"We should go there."

"I know. We just need to get your little 'identity crisis' resolved."

Monica shook her head. "It's more than just that."

"Someone's feeling reflective. It's the Arch, it makes you look at the big picture. I told you it was a worthwhile endeavor. Hey, give me a hit off of that." Angel stretched lazy and cat-like and seemed to be on the verge of going to sleep when she reached her hand out for the cigarette. Monica placed it between her friend's fingers and watched her take a deep drag without so much as opening her eyes. "I'm thinking dinner then a big comfy bed. How much exactly did you steal from Lisa's heirs?"

Monica cocked her head. "It's just a loan, and that's really cold, you know."

Angel shook her head. "Uh huh. You lifted her credit cards, money, and took her car. She may be dead, but isn't that still grand theft auto or something? In your defense, I guess someone did just try to kill you. Then there was the whole FBI thing. By the way, that name they gave you, Susan Rosenberg, that was just appalling. A little funny, but still appalling." Angel's reflectiveness permeated the night air. "Guess having taste has nothing to do with being accepted into the Bureau. Maybe you could plead severe annoyance?"

Monica sighed. "That's not a thing."

"It should be. Also, I'm glad you are growing your hair back out. You can't pull off the badass, black-haired chick thing. You're definitely a blonde. Me? I could totally do it."

Monica stiffened. "Hey! I look smoking hot with my black hair."

"Oh, no doubt, if I were a guy, I'd totally do you," Angel replied. "I'm just sayin' you can't pull off ninja chick the way I can." She made chopping gestures without opening her eyes or relinquishing her relaxed, prone position on the lawn. "Wha-cha-cha," she said under her breath as she puffed on the cigarette perched between her lips and swiped at invisible foes.

Monica sighed. "What do you want for dinner, ninja girl?" She snagged the cigarette back.

"Now you're talking. I'm thinking pizza. Do they have pizza in France? *Ont-ils la pizza en France?* It's been a few years since Ms. Roth's French class, but I still have it. Don't you think? Mon?" Angel opened her eyes, rolled over onto her stomach, and froze.

"Hello, bitch. I've been looking for you."

A small, cold circle, which could only be the barrel of a gun, pressed to the back of Monica's head. "Well, it seems you found me." A calm resignation settled over her as the survivalist took control.

"Who…who is that?" Angel asked.

The voice was one Monica heard in her nightmares. "Does he have a scar on his face?"

"Yeah. He's kneeling behind you. He's got a gun, Mon."

She nodded. "Then it has to be Joe Pesci's evil henchman."

A light chuckle emanated from the man behind Monica. "I wouldn't let him hear you say that."

Monica raised her hands. "Or what? He'll send someone to kill me?"

"There are things worse than death. This is what's going to happen. You're both going to stand up, and we're going to head toward the east entrance of the park. I have a car across the street, then we're going to take a little ride. Ready?"

"Like we have any choice." Bitterness rolled off Angel.

He smirked. "Good. If you do exactly as I say, things will go a lot easier."

Angel raised her chin. "For you, maybe. We're dead either way."

The murderer sighed. "Unfortunately for me, I'm in a bit of rush, so we don't have time to play. Now if you don't mind." He got up and indicated the east entrance with the gun.

He took an extra step back, concealing his gun in his pocket, as Angel and Monica stood. They started meandering toward the side of the park. "Not the main path," he instructed. "Too many people. Cut through the trees next to the lake."

"Anything else we can do to make killing us easier on you?" Angel turned to Monica. "Can you believe this guy?"

"Just do what he says," Monica told her.

"You can't be serious? He's going to kill us. You know that, right? A couple shots to the head and a trip down the river."

"Don't be so melodramatic."

Angel gaped. "Melodra... You're kidding, right?"

"Honey," Monica said as they entered the canopy of trees, "listen to me. Do you remember the story about when I was a girl and my mom brought the guy home?"

"Yes, but what..." Angel paused, understanding dawning in her eyes then her voice grew louder. "I know what's going on here." She planted her feet, ceasing all forward momentum. When she did, the entire party stopped too. "This is one of your guy friends from back in school, right? Play a trick on the simpleton from the little town? You and your big city friends! Well, screw you!" She raged at Monica and then turned to the mobster. "And screw you too——" Before she got the words out, he hit her in the side of the face. Angel's head snapped to the side, and she crumpled into a heap.

"You didn't have to do that!" Monica crouched beside her fallen friend.

"Get up," the man hissed. "Get up, or I'll shoot you right here and leave your bodies for the birds."

Monica stood, puffing hard on the cigarette still in her mouth. Lazy smoke wafted into the air and drifted away on the light breeze blowing in from the river. She stepped toward the hitman. "You're the man I saw with Joe."

He stared into her eyes but didn't say anything.

She reached out and traced his scar with the tip of her finger, from the edge of his ear down his jawline. "If you're going to kill us, I should at least know your name, don't you think?"

He appraised her but didn't say anything.

Monica moved closer. "What harm can come from that?" They stood almost nose to nose, and she smelled his Old Spice aftershave, saw the flecks of gray in his yellow, bloodshot eyes. She'd recognize an alcoholic anywhere. She should, after all, having grown up with one.

"My name is Tyron." He removed the gun from his pocket, keeping it close to his body and trained on Angel, who still lay on the ground, unmoving.

"Tyron," she purred. Smoke passed out her lips as she spoke.

"Put that out. They make a girl's mouth taste like an ashtray. I hate that."

"Oh, I don't blame you," she said and took it from her mouth. "Better?" She leaned in closer.

"Yes. Now do as I said and——" He didn't get the words out before Monica jabbed the smoldering end of the cigarette into his eye. Tyron shoved her back, screaming, his hands cradling his face. Monica didn't give him a chance to recover; she stepped forward and kicked him in the groin. He doubled over, the hand holding the gun performing double duty as he used it to also clutch his testicles while the other remained attached to his eye.

Angel popped up, a large branch, about the size of a Louisville Slugger, in her hands. She pulled the stick back over her shoulder, took a tremendous swing, and conked the thug in the back of the head.

Though not as hard as the baseball bat from Monica's youth, Angel's makeshift weapon nevertheless stunned the would-be assassin, knocking him from his feet. He thudded on his side in the thick grass. Monica grabbed the gun, but Tyron clung to it. Maybe in their struggle he would shoot his own nuts off.

Angel brought her foot down on his wrist, and he screamed in pain. Monica wrenched the gun from his grasp, and they sprinted for her car.

As they ran from the park, Monica threw the weapon into the lake. They scrambled into the vehicle. Angel started it, and with a slight squeal of tires, they pulled out into the light, evening traffic.

Tyron pulled himself to his feet using a nearby tree in time to see the Audi merge into the flow of cars. He leaned against the maple, the pain in his eye pulsing to the beat of his heart. Tears streamed from the burned orb, his wrist throbbed, a large knot had begun to form on the back of his head, and he wheezed from the blow to his crotch. All of his injuries combined didn't come close to the beating his pride had taken.

Barry could go screw himself. When Tyron caught these two cunts, he'd make them pay.

He limped to his car and settled into the front seat. He moaned, jammed the key into the ignition, started the engine, and headed the way they had gone.

Chapter Forty-Two

S o," Angel said through a mouthful of veggies and cheese, "this looks pretty simple. We just get on the Seventy here." She smudged grease across the screen as she traced the freeway from St. Louis. "It'll take us into Indiana then Ohio, and then we turn left in Pennsylvania."

"Lisa's going to be pissed you dirtied up her screen. She hates that."

"Well the next time we have a séance, she can talk to me about it."

Monica's face darkened. "Wow, with everything happening so fast, I hadn't even really had time to digest the fact that she's gone."

"I thought you hated that town and everyone in it?"

"I suppose that's true, and Lisa was probably the highest maintenance person I'd ever met. Self-centered. Artificial. But she was still my friend. She gave me my first job... Okay, sure the FBI arranged it somehow, but still."

"Honey, I know this is tough, but we almost got shot and dumped into the river this afternoon. At least one crazed lunatic is searching for us, maybe more. I get you need to mourn her and all, but right this minute is not the time. I promise, no more dead Lisa jokes, okay?"

Monica nodded. "You know how to get there?"

"I think so, though I'm not entirely sure where we are, and I hate to disturb Mr. Congeniality." She flicked her eyes toward the man behind the counter. They chatted while Angel finished her food and wiped her mouth. "I'm stuffed. Okay, no more stalling. I'm going in." Angel stood to go talk to the proprietor when Monica grabbed her arm, stopping her.

"Wait," Monica said, her eyes fixed on the front of the restaurant.

"Why? What's wrong?"

"I think I saw him."

"Who? The bald mobber?" Angel tried looking through the windows, but the darkness outside intensified the internal reflection. She could only see shadows on the street.

"No. Peter."

"Peter? As in Peter, the bastard and hitman from Walberg? *That* Peter?"

"Yes."

"Are you sure?"

"No. I saw someone on a motorcycle, and it kinda looked like his. He drove past, and I swear he looked right at me."

Could the stress be making her friend see danger around every corner? No one could possibly know where they were.

"I know it sounds crazy, but I swear that's what it felt like."

She held up her hands as if in surrender. "All right, I believe you. So say it was him. Do we wait and see what he wants?"

"Huh? No!"

"Okay, then let's get out of here."

They stood to leave, but just as Angel reached for her coat and the laptop, someone pushed through the door. For a second, she thought it would be the man on the motorcycle, but the figure that entered wore a gray leather jacket and a baseball cap casting a shadow on his face instead of the standard motorcycle riding gear. She started to turn back toward Monica when the light caught the scar running from his ear to his jaw, and her stomach clenched. The pizza she'd eaten turned to a lump of lead in her gut.

Tyron stepped into the little restaurant, closing and locking the door behind him.

"Hey!" the large man behind the counter shouted. "You can't do that!"

The mobster raised his silenced pistol and shot the proprietor in the forehead. The cook went right on flipping onions and peppers—swords clashing on the grill like a samurai, oblivious to his coworker's death—until the huge dead man fell on him. He screamed and pushed the proprietor to the floor, terror registering on his chubby face. He then raised his eyes from the murdered man to the mobster, staring into the dark infinity of the killer's gun.

A quiet "pumpf" from the gun, and a spot appeared into the middle of the cook's forehead, a twin of his coworker's. He fell forward, bending at the waist, landing face first on the grill where his skin began to sizzle and pop right alongside the peppers and onions.

"Good evening, ladies," Tyron said. "I believe we have some unfinished business. No chances this time. Put your stuff down, and hands above your heads." When they hesitated, he motioned with the gun. "Go on, or I end this now."

"I wish you hadn't thrown that gun away," Angel stage-whispered to Monica as she set her bag down and raised her hands.

"I don't know how to use one," she whispered back. "Do you?"

"No. But right now I'd try and figure it out."

"Tsk tsk. No forethought. No planning. You didn't think you'd see me again. Unforeseen things unfold when you are unprepared. Now, here's what's going to happen." He tossed a pair of handcuffs onto the table. "You"—he waved the gun toward Angel—"are dispensable. It's your snitch friend I'm really interested in, so you will be my little helper."

"Go bang yourself," Angel said.

Tyron shot the table to Angel's left.

She jumped as though electrocuted.

"You don't understand," he said. "I'm the one holding all the cards. I have both your lives in my hands. Now unless you want me to start shooting little pieces of your friend off one bit at a time, you will cooperate. Now, cuff her."

Angel looked at Monica.

Monica nodded. "Just do it. Maybe if you help, he'll let you go."

"Mon—"

Monica put her hands in front of her. "Ang, please. It's been coming to this for over a year now. I thought I could outrun these bastards, but it's not going to happen."

A tear spilled from Angel's cheek as she clicked the cuffs shut around Monica's wrists—the meshing of the metal teeth as ominous as the blade of a guillotine being slid into place.

"Okay, you've got me. Now let her go," Monica said.

His quiet laugh mingled with the sound of the frying cook and vegetables. "No, I don't think so. She's going to be my driver. Besides"—he rubbed the back of his head—"there's a little payback in order. So here's what's going to happen, you're going to wrap her coat around the cuffs—no need to draw unwarranted attention to ourselves—then we're going to go across the street to my car. You and I will get in the back seat, and you"—he looked at Angel—"as I said, will drive. If you so much as turn the blinker in the wrong direction, I'll shoot a piece of her off, starting with her kneecaps and working my way to more painful, intimate, places."

"Where are we going?" Angel asked.

"Someplace private. You will find out in good time; it's all about proper planning. You'd be wise to keep that in mind next time." He chuckled at his own little joke. "All right, let's go."

Angel wrapped the coat around Monica's hands.

Monica's eyes dropped. "I'm sorry."

"It was my choice to come with you. I knew the risks."

"Did you? Are you sure? Would you have still come if you knew this was a possibility?"

"A million times over," Angel assured her.

"Enough!" Tyron shouted. "Let's go."

☆☆☆☆

As they made their way toward the front of the restaurant, a burning stench saturated the air—scorched vegetables and searing fry cook. Monica glanced at the sickening sight of the dead man blackening on the griddle.

Tyron followed her gaze. "Unfortunate." He stepped aside, and for a moment, they clustered together. If she had planned to do something, the time had come, but she didn't have any tricks left in her handbag. In the park, the pompous mobster had underestimated them, and they had used that to catch him off guard. But this time…

Maybe when they got outside, she could start screaming for help? If she threw herself on top of him, maybe Angel could get away? But as each new thought formed in her mind, she realized her friend would never abandon her, even if it meant their deaths. Resigned, she plodded toward the entrance of the small eatery.

A dull "Pop! Pop! Pop!" emanated from the front of the restaurant. The trio froze, staring as the big picture window overlooking the street spider-webbed and became frosted. A dark figure approached, like Death had decided to pay them a visit from another dimension.

The huge window exploded. A dramatic shower of safety glass rained down on them, and they had to turn away to shield themselves. Monica looked up in time to see a black-clad demon sail through the air. She and Angel stood just behind the bald mobster, when it—he—slammed into their assailant, and the four of them toppled to the floor in a heap of arms, legs, and miscellaneous restaurant paraphernalia.

Monica landed on top of Angel but underneath Tyron, along with what seemed like half a dozen busted-up chairs. Though she struggled to get free, the dead weight of the heavy assassin kept her pinned. Had the thug planned for this particular contingency?

Chairs lifted off her, and the killer's weight vanished. The man in black picked up Tyron and threw him aside. Monica tensed, ready to fight, as she saw Peter reach down for her. Instead of grabbing her by the throat, he grasped her hands and pulled her to her feet. He did the same with Angel.

"Peter, what the hell?" Monica asked.

"Get out of here," he commanded.

"I don't understa—"

"Now!"

Angel, as unsteady on her feet as a newborn fawn, grabbed their purses and the laptop, and the two women started to leave.

"Wait. Not this." He grabbed the computer from Angel, withdrew a gun from his coat pocket, threw the PC into the air, and shot it. Turning back to Monica, he said, "Don't ever log on to that email again. Understand? It's been compromised."

"No, I don't understand any of this." She started to say something else, but she didn't have a chance before a chair broke over Peter's back. The simple piece of furniture dissolved into splinters of wood and bits of plastic. Tyron grabbed Peter, spun him around, and hit him in the face. Peter responded by grabbing the man in a bear hug and piling on top of him.

Monica didn't see how things ended because Angel grabbed her cuffed hand and tugged. "You heard the man, let's go, sister!" Angel yanked her through the now-empty window frame of the front of the pizza joint and into the cool night air.

They got in their car and drove off, making their second escape from the deranged killer.

Chapter Forty-Three

S am hoped the girls did as he'd instructed, but he didn't have time to look. His full attention remained on the bald man as they rolled around on the floor, each trying to gain the advantage. Tyron had lost at least two of his guns. Sam heard them skitter across the floor in the melee.

Tyron wrapped his hand around Sam's throat. The man's vise grip squeezed until black roses encroached on the periphery of Sam's vision, and his heart pounded in a desperate attempt to force blood past the blockage. He tried to pry the man's fingers from his esophagus, but Sam didn't have the leverage. The mobster bore down with all his weight. Sam reached down and tried to push the vicious killer's torso from his but again found himself at a disadvantage.

> **Rule #37:**
> **The unexpected will always gain you the advantage.**
>
> —*122 Rules of Psychology*

Instead of pushing, Sam wrapped his arms around the other man and pulled, lifting himself up into Tyron. Snaking his hand into the mobster's back pocket, Sam fumbled for a weapon, any weapon, and discovered a hidden treasure when his fingers found a knife sheath on the other man's belt. He pulled the blade out and raised it up so he could drive it into his assailant's ribs. But he didn't have the right angle for it, so he brought the blade down, burying it up to the hilt in the man's left butt cheek.

Tyron let out a wail of pain and relaxed his grip enough for Sam to thrust his forehead up. The other man's nose cracked, the sound both gruesome and satisfying. Sam threw the mobster off and rolled out from under him. They stood facing one another. Tyron wiped his nose, glanced down at the blood on his fingers, and shook it off. "You damned bastard, you stabbed me in the ass. You will pay for that, and when I'm done with you, I'm gonna go slice me a piece of snitch pie." He reached back and pulled the knife out. Blood covered the blade, but it looked wicked sharp as glints of silver shone through.

"Like you did with that waitress? You're a one-trick pony, sadistic and predictable. But as payments go, it's your turn to pony up."

"You'll find me full of surprises." Tyron snarled as he charged. Sam grabbed the arm holding the knife to keep from being lacerated. This action left him open, and the mobster collided with him. The two flew up through the glass partitioning the kitchen and dining area, over the counter, and onto the greasy floor. Sam held the wrist with the knife with one hand while pummeling the man in his stomach with the other. Tyron bucked him, flipping over and landing on top of him again. Sam lost tension in the arm holding the knife and struggled to catch it before Tyron shoved it into Sam's eye. Locked in a stalemate, each waited to see who tired first.

Sam had been riding hard for three days, sleeping or eating when he could, though not often enough. In spite of the huge surge of adrenaline pounding through his veins from the moment he shot out the front window, his strength waned as he fought the exhaustion that threatened. Their faces pressed close together, Sam could smell the hitman's vile breath and see the deep red of his left eye where it should have been white.

One of the guns had slid under the counter and lay next to Sam's face, just out of reach. With the last of strength, he strained his neck forward and bit down with every ounce of energy in him on Tyron's broken nose. When the mobster tried to pull back, Sam's jaws slipped off the boney nub of the bridge and caught on the bulbous tip. He clamped down tighter and felt cartilage and skin succumb to the force of his incisors. He twisted his head and ripped it off, the flesh coming away in Sam's mouth in a large bloody chunk of pulp.

Tyron scrambled off, jumping to his feet screaming. He backed into the wall, holding his ruined face. "Oh, you sonofabitch!" The mobster should have reevaluated and taken stock of the situation. But he didn't.

Rule #45: Frustrated people do not think clearly.

Rule #46: Angry people do not think rationally.

Rule #47: Furious people do not think at all.

—122 Rules of Psychology

Instead, Tyron re-gripped the knife and charged.

Sam grabbed the gun next to his head, brought it around, and fired. The shot hit Tyron's cheekbone, dissolving the side of his face in a spray of blood, skin, and bone. The force of the impact spun the mobster around. He flew back, slamming into a cupboard, then slid down to the floor, his feet tangled with those of the fallen cook.

In the aftermath, Sam thought he could detect the sound of sirens in the distance. But the sizzle and pop of the dead guy frying on the griddle, mingling with the ringing in his ears from the gunshot concussion, made it impossible to know for certain.

He did not want to be there when the police arrived, so he took one last look at the hitman on the floor, forced himself to his feet, and stumbled out the front window. His back throbbed. Deep cuts in his face bled, and he knew he'd find more injuries as the frenetic energy of the moment seeped from him. But he'd deal with those problems later. He pushed through the small crowd gawking through the window frame, climbed on to his bike, and gunned the engine.

In a display of brilliant timing that would have rivaled the best nighttime cop show dramas, he exited the scene before the first of the squad cars arrived. By the time the police secured the premises and realized a suspect required pursuit, Sam had slipped away into the night.

Chapter Forty-Four

As Angel navigated the nighttime traffic, Monica kept her eyes fixed on the rear window, trying to ascertain if anyone followed them. The headlights all looked the same. Someone could be trailing them, and she wouldn't know it. Besides, the bald mobster had already found them once. Distance would be their greatest ally.

On the edge of St. Louis, Angel guided the car down an off ramp. They had been driving for almost an hour, stunned silent most of the trip.

Monica broke through the monotonous drone of the car's engine. "Why are we stopping? Ang, we should just keep going." Exhaustion and fear nipped at her frayed nerves, and she tried to keep the agitation and irritation out of her voice.

"We need to get the handcuffs off you. If we run into more trouble, you'll be helpless. Besides, at some point you're going to have to use the john. And honey, I'll die for you, but friendship only goes so far."

They approached a neon-orange home store sign that jutted so high, low-flying aircraft had to be diverted around it.

Angel parked as close to the entrance as possible, and the women piled out. Only a smattering of patrons occupied the store. To hide her restraints, Monica wrapped her coat around her hands. A chipper employee, wearing an apron the same bright orange of the store's mile-high sign and carrying a clipboard, asked if she could help them find something.

"Bulk chains?" Angel asked.

If the woman thought the request odd, she didn't let on. "Aisle thirty-three, clear on the back, left-hand side." She pointed and smiled.

They followed her directions, passing hammers, drills, and heaters. Just beyond the screen doors, Angel stopped at the section containing various gauges of chain wrapped around large bolts. A long, flat bench, with an embedded yardstick to measure the desired length of chain, sat in front of the huge, thick coils. Angel examined the heavy-duty pair of bolt cutters tethered to the bench and nodded.

She started to remove the coat from around Monica's shackles when a voice broke the quiet. "Can I help you?" Another orange-aproned, way-too-chipper employee had slipped up behind her. In haste, Angel rewrapped the handcuffs, but he must have already seen Monica's bound hands because his smile faltered.

"Hi, no, thank you. We're just browsing." Angel grabbed a length of chain between her hands and tugged it as if to test its strength. "I think this will be strong enough."

"Oh, what is your project? Maybe I could help you pick out a gauge?" The robotic words, home-store-employee correct, poured out of his plastered smile, but his eyes never left Monica's wrists.

Jesus. Exhaustion pervaded every one of Monica's pores, and they still had a long night of driving ahead. They had almost been killed twice. She didn't have the patience to deal with this I'm-applying-for-a-job-at-Disneyland wannabe. She'd been about to tell the little prick to mind his own business when Angel interrupted her.

"Look, it's an S&M thing. I'm her dom." She turned to Monica. "Eyes down!"

Monica didn't hesitate, dropping her gaze to her feet.

Angel sighed.

Her face toward the floor, Monica dared to raise her eyes to watch the ensuing standoff. If this man called the police, it could destroy everything they'd worked so hard for. She surreptitiously scanned their immediate surroundings, searching for weapons. If she could get her hands on something, she might be able to disable him long enough they could make their getaway. If Angel couldn't wriggle them out of this, Monica had her own plan.

Angel turned back to the employee whose badge identified him as Todd. "So much spirit in this one. Do you know what I mean?"

"I...ummm...well..." His mouth hung open like a guppy, and when he swallowed, his Adam's apple bobbed up and down like a cork in the water.

Angel stepped closer to him and lowered her voice. "She seems to think she's an equal, Todd. Can you believe that? I'm tired, but there is much discipline ahead of us tonight. Such is the life. Anyway, if I can manage her, I think I've got this covered too, but if I need anything, I'll ask for you personally." She made "walking fingers" at him and raised her eyebrows. Then she turned her back, focusing once again on the chains.

"Ummm, yeah, sure. Okay." He backed away. "Have a good night."

Angel pulled a length of chain taut and stared down the links. She shifted her focus back to the kid in the apron, gave him a lecherous smile, and said, "Oh, we will." And she dropped an exaggerated wink. He stiffened and left, not quite breaking into a run. Monica giggled as she imagined the conversation in the break room tonight.

"Silence!" Angel barked, but amusement danced in her smile.

Monica laughed again as Angel started to unwrap the handcuffs and placed them on the big table.

"Okay," Angel said, "let's see if we can get this done before Todd has a change of heart and asks to join us."

"I think if he could, he'd be headed over the hills and through the woods."

"Quiet, slave." Angel bit her lip as she concentrated on getting the large cutters as close to the left cuff as possible. She pulled down. The blade bit into the metal and seemed to get stuck. But as Angel continued to press, it slid down, and the chain parted. She repeated the process with the other cuff. "Well, you've got some wicked looking bracelets, but at least your hands are free. Hopefully your friends at the FBI can help with this."

They quickly re-wrapped her hands and headed back to the front of the warehouse. Todd leaned against a counter, whispering with one of the cashiers. They both stared at the women as they made their way toward the exit.

"Did you find everything you needed?" he asked them.

"You don't carry anything heavy enough. It's okay; I know a guy. Thanks anyway." She blew them a kiss as they breezed through the large sliding glass doors.

"Okay, thanks for shopping at..." The no-longer-so-chipper employee's store-appointed farewell faded into the background as they hurried into the night.

Chapter Forty-Five

S am stared in the steel mirror, gathering himself for the task ahead. The front window of the pizza place had been made of safety glass, but the partition had not. When he and Tyron went over the counter, the barrier had shattered into sharp jagged pieces of shrapnel. His thick leather jacket protected him, for the most part, but the seam connecting the arm and torso sections, comprised of a simple, thin material, offered little protection. A long piece of the heavy glass, as sharp and wicked as an assassin's knife, stuck out of the muscle in his chest. Blood dripped from the wound saturating his shirt. When he pulled it out, the injury would bleed even more.

He had stopped for hydrogen peroxide, bandages, and a bottle of painkillers and asked the store attendant, in his most casual voice, for the bathroom key. He popped five of the dusty white pills. Stripping to the waist, he stood in the dull light, examining the shard.

The shrapnel had entered at an angle with an inch of it jutting out from his flesh. He shoved a rag in his mouth. Careful not to cut his fingers, he pinched the glass and pulled. He bit down hard on the rag as the searing agony ripped his chest apart. Resistant at first, the shard gradually released its hold on his muscle. He dropped it into the wastebasket and leaned on the counter, waiting for the worst of the throbbing to pass.

As gently as his shaking fingers would allow, Sam pressed around the injury. With each touch, the wound sent angry bolts of fire through every nerve in his torso, but he carried on. He stopped, examining a small bulge just beneath the skin. Just as he feared, a piece of the glass had broken off when it entered. In addition to the purchases, Sam had also retrieved a Swiss army knife and a pair of needle-nose pliers from a small toolkit on his bike. The truck stop didn't have much in the way of surgical supplies, but he made do, setting everything on the counter. He poured the disinfectant over the blade of the knife. Steeling himself, he cut the tissue around the edge of the glass. When he set the tool down, his hands shook so hard he missed the counter, and the blade toppled to the floor.

Sam disinfected the pliers next and grasped the edge of the glass. He needed to focus. If he squeezed too hard, the shard would break into smaller pieces, and he'd be forced to dig those out as well. He took a deep breath, settled himself, and gave a slight pull, encouraging the glass to move rather than forcing it from his flesh. Pain radiated from the injury, traveling the length of his body, but he continued to work the piece out. When the edge pulled free of his skin, he set the pliers down and continued moving it back and forth with his fingers until it came out with a sickening rip. He bit down on the rag so hard, there was a chance he would just bite through it. Blackness encircled his vision and pulsed with every beat of his heart, and he leaned against the sink. After a while his sight cleared, the pain faded, and he could breathe again.

Pouring hydrogen peroxide over the wound filled it with liquid fire. He applied a bandage, securing it with tape, and then loaded everything back into the plastic bag. He walked out to his bike, stowing the items in one of the saddlebags, then filled his gas tank.

The effort to climb on then start the big bike drained what little energy he had left and sent a fresh wave of pain radiating from his injury. His entire body ached, and he slumped over the handlebars trying to recover some of his strength while the motorcycle's heavy engine idled underneath him like a purring dragon. Taking a deep breath, he sat up, dropped the bike into gear, and headed out into the night.

Though exhaustion dogged him, Sam drove on. At one point, his vision blurred, the headlights coming toward him appearing through a prism. When his eyes tried to close, he pulled into a state park, slept for two hours, then got back on the road.

Pocahontas led him to the address Armon had given him, until she pronounced—in a computerized, pompous voice—that he had arrived.

His eyes took in the details of his "destination"—a large, abandoned-looking gray concrete building on the edge of the city's industrial district. A ten-foot cyclone fence, topped with razor wire angled to make it difficult for people to enter, surrounded the bunker. Sam drove around the lot to the gated entrance, noting the men on the roof with automatic weapons.

A large lock secured the gate shut. He waited. Sam had faced drug lords before but never anything on as grand a scale as this.

The sun had just started to rise in the east; early-morning shadows still lingered in the pockets of the land. If he tried to climb the fence, he had a very good chance of being shot, so he did the only other thing he could think of.

"Hey!" he yelled. "Anybody home?"

Everything remained motionless.

You're being watched, Chet said. His alter ego had been almost silent the last few days.

Yeah, I know, but from where?

Not sure, but they're there.

"Hello?" Sam yelled again. "Anyone want to buy some Tupperware?"

He waited, then a door opened. Sam heard the squeak of its rusty hinges all the way across the yard. Three men brandishing large weapons exited the building, accompanied by a big black Doberman.

Don't do anything they will perceive as threatening, Chet informed him.

Yeah, no shit. Is this the type of advice I pay you for?

You don't pay me at all, so eff off.

Though Sam raised his hands to show he held nothing in them, the action did not seem to endear him to the large men as they approached.

"What do you want?" the first one asked. He had huge shoulders, a handlebar mustache, and, to round out the outfit, a large gun aimed at Sam's chest.

"I need to talk to your boss."

"Oh, really? What about?"

"I have information he will be interested in."

"Uh huh. And what would that be?"

Sam had thought about this exact situation on the way. He had to convince these guys to let him in. "It's not for you, it's for him. It's business."

The man sneered. "Look, I don't know what you got or who you think we work for, but I suggest you get on your little bike and pedal your ass out of here before I get even more annoyed than I already am." He turned and started to walk away, the others following.

"I have inside information on Laven Michaels. I could go to the authorities with it, I suppose, but I thought your boss might be more interested."

The mustached man turned and came back, regarding Sam. "What exactly do you have?"

"I'm not going to stand out here handing out all I know to some two-bit thug. Now, are you going to let me in or not?"

The man stared at Sam for a long time then motioned to one of the other men to unlock the gate. The third man, who now had the dog on a leash, kept the gun in his free hand trained on Sam. As the gate slid open, an indignant squeal of un-lubricated steel on steel pierced the vacant yard, and Sam pushed his bike through.

"No, the bike stays out here."

Sam looked around. "In this neighborhood, it'll get stolen. Besides, what I need is in the bag."

"Well, that's just a chance you're going to have to take. You want to see my boss, you're going to do it my way. Get what you need, but the bike stays." Sam had expected a confrontation about his bike and been prepared to leave it behind. He wanted to make the thugs feel in control and less apt to pull the trigger.

Sam got the file he needed from the bike and stepped through the gate. The man with the dog frisked him, relieving Sam of his Sig Sauer.

Metal grated as the remaining men closed and locked the sliding gate. "Let's go." They surrounded him as they marched toward the door.

The gloomy light inside the building felt like a weight as the men marched Sam down the hall. The peeling paint revealed large, origin-unknown stains that reminded him of Rorschach tests.

Chet observed each of these inkblots with his usual tact. *Dead guy. Murdered guy. Gutted guy. Why do people make such a big deal about this? Seems pretty straightforward to me.*

The thugs led Sam to an open door. Inside, a large man sat at a huge wooden desk, reviewing papers that were strewn helter-skelter across its surface.

Sam added the file he had brought with him to the jumble. "I think you should look this over."

Without looking up, the boss picked up the file and started reading. The room remained silent except for the occasional sound of turning paper. Finally, he said, "So

you have a lot of information on my friend Mr. Michaels'
organization." He looked up. "All very interesting. How
did you come by such information and why did you bring
it here?"

"I need a favor. Something that needs to be done in
exchange."

The man laughed quietly. "I see. Well you are not in a
very good position to negotiate. I have all that I want, and
you have...well, nothing." He shrugged his meaty shoulders as if to say, "What can you do?" Sam did not reply,
so the man continued, "Mr. Michaels is, of course, being
released soon. The case against him is falling apart, and I
see that there is information about that in here too." He
paused and appeared to be thinking.

This was the tipping point, and though Sam kept his
face impassive, his heart picked up its pace.

The man behind the large desk regarded Sam for a long
time. "Tell me what you want."

Relief flooded Sam's veins, and he began to talk.

Chapter Forty-Six

Angel and Monica stopped at a joint only a little nicer than the Stardust Motel Monica had stayed at the night she'd fled the explosion. At two in the morning, fatigue had overwhelmed them, so they'd chosen it at random. Monica lay in bed, listening to the night in search of a threat, but sleep beckoned.

To her surprise, she awoke—alive—at eleven the next morning to drizzly skies. With all that had happened, she'd half expected Tyron to find and kill them during the night. Maybe Peter had taken care of him. Or maybe Peter lay dead in the middle of the restaurant, and even now the madman sought to tie up the little loose end.

She nudged her friend. "Ang, wake up."

Angel had her arm wrapped around Monica's waist, a little puddle of drool collecting on the pillow. The corner of Monica's mouth turned up in a half smile. At fifteen, she and her best friend had slept in this same position, except now they huddled together in a hotel somewhere south of New York while a murderer, with death inked on his heart like a tattoo, stalked them.

"Hmmm," Angel murmured without opening her eyes.

"It's late, hon. We should get going."

"Are we dead?"

Monica smiled. "Not yet."

"Is Tyron or whatever his name…is he at the door?"

"No."

"Good. Okay, give me ten more minutes." She snored, light puffs of air emanating from her slack face.

Monica chuckled and stroked her friend's hair. The girl had given up her life in The Cove and had then put that life at risk for Monica several times now. Ten minutes didn't seem like too much to ask.

An hour later, Monica and Angel picked up a map of New York City and made a plan to get to FBI head-quarters.

Then comes the hard part. "So," Monica started, "what are we going to do when we get there? It's one thing to say we're gonna waltz in and demand to see Jon, but actually getting results is a completely different matter. They'll probably just throw us out. Then what?"

Angel shook her head. "Don't overthink it, Mon. We'll just walk up to the front desk, tell them who you are, and ask to talk to Jon."

"Just like that?"

"Just like that."

Monica gave her friend the once over as if really seeing her for the first time. "You know, you're pretty good at this sort of thing."

"I know, right? These last few days, I've been thinking about going into law enforcement. I could do a hell of a better job than Crew Cut."

"That wouldn't take much. But honestly, I'm really proud of you. No matter what happens and how this thing plays out, you need to go to school and follow through with it."

"I will." Angel sounded business-like, but a satisfied smile played on her friend's face as she started navigating the busy New York City streets.

☆☆☆☆

The area around 26 Federal Plaza had been cordoned off, so Angel and Monica parked the car several blocks away. Angel strode with purpose. She didn't hesitate before barging through the door of one of the most powerful law enforcement agencies in the world.

They had to pass through a metal detector then watch as burly and well-armed security guards went through their purses before being allowed in. Monica trailed in Angel's wake as she marched up to the front desk.

A middle-aged woman, hair in a tight bun and wearing way too much blue eye shadow, asked if she could help them, though her severe face told them she would prefer to do anything but.

Angel looked her in the eye. "We need to talk to Jon. Can you call him down please?"

The receptionist gave them a placating smile that said she dealt with crazies and egomaniacs all day. "We have several Jon's. Do you know his last name?"

Angel looked at Monica. "He told me it's Smith," she said, "but somehow I don't think that's his real name."

Angel turned back to the receptionist. "Then no."

"I see. So what is this in regards to?"

"This woman"—Angel put her hand on Monica's shoulder—"was in the Witness Protection program. Only your agents screwed up and let someone almost kill her, several someones actually. She got away, with no help from anyone here I might add, and"—she flicked her hand toward the woman's desk—"shouldn't you be writing this down?"

The receptionist shot her a condescending look. "No, I think I can remember it. So your...what? Client? Are you her lawyer?"

"No, she's my friend."

"Okay, so your *friend* was in Witness Protection? What is your friend's name?"

"Her real name is Monica Sable, but your goons gave her the ironic name Susan Rosenberg."

"I see. And why was she in the Witness Protection program?"

Angel sighed. "Is it really relevant? Seems like we should be telling this to an actual agent." She paused for emphasis. "Not the secretary."

The woman bristled, but, to her credit, remained calm. "I need to have a little more information before I know if I am going to call one of our 'actual' agents or if I am going to ask my uniformed friends to escort you from the premises."

Angel scoffed, the words failing to intimidate her. "Fine. She overheard some mob guys planning a hit, and the FBI needed her as a witness so they could put them in jail.

Only instead of protecting her, they stuck her in a shitty little town in the middle of nowhere. The bad guys found her and blew up her house."

"So you're telling me she survived being blown up in her house?"

"No." Angel huffed and rolled her eyes. "*Obviously* she wasn't in the house. Her boss, Lisa, was. Look, we've been driving for days. Someone from the mob almost killed us, twice, and for all we know, he's still out there. Are you going to call someone to come help us or not?"

The receptionist's pinched face spoke to her exasperation, but instead of asking them to leave, she sized Monica up. "Who was the defendant you were testifying against?"

"Laven Michaels."

For a second, the woman's eyes widened. She picked up a phone and whispered into it, then returned the receiver to its cradle. "Someone will be down in a few minutes. Please take a seat." She pointed to a bench on the other side of the foyer.

Once they made it out of earshot, Monica leaned over, giggling. "'Shouldn't you be writing this down?' Girl, you have balls. Big, brass ones."

"It's all about intimidation with these people."

"How do you know all this?"

Angel shrugged. "Haven't you ever watched TV?"

A few minutes later, a nondescript man in a dark suit approached them. "Hello, ladies. I am Special Agent Martin, please come with me." He led them to a handle-less door.

Fear and trepidation gripped Monica's heart as their new friend typed in a number on an inset keypad.

"What is it?" Angel asked her.

"*Déjà vu.*"

"Well, love, it's what's gotta be done. I'll be with you this time."

That helped, though it didn't entirely quell the quaking in her heart.

The lock buzzed open, and they stepped across the threshold.

Chapter Forty-Seven

Monica's sense of *déjà vu* deepened as Martin lead them down a familiar white hallway and back to a small room that could have been the twin of the one she'd been in before. The sensory recall slammed into her like a speeding New York taxi.

He set up three chairs around a small round table and left.

Monica couldn't sit and began pacing. "Ang, are you sure about this?"

"It's a hell of a time to have second thoughts. You know there really isn't any other choice. What else are we going to do? Keep running for the rest of our lives?"

Monica stopped. "It's an option."

"It's *not* an option. Besides, this time you're not alone. Between the two of us, we'll kick their ass."

She frowned. "You mean like at the restaurant?"

Angel took a seat as though she had the whole thing figured out. "Look, we had it under control. If that Peter guy hadn't shown up, we'd have thought of something. Besides, compared to the mob, these FBI guys should be a walk in the park. At least they have to follow the rules."

Monica heard Angel's words, but she didn't believe them. The FBI had been in control of her life—dictating what she could and couldn't do, flying her in to testify, questioning her every move, listening in to her conversations, herding her like they were sheepdogs and she the only member of the flock—for so long, she didn't remember how it felt to not be under their thumb. They made the rules and seemed free to change them at any time to suit their needs.

A half hour later, Martin returned, carrying a clipboard and a pen. He took the empty seat. "Hello, ladies. Sorry for the wait."

What had taken thirty minutes? Another intimidation technique? A chance for them to change their minds?

Angel must have wondered the same thing. "Where have you been? Why did it take you so long to get something to write on?"

Martin stared at her. "I didn't catch your name."

"Angel Humbolt, and I don't like being kept waiting unnecessarily."

"Noted." Martin wrote something on the clipboard. He turned to Monica. "I understand you are Monica Sable?"

She nodded.

"And you are in Witness Protection?"

"Yes. My new name, my alias, is Susan Rosenberg."

"I see." Martin scribbled some more on his clipboard.

"We are here to see Jon." Angel tapped the table, an impatient look broadcast on her face.

"So I've been told."

Angel held up her hands. "Well?"

"Well, I need to confirm your story before we can contact him."

Angel pushed Martin's clipboard onto the table, staring him in the eyes. "It's not a story. Your agents screwed up, and if it weren't for her quick thinking, she'd be dead."

He continued to stare at Angel, but asked Monica, "Where were you relocated to, Ms. Sable?"

"Walberg, Arizona. It's a total shithole."

"Do you have identification?" The agent turned his attention to Monica.

She dug out her Arizona driver's license. "I don't have my real one. The agents took it."

"I will need your identification too." He spoke at Angel but did not bother to look her way.

Angel frowned at Martin. "Why?"

"Standard procedure."

"It's the line they use for everything illegal they do," Monica informed her.

Angel pulled out her California driver's license and handed it to him.

Martin studied their IDs then stood. "Please be patient, ladies. I'll be back." He opened the door to leave.

"Wait," Angel called.

He turned, his eyebrows raised as he regarded her.

"Can you do something about these?" She picked up one of Monica's hands, showing him the handcuffs.

"Probably. Once we run the police reports to verify you aren't wanted, we'll talk about it." With that, he left.

"Jesus, really?" Angel flipped off the closed door.

"Really. This is pretty much what happened last time. I was pissed the first time too. I think they leave you in here to wear you down."

According to Angel's watch, which they had to rely on this time, Martin had been gone for over an hour when the door opened again.

"It's about time..." Angel's eyes grew wide when a different agent entered the room. "Who are you?"

Amusement flicked across the man's face. "You must be Angel. I've heard so much about you. My name is Jon."

"You're Jon?" Angel appraised him. "You're shorter than I pictured."

He chuckled. "And you're *exactly* the way I pictured."

They sat opposite each other, squaring off in silence for a few heartbeats.

He then turned to Monica. "You surprised me. First of all, we closed your case because we thought you were dead. If it wasn't your ashes they pulled from that house, whose were they?"

Angel threw her hands up in the air. "Seriously? You don't know?"

"Well, sometimes even we don't know everything. See, that's why we interview witnesses, to gather all the information." He turned back to Monica. "So, if you know the answer, please enlighten me."

"That was my boss, Lisa Bunder. She owns...owned the lawyer's office where I worked."

"Ah, that explains that."

"That explains what?" Angel leaned in as she had done with Martin. "If you want information from us, it has to be give and take. Monica was kept in the dark too long."

Jon's eyes lit up with an emotion resembling amusement. "It explains the missing persons report filed by Lisa's husband. He was the primary suspect in a foul play investigation. Seems they had a very…tumultuous relationship. We had a working theory he got tired of her and did something about his little problem."

Monica nodded. "Yes, she and her husband had issues, and sometimes she stayed the night with me. She was a pain in the ass, but she was my friend. Your agents messed up, and because of that, she's dead."

"That may be true, but it seems that *you* were the one who messed up."

Angel slammed her fists down on the table. "What are you talking about? It's the job of the——"

Jon held up a hand and turned back to Monica. "See, my people tried to keep you safe, but you tried to escape on several occasions. You were mean to the agents, hid information, emailed in secret."

"How did you——" Monica began.

"Others in town, unlike you, are very forthcoming with information."

"Mary Beth," she said. "I should have been more careful around her."

He neither confirmed nor denied her accusation. "So." He pierced her with his cutting eyes. "Not only that, but as soon as you got your tracking device off you left town with some guy, then told him your actual name."

"Hey!" Angel grabbed Monica's hand and squeezed. "Look, she was in a hard spot. You stuck her out in the middle of nowhere, and she had to leave everyone she knew. She did everything—well almost everything—you asked her to. *You* needed her, not the other way around. I expect you to treat her with respect. *She's* not the criminal here."

Jon shifted his gaze back to Angel. "Well, because of her, someone died. That sounds criminal to me."

"No. Someone died because she was helping you," Angel bit back.

Monica sighed. "He's right. Lisa died because I told Peter my name, and he tried to kill me but missed."

"Mon, no."

"It's like you've been telling me all these years. I fight the system, and this time someone besides me got hurt."

"Please, Monica," Jon said, "it would help us greatly to know about the man you met."

Monica gave a brief synopsis of the night she and Peter had spent together.

"So, you don't have a picture of this guy?" Jon asked.

Monica shook her head. "We were only together that night. It wasn't like I was asking for mementos or anything. I told him to leave, and he obliged."

"I see." Jon added more to the pages of notes he'd been taking. "Well, we'll run Peter Morrell and Tom Phillips through the system, but my guess is they are both aliases. We'll see if there is any video footage, maybe a traffic cam, but Walberg probably doesn't have any."

"I don't believe in coincidences." Angel, who'd been quiet, reinserted herself into the conversation.

"Nor do I. But his physical description doesn't match anyone we have on file. It could be he's a new player. He could have been the one to plant the bomb."

Angel shook her head. "That doesn't seem likely."

"Oh? And what makes you think that?" Jon folded his hands into a triangle against his lips.

"Well, because," Angel informed him, "the most likely culprit was Tyron, the mobber."

"Excuse me? You mean Tyron Erebus, Laven Michaels' hitman?"

Monica considered jumping into the middle of the conversation, but Angel seemed to have it well in hand. "You tell me. All I know is that he almost killed us twice yesterday. If you're looking for who probably planted the bomb, I'd start there."

"You survived an encounter with Tyron? That seems highly unlikely."

"Where exactly do you think she got those?" Angel pointed at the handcuffs. "Tiffany's? Look at my face. Do you see the bruises where he hit me? God, you're such a moron."

Jon sighed. "All right, tell me what happened."

So Monica began a monologue, with interjections and clarifying remarks from Angel. Jon looked suspicious at first, but as their story continued, he resumed his note-taking.

"This was last night?" He glanced up from the paper.
"Yes."

"And you said he killed the two guys at the pizza place?"

"One of them fell on the griddle," Monica said.

"It was nasty." Angel shivered.

"Then this Peter shot his way in and tackled the guy?"

"Yes."

"Then you ran away."

Angel held up a finger. "Yes, but not before he shot Lisa's laptop."

"Oh, right." Monica nodded.

"He shot your computer?" Jon scribbled in his notebook. "You mean Lisa Bunder's laptop?"

"She left it in the car. We were using it to get directions," Monica explained.

"But before we left, Peter grabbed it and threw it in the air and shot it." Angel made a firing motion. "Blam! Told us it had been compromised. Then we left."

"No." Monica bit the inside of her lip as she recalled Peter's exact words. "He said not to log on to my email account any more. *That* was what had been compromised."

"Oh, that's right. It all happened pretty fast."

Jon rubbed his forehead.

"Okay, so now you have what you need." Angel crossed her arms as she settled back against the seat. "What can we do about getting Mon's life back? You got your guy, now she should get what she's earned."

Jon shook his head. "That isn't possible. I know you were hoping that eventually you could go back to NYU and pick up where things left off, but that isn't going to happen."

"And why not?" Angel cocked her head to the side and narrowed her eyes.

"Let me lay this out for you. Tyron Erebus and Peter Morrell are just the first in a series of people who will try to silence you. There's no way we can protect you forever if you go back to your old life. You will be too exposed."

Monica ground her teeth in frustration. "So, it's back to being alone in Witness Protection?"

"No." Angel, who still held her hand, patted it. "You're not going to be alone because I'm going with you."

Monica's eyes grew misty. "Oh honey, no."

"That's not possible. Sorry. It isn't going to happen." Jon snapped his notebook shut. The sound ricocheted around the tiny room.

"Yes, it is. See, you used her. You wanted her to give up her life and testify. She did that. Besides, I know too much."

Jon stared at her. "You know what you are asking? You will be giving up everything."

"Yes." She held up their intertwined hands. "Where she goes, I go."

"Let me see what I can do."

Chapter Forty-Eight

Monica kept looking at Angel's watch as Jon stayed gone for over an hour. Once he settled himself in the seat across from Angel and Monica, he placed his laptop on the table. "There has been a development."

"What now?" Monica asked.

"All in good time. First, I checked on the story in St. Louis. There was indeed an incident at Papa Pelone's Pizza last night. Two men were found dead. Ricardo Pelone, the owner, and his brother the cook, Belivo Pelone."

"There has to be one other person, either Erebus or Peter," Angel said.

"There were eyewitnesses that say a man left the restaurant, got on a motorcycle, and drove off. One of the witnesses reported injuries to the escapee. But there is more."

"Just spill it already!" Monica blew a piece of stray hair out of her face and wished she could just punch frigging stupid Special Agent Jon. "Why do you have to make everything so dramatic?"

Jon just shook his head and unfolded the laptop. He clicked a few times then flipped it around for them to read. "Here is a preview of a news article that's set to go out in the *Times* this evening."

Associated Press
September 17

Four men were gunned down on the steps of the City Courthouse this morning following the release of Laven Seth Michaels, who was suspected of leading a local branch of the mob. Mr. Michaels had been arrested on multiple charges including murder, bribery, conspiracy, drug trafficking, and assault. Full details of his release have not yet been disclosed, however rumors abound.

He and three other men, suspected of being key players in Mr. Michaels' organization, had just left the courthouse when a dark SUV pulled up. Two unidentified men fired a series of shots.

The four were fatally wounded, but no one else was injured in the attack.

Brett Wells, lead NYPD detective on the case, believes a competing organization committed this act as the result of a turf war, though no evidence has surfaced to support the claim.

Police are looking into the shooting. Citizens are asked to contact authorities if they have any information regarding the incident.

Monica sat back against the seat with a resounding thud. "Does this mean what I think it means?"

"With Laven dead, we no longer need you to testify…until, of course, we catch Tyron Erebus. But for now we believe you're out of danger." Jon paused. The air thickened as the two women waited for him to speak again. "But there is something else."

Angel hissed out a curse. "Of course there is."

"The paper speculated a rival gang might be responsible for Mr. Michaels' untimely demise, but we know exactly who that is. In fact, even as we speak, this other group of individuals is systematically destroying their competitor's operation. It was as if someone provided them with the information to take them apart. You wouldn't happen to know anything about that, would you?"

Monica and Angel both shook their heads. "It seems like a good thing, right?" Angel asked. "I mean, a whole drug operation is getting shut down."

"Only to have a new one put up in its place." Jon frowned, his brow knitting together. "We had contacts and informants in the old operation. Now we're going to have to start from scratch."

"So we're done here? I can finally go back to my life?" A wide smile spread across Monica's face.

"No. No, we aren't done yet," Angel said. She swiveled sideways in her chair to face Monica. "There's still the matter of what happens next. What do you want to do?"

"Well..." Monica stared at her friend, trying to imagine her future. "I need to finish school, get a job, and get on with my life. Really, I just want to put this whole thing behind me."

"No." Angel patted Monica's leg. "That's not all that's going to happen. Tell her what you are going to do, Jon."

He cocked an eyebrow though a grin played on his lips. "Who's running the show here, exactly?"

Angel just shrugged.

Jon sighed and started talking.

☆☆☆☆

Hundreds of miles from New York, a man sat a secluded table in an outdoor café. He scrolled through the news reports about the death of Laven Michaels and the subsequent takedown of the mobster's organization. He smiled as he closed the computer.

Now that he had officially started his vacation, he had no place urgent to be, so he sat staring at the flow of the traffic and the pedestrians meandering by. For once, his inner conscience remained quiet, allowing them both this moment of peace.

He finished his coffee and gathered up his belongings. Stuffing the few items into the saddlebags of his motorcycle, he winced at the pain that radiated from his chest.

He climbed onto the big bike and started up the music linked to his helmet. Though the artist had long ago been put in the ground, the gifts of these melancholy guitar riffs remained as alive and vibrant as the day the tracks had been recorded.

Sam smiled, satisfied and content in a way he couldn't ever recall, as the Triumph—and the music—carried him home.

Epilogue

Monica and Angel went on a two-month trip to Paris, funded by the taxpayers. When they got back, they rented a car—the bashed-up Audi had been returned to the estate of Lisa Bunder—and drove to Alabaster Cove. Angel needed to give notice on her apartment, close out her bank account, and all the other little details that accompanied a major lifestyle change.

They planned to share an apartment in New York City, paid for by a generous stipend from the government, and go to school—this too funded by the taxpayers of a grateful nation. Jon had offered to assist Monica in her education, but she wanted to finish what she had started.

Angel had her mind set on getting a degree in law enforcement. She and Jon spoke often about the requirements for joining the FBI. He told her that after she finished school, he would assist her in getting her foot through the proverbial door.

"Once you're through though, you're on your own," he warned her.

"I can take care of myself."

He'd looked at her appraisingly. "Yes. Yes, I think you can."

Angel guided the car across the bridge into Alabaster Cove, well after midnight.

As the two women climbed the steps of the apartment building, Angel said, "I'll be glad not to have to…" She stopped. The door to her flat lay partially open, its frame split. "Shit."

Fear raced through Monica. She whispered, "Come on, let's go." She turned to leave. When her friend didn't follow, the fear transformed into panic. "Ang, what are you waiting for? Let's get the hell out of here. Whoever did this might still be inside."

"He's not."

"What?" Monica glanced at the door, certain that at any second it would creak open to reveal a murdering psychopath with glowing yellow eyes. She shivered. "You can't know that."

"There are leaves in the doorway."

"Pardon?"

"Leaves. See? There's more in the living room. Old newspapers on the landing too."

Monica could not wrap her brain around the point, but before she had a chance to raise an objection, her friend pushed the door and stepped across the threshold.

Cringing against the inevitable *pumpf* of a silenced gun and Angel's body falling to the floor, Monica followed. The apartment, draped in shadows, looked as though it had been attacked by a pack of rabid wolves. The furniture had been smashed, the pillows from the couch torn to shreds, and the dishes lay shattered on the floor. Aside from the chaotic ruins of Angel's belongings, an abandoned vacancy permeated the small space. Her friend had been right; no one waited for them.

"This place is a wreck." One side of Monica's nose turned up as she surveyed the damage. "I hope you're a better housekeeper when we're roommates."

Angel snorted as she righted lamps and flicked on the kitchen overhead. The light cast an eerie yellow glow on the carnage. Oddly calm where others might have broken down, Angel studied the damage but did not comment.

She stepped over broken teacups and strewn canned goods toward the far side of the kitchen. Monica followed, and together they moved down the hall to the small bedroom. The door had been partially ripped from its hinges and lay cockeyed against a divot in the wall. Two large holes, about the size of man's fist, had been punched clean through its softwood skin and hollow core, revealing patterned innards of cardboard and glue.

Monica's eyes traveled over the shards of a broken mirror, the ransacked dresser, and the pile of shredded dresses and shirts, then stopped on the knives—three of them—protruding from the bed. Two handles skewered each of Angel's pillows. The third had been buried up to the shaft in her mattress—in the exact spot her friend's heart would have been if she'd been asleep upon the padded surface.

A bloom of reddish-black, as large as a dinner plate, blossomed at each entry point where hilt met fabric.

Monica stared at the malignant roses. No one had died here. The human body contained over five quarts of blood, and the bed would have been saturated in a sea

369

of red had the blades of this dinnerware-turned-weaponry punctured flesh. But the morose tableau had been laid in anticipation of their arrival, both premonition and promise of unspeakable violence and unsatiated rage.

As they returned to the living room, Monica said, "This had to create a hell of a lot of noise. Why didn't anyone call the police?"

Angel's face dropped. "There're only two units in this building, mine and Mrs. Anthony downstairs. She's about ninety and wouldn't hear it if you drove a car through her front window."

"But…" Monica prompted, dread uncoiling in her belly.

"If we went downstairs, we would find that before he came up here, our madman stopped there first."

"Our madman…" Monica shook her head.

Angel looked around one last time. "Come on, we're getting out of here."

"That's the best news I've heard all evening."

Angel shut off the lights, and they stepped past the busted frame and out onto the front landing.

Rain. It had begun shortly after they'd arrived, but at the time, Monica hadn't paid it any attention. More than just a passing shower, cascading sheets of water fell, and the wind howled just beyond the covered stairs.

Angel pulled out her phone and clicked a few buttons. "Storm's coming. It'll be full on in just a little bit."

Monica shrugged. "So what?"

Angel raised her eyebrows. "They're predicting flash floods."

Monica gestured toward the apartment. "The bastard that did this could come back at any minute. He might be watching us right now. I don't want to just sit around waiting for him."

"You think he's watching us through that?" Angel pointed at the waterfall just a few feet away.

"I wouldn't put it past him. Come on, it's just a little rain. We faced worse on our trip to New York."

As if in disagreement, thunder boomed, vibrating the concrete foundation under their feet. Debris protested as the winds whipped it about and slammed it into the side of the building.

Monica's shoulders slumped. "Son of a bitch." They returned to the ruins of the little apartment.

Angel turned the lights back on then moved the refuse from the entryway so she could close what remained of the door. The latch had been fractured and wouldn't keep it in place, so they slid her desk against it, piling it high with anything they could find.

In unspoken agreement, neither went back to the bedroom; instead, they cleared a space on the living room floor and piled it with blankets. As they lay in silence, Monica held Angel's hand while staring at the ceiling and listening to the rain as it pummeled the building. In spite of her anxiety, fatigue won out, and she drifted off to sleep.

☆☆☆☆

The next day, the storm still raged. They spent most of the morning lying in their makeshift bed, drinking cold instant coffee, and talking. Had the power not been out, they might have watched TV, but that, along with the stereo, had been smashed.

Angel paused in looking through a pile of newspapers and said, "I just wish we'd been able to find Peter. I still think he told those thugs where you…"

"Where I what? Ang?" Monica looked up.

Her friend held a copy of the most recent news rag, incredulousness spread across her face.

"What? What is it?" What else could possibly be wrong?

"Dead."

"Huh? Who? Who's dead?"

"You are." She held up the paper. Monica's breath caught in her throat as she saw her own face peering back at her under the glaring headline:

MURDER IN THE COVE.

They sat down together on the floor and read the article.

"Geezus." Angel lay back, her arm over her forehead.

Monica flopped beside her. "Holy shit. This article says they identified 'me' by a piece of jewelry 'I' was wearing. What are they talking about? How would this dead girl get some of my stuff?"

Angel shook her head. "I don't know."

"Gawd, the police and FBI are so egotistical. Even when they get shit wrong, like, oh yeah, I'm *not* dead. They don't confirm their facts or bother to call, just keep chugging right along. Posting my picture in the paper and telling the world I've taken the big snooze."

"Actually, they said you took the big swim. In the ocean to be exact."

Monica rolled onto her side and poked Angel in the chest with her finger. "You join these goons and you sure as hell better be right before sayin' someone's dead. If you don't, I'll track you down and kick your ass so hard your grandchildren walk funny."

"Okay, okay." Angel held up her hands in mock surrender. "Fine. I'll straighten out the lot when I get some power."

"So after he got done here, he left and went and took his anger out on someone else?"

"That or the other way around. He might have killed the wrong person, gotten so pissed he came back here and threw the grand mal of temper tantrums. It's either Peter or that freak that worked for the mob. Ebenezer or whatever."

"Erebus," Monica corrected.

"It doesn't really matter." Angel thumped the paper. "This information had to come from the police, so obviously it's either a complete lie or unreliable due to extreme incompetence."

Monica sighed. "I thought we were done with all of this."

"Well, apparently not. But we can't just sit around waiting for the bastard to find us. We need a plan."

"I'm open to suggestions."

"First, we tell the cops that it isn't you." Angel held up the newspaper.

"No." Monica crossed her arms and huffed. "That's not happening. I'm done with the cops and the FBI."

"Unless you have a better idea? Look, they think it's you. The sooner you tell them you're not dead and they start figuring out who it really is, the better."

"Fine." Monica flopped back on the blankets. "Then what?"

"Then we beat feet. Let's just get on with gettin' on."

"Now that's a plan I can get behind." Monica looked out the window as the storm railed and flailed. "As soon as the storm is over, we make way for greener pastures."

Angel nodded. "Deal."

☆☆☆☆

The next morning, the sun shone as if it didn't have a care in the world. The women stuffed what remained of Angel's belongings into the car and headed toward town.

They talked quietly as they navigated the city streets, then Angel said, "I have a headache. We haven't eaten yet. Let's grab something on the way."

"Really? You're hungry? Now?"

"Yes, now. Look, there isn't anything outside of the city for miles and miles, and once we pop into the sheriff's office and say howdy do, we are headed straight out."

"Okay, fine."

Angel changed course to the 50s style diner in the middle of town. As they got out of the car, Angel kept glancing around like at any second hell would descend upon them.

"Change your mind?" Monica asked, smiling at her friend's disconcertion.

Angel didn't reply. Her gaze remained fixed on something across the street.

Monica followed her gaze. Separated from the usual flow of city dwellers and beach bums, a man stood looking into a store window. Something about him struck her as familiar—his stance, the set of his shoulders, his build. Something.

"Mon, get back in the car," Angel whispered.

"What? Why?"

"Now!"

Monica did as she had been instructed. After they closed the doors, she asked, "What is it? You look as white as a ghost."

"That man. Does he look familiar?"

"Yes, but I don't know why."

"Take a good look." Angel pointed to the sidewalk on the far side of the road.

They both craned their necks to gaze out the back window. The man turned, and Monica gasped. "Oh shit! We need to get to the police and get out. Now."

"Yes, I think you're right." Angel said. She started the car, dropped it into gear, and tore out of the slant parking space. Pedestrians dove out of the way as she floored the gas.

☆☆☆☆

The man on the sidewalk adjusted his ball cap as he watched the car accelerate down the narrow road. He thought he had seen someone familiar staring at him through the glass. The glare of the sun, however, prevented him from getting a clear view of the vehicle's occupants. But still, he wondered…could it really be?

The car sailed down the street, taking the corner so fast it almost ran up onto the curb, and disappeared out of sight. He stood for several minutes, long after the revving engine and squealing tires faded and traffic had returned to its regular cadence.

Finally he turned and walked away. His plans had just changed.

The End

Acknowledgements

First and foremost, I'd like to say thank you to my readers. It means the world to me that you've spent some of your valuable time in my crazy little world. I hope you enjoyed reading about it as much as I did writing about it.

To all my friends and family: This book has been many, many years in the making, and I'd be nowhere without your love and support.

To Paula: You maybe forgetful, but I won't forget all your support and the many times you read and reread this manuscript.

To my Ninja Girl, Erin: we had some of our first conversations in the margins of this book way, way back. Even if I don't sell a single copy, I'll always be a smashing success because this novel led me to you and our life together. My heart and my life will forever be rich because you have touched it with your gentle soul.

You are my Ideal Reader; when I write, I hear your laughter, see your smile, and feel your emotions. This pushes me to be more than my potential.

Erin, you are my best friend, my lover, and, even better, you are my beautiful bride. You make my cloudy days sunny, and the unbearable bearable. You have taught my soul to dance. I love you more than words could ever express. #Always

About the Author

Deek may or may not be a cyborg.

Though he won't say for sure, he did (allegedly) escape the Pacific Northwest to protect his gears from rusting in the rain. He now lives on a Southern beach where the sand grinds his cybernetics and the salt air erodes his pneumatics, but the sun and surf are worth the frequent repairs.

When he's not writing sci-fi, futuristic military, and adult thrillers, he and his brilliant but stunning author bride, Erin Rhew (a non-cyborgian geek), are adventuring the beach life. Being part computer, it's only natural Deek has spent a lot of his adult career—outside of writing—engineering and nerding over technology.

You can find him on Facebook at Deek Rhew – Author, visit his web site www.DeekRhewBooks.com, and write him at Deek@DeekRhewBooks.com.

One of my favorite things about being a writer is building relationships with readers.
I occasionally send out newsletters with details on new releases, information on how to become part of my advanced reader team, as well as subscriber-only material.

If you sign up to the mailing list, you'll get a Tenacious Books Starter kit which includes two **free**, award-winning novels.

You can get both books for free by scanning the above QR code with your smartphone.

Alternately, you can register at:
www.DeekRhewBooks.com/contact.html

Thank you for being a
Tenacious Books Reader!